Boulong's Cheese

Ricky Ginsburg

Black Rose Writing | Texas

ISBN: 978-1-68433-771-2
PUBLISHED BY BLACK ROSE WRITING
www.blackrosewriting.com

Printed in the United States of America
Suggested Retail Price (SRP) $18.95

Boulong's Cheese is printed in Garamond

*As a planet-friendly publisher, Black Rose Writing does its best to eliminate unnecessary waste to reduce paper usage and energy costs, while never compromising the reading experience. As a result, the final word count vs. page count may not meet common expectations.

With Many Thanks To...

Carol Miller, proofreader extraordinaire, grammarian, and girlfriend, is without question my most valuable writing asset. All the tiny words my brain misses, she finds. Every plot-hole that needs to be filled is found by her careful assessment of the action as it unfolds. And when I wake at two-forty-five in the morning and need someone to discuss a scene, Carol rolls over and together, we solve the mystery. Every writer should have someone with her talents. No, sorry, I'm not sharing.

Scarlet Sparkuhl Delia, John Hazen, Cory Swanson, and Sue Tokuyama, a fine group of fellow authors who poured over the manuscript with magnifiers, spell checkers, and a punctuation manual that must have been written in Cyrillic. Editorial excellence I couldn't buy with a Gold Card.

"You've got to be very careful if you don't know where you are going, because you might not get there."
–Yogi Berra

Photo by the author

Also by Ricky Ginsburg

The "Bird" series featuring Detective Valarie Garibaldi:

The Blue Macaw - October 2020

Shooting Limpkins - April 2021

Clouds Full Of Ravens - December 2021

Castro's Pelican – 2022

Herons Die Slowly - 2022

Boulong's Cheese

Chapter One - History

This is a story about cheese. Of course, there will be wine since they pair so well together and one wouldn't want to be considered a poor host. Throughout most of the universe, wine and cheese invariably lead to sex which begets love or vice versa, depending on whether the scene is written by a poet or a movie director. Several passionate love affairs will take place and there will be the occasional tryst involving a cow. But mostly, this tale is about cheese.

However, before we get to the actual conflict, a bit of history is necessary.

. . . . .

With the pandemic raging and bodies literally falling by the wayside, the major pharmaceutical companies threw caution and profits to the wind to find a vaccine. Every molecule from ape droppings to zebra snot was tested on volunteers, with the only result being rashes and strange dietary changes. From tropical plants dug near the equator to mosses collected on the ice of the Arctic Circle, the foliage was broken down into its component parts and distilled to fill a syringe. Even the moon dust stored in the basement of the Smithsonian was hauled out and swirled into a saline solution.

The results weren't worth cataloging. Brilliant scientists were stymied until they noticed the low mortality rate in states where cannabis had been legalized. Conservative governments had prevented testing with the still illegal plant, despite millions of anecdotal reports of cures from jock itch to cancer. The solution had been in their bottom desk drawers all that time. One toke was never enough, and the flowering top of the heroic plant from the sixties was about to unfurl its cape once again.

A vaccine was produced and injected into ten-thousand people who showed no symptoms and tested negative for the virus after four months of reporting. The CEO of the drug company that discovered the silver bullet was inoculated on live television. Cameras followed him across the street as he walked into a hospital and through its intensive care ward the following day without a mask. He shook hands with all fourteen patients there–conscious or not–smiling for the cellphone cameras held by the nurses and doctors.

Daily tests for the next thirty days on the overweight, sixty-two-year-old diabetic came back clean. He had walked through the valley of the shadow of death and survived.

In the early spring, all of the first three million doses of the vaccine that were produced went to the military, the government, and the lobbyists who supported big pharma. Wars were still being fought. Our borders needed to be protected. The donkeys and the pachyderms had arguments to settle and exorbitant lifestyles to maintain. Police officers got their injections at roll call.

In one month's time, every dose was injected into an arm. The next supply of the vaccine was promised before summer. It never came.

.   .   .   .   .

The vaccine had a side effect that most described as miraculous. However, the three million people who received the injection were aghast. The molecule that attacked and killed the virus also reacted with cells of the human lung and the microbes that lived there, forming a new bug that was exhaled with every breath. This new, single-celled organism grew regardless of whether or not the host had the virus. And once released into the atmosphere, the tiny invader multiplied faster than a hutch of drunken rabbits.

This microscopic speck of life did no harm to any other living creature. It didn't grow mold on indoor plants or spoil the citrus crop. Beaches were never shut due to some bizarrely tainted tide or dead marine life washing up on the shore. All the tiny collection of atoms wanted was to eat.

And its diet? Glad you asked. Gunpowder and nitrocellulose–the modern version of black powder. The subminiature creature had a voracious appetite for the propellant that pushed a lead bullet out of a gun. It was small enough to squeeze between the crimps that held the projectile in place until the hammer struck the primer which exploded the powder. The bug–named Dud because it turned all the ammunition in the world inert—worked at subatomic speed. Within a month, every pistol, semi-automatic, rifle, shotgun, and cannon were rendered useless.

On submarines, the torpedoes could be launched, but their explosive charges were nothing but gray dust thanks to the sailors who breathed on them as they were loaded. They would strike their target and bounce off, sinking harmlessly to the bottom of the ocean. Several were inadvertently swallowed by passing whales as they descended. One, in fact, was disgorged by a sperm whale into the stern of a very expensive, transatlantic yacht. It was the first recorded case of marine life taking sea pollution into their own fins.

Missiles mounted on fighter jets could still do major damage to another aircraft, but they would never again explode. Air-to-air combat was reduced to kamikaze attempts at glory. Helicopters still proved formidable, lifting large boulders in their rescue nets and dumping them on strategic targets. However, even the fastest chopper was a plodding attacker when it was loaded down with rocks. An enemy could walk out of the way of a falling chunk of granite.

Privately owned weapons were as useless as a fire hose without water. Even stocks of tightly packed ammo down in a survivalist's bunker turned to lead paperweights as soon as they were torn open and shoved angrily into a weapon. Gun collectors wept. Major weapons and ammunition manufacturers closed their doors and sent their workers searching for new jobs. Macy's Fourth of July fireworks celebration was replaced by massive LED displays hanging from any available helicopter not carrying rocks.

. . . . .

A wave of pacifism, the knee-jerk reaction to the wars, cries of battle, and threats of nationalism that had overtaken the world, celebrated the death of guns. Long before a small group of inventors had tinkered together a pistol that worked on high-pressure air cartridges, they were outlawed in anticipation by all the major governments. Knives, swords, bows and arrows were all that were left.

The military retooled itself with crossbows, catapults, and slingshots. Officers were once again seen wearing scabbards. Hand-to-hand combat, already popular thanks to a series of coming-of-age karate movies from the infamous year of 1984, was taught in all public schools. (What would Orwell have thought about the Dud?)

Violent crime plummeted. A robber with a switchblade against a bodega owner with a baseball bat had become an even match. Bank guards with Tasers had little to fear from a sword-wielding criminal. Every one of the electrical gadgets had been snapped up by financial institutions for protection. Pocket knives replaced fountain pens as the most common Bar Mitzvah gift. Around the globe, police officers shed their Kevlar vests and began twirling nightsticks again.

Wars came to an end. Sure, minor skirmishes still took place. On both sides of the 38th Parallel, Koreans had constructed trebuchets and dug tiger pits filled with pointed stakes. But sentries spent their time playing sudoku puzzles and stuffing kimchee into mason jars. Soldiers came home and were tasked with the rebuilding of their countries. New bridges, highways, and airports were constructed by the former warriors. The Union of Nuclear Scientists rolled the Doomsday Clock back to noon when it was announced that all the explosive triggers in the atomic warheads had been rendered inert.

Religious fanatics from the Middle East to the Midwest came to the realization that their killing days were over. The promise of virgins and cultural supremacy was never going to be fulfilled. While they still prayed fervently for their tribe to be the one and only in the eyes of God, Allah, Jah, or Sponge Bob, they turned their efforts inward and closed the doors to their temples.

. . . . .

The microscopic solution to the worst pandemic in man's brief history made the cover of *Time* magazine. The scientists who had worked on the project were offered movie deals, penthouse suites, and fast cars. It became much cooler to be a pharmacological researcher than a rock star. It was rumored that the Rolling Stones were working on their fourth farewell album titled *"Let It Feed"* with a pixelated image of the new bug on the cover.

Nightly news broadcasts featured nothing but positive announcements: the economy was booming, the murder rate was plummeting, and the cannabis yield was expected to be five percent higher than last year. With the threat of the virus eliminated, life on planet Earth had been reborn with a better "normal" than before.

People hugged, walked up to strangers on the street and chatted about the weather. Restaurants were once again serving packed tables. Bowling alleys lit all their lanes. Outdoor target ranges were filled with picnic tables. A feeling of euphoria unknown since the repeal of prohibition spread across the globe. Dud was the savior, not some mysterious hippie type in a flowing robe that was still rumored to return even now that peace was restored.

. . . . .

On the Isle de Boeuf located in the middle of the Doubs, a river forming the boundary between France and Switzerland, lived a farmer named Boulong who had never needed a gun. The island, just over fifty-seven acres, had a Swiss chalet, a barn large enough to fit a ten-cow milking machine with an attached cheese processing plant, an eight-foot diameter hot tub, and a wooden dock.

Boulong's great-grandfather had settled on the Isle de Boeuf when the island had no name. He claimed the land for his family and began raising cattle, hence the French version of the moniker. Boulong's father had built the chalet and hot tub. The current owner had installed the modern equipment to handle the manual tasks his family had performed before him.

Average height and a bit overweight, Boulong was a dairy farmer who did nothing to hide his station in life. Even though he bathed regularly, the bovine stench had impregnated his skin and could never be removed. His legs were muscular but not half as developed as his broad shoulders and powerful arms. He'd stopped shaving and began trimming the day his wife left him.

Both his mother and father were long in the ground. He'd added their ashes to the cow's daily food and let the bovines decide where to lay them to rest. It was in their Last Will and Testament. Just as it had been for generations. Boulong's ancestors never left the island.

Sabrina, his ex-wife, had left for that reason alone. The thought of her earthly remains passing through the digestive system of a cow was too much to handle. She'd given birth to the twins, waited a year, and then left with a German tourist who remarked that she had, "A smile befitting an angel with blue eyes that were truly windows into heaven." Of course, he'd said it as he overpaid nearly a hundred Euros for a five-Euro block of Boulong's cheese.

And thus we have our first appearance of cheese...

. . . . .

During the time in Earth's history when the largest dinosaurs roamed the area, the Isle de Boeuf didn't exist. The Doubs was part of a glacier and the land below it flat. The area that would one day be Boulong's Paradise was transformed into the huge creatures' favorite feeding ground with lush vegetation and cool, clear drinking water as the glacier receded. Daily, a congregation of beasts stomped in for a meal, spreading whatever news dinosaurs discussed while they dined. And being the largest creatures on the planet at that time, they emptied their bowels right where they stood. No one complained.

On the day of the great meteor and moments before the soon-to-be extinct animals had a chance to wonder why it had suddenly gotten so hot and bright, there were thousands of prehistoric creatures munching on trees and relieving themselves. Boulong's Paradise was full of crap long before it was full of cows. One bright flash and the dinosaurs were museum-ready. Only their super-enriched, completely baked poop was left behind.

Over several millennia, the dinosaur poop mixed with the developing soil, adding minerals to it that wouldn't be found anywhere else on Earth. By the time Boulong's ancestors had settled on the Isle de Boeuf, the grasses that grew there were among the most potent cow food on Earth. Boulong had two hundred milk-producers and twin sons that churned the milk into butter and cheese. The flavor of Boulong's cheese, unlike any other known to man, along with a perfect texture for spreading, won his products every award in the book.

. . . . .

The farmer loved his cows. Of course, not in the same way a husband loves a wife or a Liverpool resident loves the sun. He'd never given them names, knowing that one day they'd be dinner, but could tell them apart at fifty paces. Right now, his two sons made up his universe. The unpleasant experience with Sabrina had left him with no desire for another star in his personal sky for over a year.

The best dairy products in Europe were his only goal. Butter so smooth and creamy that it spread on toast with the ease of jam. Cheese that not only complimented an entrée, it made it better. Boulong had given up heating the hot tub and drinking wine for over a year to save enough money for state-of-the-art milking equipment. He knew that if he gave his cows the best, they would respond in kind, and it worked.

For more generations than anyone could remember, there had been only boys born in the Boulong family. The women came from off the island and were usually French. Mookie and Mikey, Boulong's twins, were destined to carry on the dairy production and began training in the barn when they were still in diapers.

The love and respect the farmer had for his children was greater than his passion for cheese, but not by much. He often saw the boys as employees and was prone to pushing them beyond the limits a father would expect from a family member. Having raised them without a mother around, they in turn saw no distinction between "dad" and "boss."

The trio worked from Monday at dawn until after midnight on Thursday, converting fresh milk from their herd into cream, butter, and cheese. Mikey handled the roundup, chasing down lost cows with their six-wheeled Gator and moving them into a holding pen next to the barn. His brother, Mookie, was the milker, bringing in ten cows at a time and connecting their udders to the milking tubes.

Boulong was the master dairy producer. His father's teachings, passed down through the generations, had also been given to the boys, but the farmer preferred to have his hands controlling the processing equipment. Any one of the three could handle the other's tasks, but in military efficiency they did the same job day after day.

Retirement would come on the day Boulong took his last breath. Just as it had for his father, his grandfather, and every male who worked on the dairy farm on the Isle de Boeuf, while he was still sucking air, the farmer's first thought in the morning was always going to be cheese.

. . . . .

Boulong and his sons left his little island each Friday morning by boat, first going to the French side of the river to sell his cheese and then back across to the Swiss side with the balance. The island's French name was on most local maps, but it also had a Swiss name that had long been forgotten. Farmer Boulong called his home "Paradise" and paid taxes to neither government.

Chefs from six continents (and once, a drunken cook from an Antarctic research vessel) waited onshore for Boulong every Friday along with hundreds of locals to buy his butter and cheese. He always portioned the products into two lots: one for the French and an equal one for their neighbors on the opposite bank.

Unfortunately, this coming Friday was going to be a problem. One of Boulong's sons had fallen and broken his leg while bungee jumping in the Alps the previous weekend. He was able to help his father with the cheese production, but at a much slower pace. The other son had gone to Paris early in the week and was still missing. Boulong had called and texted, but there was no response. He would have less than one-quarter of the normal cheese production to sell.

To make matters worse, his girlfriend—an American tourist who'd checked out of her AirBnB seven weeks prior—had missed her period and her parents were insisting that she fly home for proper medical care. Despite the thirty-year difference in their ages, Boulong had been having the best sex of his life. *Certainly better than that bitch, Sabrina.* He was torn between having another child with his sixtieth birthday only a few years away and losing the girl's passionate lovemaking. It was a conflict that was not only keeping him up at night, but occupying his days as well.

Boulong had worked until dawn, processing the milk into butter and raw cheese. Earlier in the day, he'd cut and wrapped two-hundred-and-nine five-Euro chunks of the aged cheese and filled over a hundred tubs with his spread. Normally, he would have at least five-hundred blocks of cheese and triple the number of tubs.

I'm going to rip Mookie a new asshole when he gets home. God knows what that boy is doing in Paris. Hookers, pole dancers, dwarves? Enough of this shit. Probably went looking for his mother again. If only I knew how to cut off his cellphone...

Boulong shook his head. *I can't deal with another child.* He stared at his crotch for a moment and then spit. *Should have used a condom.*

With the first hint of sun painting the Alps to the east, Boulong loaded his skiff and looked at the much smaller than normal cargo. He could still divide it in half, but every customer would get less and some would get nothing. Boulong shrugged. *The French have wine. The Swiss only chocolate. You can't pair cheese with chocolate.* He decided to skip the Swiss this time around and just sell to the French.

The dairy farmer from Paradise didn't think it would start a war.

Chapter Two - Conflict Over Cows

General Purpose sat back in his chair, angrily shoving the cup of coffee away from the edge of the table. The text he'd just received was confusing, poorly worded, and it came through on a regular line, not his secure phone.

Swiss Guards engaged in skirmosh on French border. One cow dead, one wounded. French is requesting air support.

The General slammed his phone on the table, stressing the Muskratbox to its limit in absorbing the shock. "What the hell? Cows?" Turning to his aide, Corporal Tsunami, the General shook his head slowly. "What do you make of this, Hideo?"

Hideo Tsunami put his half-eaten hamburger on his plate and leaned over to read the text on the General's phone. "Cows? Is that a code word for something?"

"Don't know." General Purpose tapped the phone to reply. "Whose cows?" was his message.

The reply came back immediately: *Boulong's.*

"Who?" The General squinted at the word and read it again. "Boulong? Is that a king, a prime minister?"

Corporal Tsunami did an Internet search on his phone. "No. There's a Stephanie Boulong, MD in Jackson, Mississippi and Fernando Boulong from Wales who's credited with the invention of the retractable pitchfork, but no mention of cows." He picked up the burger and took another bite. "Maybe Boulong is a code word."

. . . . .

At three-hundred-and-ten pounds, Corporal Hideo Tsunami's last name was more than appropriate. Born in Holland to a Japanese father and Dutch mother, Hideo had eaten his first steak (actually gummed it, since his molars hadn't punched through yet) when he was two-years-old. He broke one-hundred pounds by his eleventh birthday and was over two-hundred when the family immigrated to the United States four years later.

The family's first house in America was in rural Vermont, where his father made an unsuccessful attempt at opening a sushi bar in-between a popular roadhouse and a gas station that also served barbecue. They sold gallons of sake and imported Japanese beer, but the only fish went out to anglers, who bought it for bait. The house was near a river that Hideo never set foot in or tried to fish. The terror of its rushing water in springtime kept him up at night, even though he couldn't hear it from his bedroom.

Having lived below sea level during his childhood years, Hideo had developed a deep-seated fear of drowning. Storms in Holland came with sirens that warned of rising tides and leaky dykes. The boy never learned to swim and even held his breath in the rain, running from their apartment in Rotterdam to the car.

Their house in the hills of Vermont had two bathrooms. One of them was in the hallway of the ranch house with a toilet and sink. The other was in his parents' bedroom and it had a tub but no shower. Hideo's solution was to wash in the backyard, holding a hose over his head. It worked until the weather turned cold, and then he switched to a watering can that he filled and dumped over himself while standing in the tub.

Hideo became an American citizen along with his parents on his eighteenth birthday. He enlisted in the Army the following day and, over the course of ten years, worked his way up through the ranks to become the solitary aide of the five-star general who was now in charge of the remaining soldiers in all U.S. military branches.

The Army let him slide on his weight thanks to his marksmanship. That, of course, was before Dud. Hideo Tsunami's natural ability with a rifle had put him at the top of his class at sniper school. He might have gone on to become the greatest shooter the Army had ever trained if it wasn't for his weight. His belly was too large for him to get into a prone position, so all his shots were taken while standing. A drill sergeant who had suggested a diet was still having dental work to repair the teeth Hideo had punched out of the man's mouth.

Cassandra, Hideo's girlfriend, was a reptile handler who'd quit her job at the London Zoo to work as an electrician's apprentice in suburban Orlando where they lived. She'd mentioned "snakes" in her HookedUp profile, not realizing that some of them were made of wire. Her employer–Shocking Electric–couldn't understand what she was saying with her heavy Liverpool accent, but hired her on her good looks alone.

They'd met online, matching over their love of children's toys. Cassandra had a complete collection of Lincoln Logs, wood not plastic. Hideo, obsessed with Erector Sets, had been buying every one of them that popped up on eBay for nearly a decade. Together, they had constructed bookshelves, ashtrays, coasters, and a metal crane that was bolted to the kitchen table. They used the crane to bring sugar to the table for coffee and silverware from the tray that sat on the counter.

Cassandra had used eleven cans of logs to make tool racks in the garage and fixed the broken table leg with a brace made out of the miniature notched pine logs. Because of the enormous amount of commercial construction in the Orlando area, the racks were empty and all her tools were in her truck.

Corporal Tsunami drove the General's car, handled his paperwork, and acted as an impenetrable wall between the civilians who were doing their best to completely eliminate the military and the soldiers who continually barraged the General with problems he was ill-equipped to solve. It was rumored that Corporal Tsunami and General Purpose had a relationship that went beyond the chain of command, but it was never proven.

. . . . .

Squeezing the volume control through the thick rubber of the Muskratbox to make it loud enough to hear over the background noise, General Purpose tried to place a call to the military command center in the White House. No one answered after ten rings and he gave up.

"What the hell is going on?" The General shook the phone and pointed it at Hideo. "Who's sending these ridiculous texts?"

"Someone who gave up their education after the fifth grade would be my guess." Taking a long drink of his milkshake, the Corporal continued his search for Boulongs around the world. "There's a Chinwang Boulong who was the first Asian mayor of San Jose."

"Nothing about his cows?"

"No, sir. It says here that he was a vegetarian." Scrolling to the end of the page, Hideo clicked off the phone and laid it on the table. "Do you think we should send in the Marines? Let them do some reconnaissance?"

General Purpose shrugged. "Let me think about it for a bit."

. . . . .

A man not quick to make a decision, the commander of the U.S. Armed Forces had his share of blunders, but his good choices far outweighed the bad ones. He would sit and weigh the options until the situation either resolved itself or no longer offered more than a single solution. Hideo was certain the superior officer could put himself into a trance just by thinking too hard.

Of course, in a time when military action had slowed to a medieval pace, decisions could be made with much greater deliberation and thought given to their consequences. General Purpose enjoyed the process but often took it to the extreme.

. . . . .

Prior to Dud, weapons training relied on cheap, simple-to-produce bullets. However, once all the ammunition in the world had become paperweights, trainees were left with learning to fire weapons that hadn't been used since the last dragon was killed. Crossbows, swords, bows and arrows were the first weapons called back into service by a suddenly unarmed military. But unlike the rifles the boot camp newbies had trained on for decades, they didn't have an unlimited supply of ammo to waste in the process.

Although the bolts fired by a crossbow were stamped out by a punch press, they had to be hand-tooled to sharpness. Thus the bolts fired during practice had to be retrieved so they could be used again. The luxury of firing a hundred rounds just for target practice had come to an end. Superior officers were told to have their underlings search for and reuse crossbow ammunition until it was embedded in an enemy's skull.

The regulations as to how many times they were actually supposed to be fired were changed as often as Hideo's drawers. It took General Purpose a week and a half to decide that five was enough. Until his order reached the troops, they had spent more time digging the bolts out of trees and mud than using them in battle. The General had chosen five as the correct usage on his first day of deliberations. In the intervening nine days, he'd vacillated between four and five, often staying up all night to consider the implications of one additional firing of a metal bolt.

. . . . .

Positioning his forces around the world to deal with the few minor details that required military intervention was another task at which the General failed miserably. His order to pull all the troops stationed in cold weather areas and move them to the tropics made sense when the Russians abandoned their bases on the Bering Strait. But ordering them to continue using the same gear was a disaster as the troops succumbed to heat stroke and exhaustion.

It took almost a month before General Purpose was able to pass on orders to resupply the soldiers with the proper uniforms. By then, most of them had shredded the sleeves and pant legs of their polar gear and looked every bit the collection of beach bums with slingshots.

Officers who sent recommendations to General Purpose up through the chain of command were promoted whether or not he read them. That he was the Commander of all U.S. military forces wasn't because he was best suited for the job. Everyone else had quit.

. . . . .

For his part, General Purpose had remained a bachelor, only occasionally seeking female companionship when Hideo was off visiting his parents, who had returned to Holland several years before the pandemic struck. He was a year past mandatory retirement from the military, but that was also before Dud and the temporary suspension of the rules. A staunch believer in healthy living, General Purpose exercised daily, kept his weight under control, and refrained from any clear alcoholic beverage. It was his belief that only liquor with color was safe to drink.

His full head of hair had turned white in his twenties but it was as thick as a sheepdog and so smooth that one would think the man invested all his money in conditioner. At six-foot and five-inches tall with a booming voice that never needed a megaphone, General Purpose was an imposing structure of a human who not only demanded respect from his men but came to expect it without question.

The General favored women who couldn't speak a word of English and were less than five feet tall. His current obsession was with a four-foot, five-inch pole dancer who worked at a club on the south side of Orlando within spitting distance of the Magic Kingdom. Tanya, who also went by Blaze, Diane, and Star, was a Native American who left the reservation after she'd been raped twice by a drunken uncle. She ate breakfast cereal for lunch and dinner, rarely getting out of bed before noon.

Tanya was fluent in Sioux, Cherokee, and Seminole. She also spoke perfect English but rarely around the General except when they were having sex and then only his name, "God," and "Oh, baby," but with a weird accent that was a cross between a French Canadian dialect and New York City slang. She never said "Yo" but called the General with "Ya" and had a constant craving for poutine. Lately however, she'd gotten tired of the charade, saving the phony accent just for sex.

. . . . .

Both officers lived on base. The Orlando Executive Airport had been converted to an Air Force staging base after a hurricane destroyed Patrick AFB. General Purpose and Tanya had a three-bedroom, two-and-a-half-bath palace with a swimming pool and helipad in the backyard. Corporal Tsunami and the snake handler turned electrician occupied a townhouse on the opposite side of the base with a splendid view of the lagoon and the Magic Kingdom which was lit up at night. They'd enjoyed watching the nightly fireworks display until Dud. Fortunately, Hideo had plenty of video footage of the gala that they watched on his sixty-five-inch flat screen.

. . . . .

The General and his aide were having lunch at a diner with a superb view of the interstate. It was one of their regular stops, the food in the mess having taken another turn for the worse. Outside, gray clouds were darkening and a distant rumble of thunder announced the incoming afternoon storm. It was a typical Florida day in early June and the tourist traffic was light.

A private, in uniform except for his cap, walked over to their table and offered more coffee. General Purpose pushed his cup closer to the boy and frowned.

"Where's your cover, soldier?"

"In...in...in my locker, sir," the private stammered. "It got grease spilled on the brim yesterday and I haven't had time to wash it, sir."

General Purpose looked over at his aide. "First, it's the guns. Now the damn uniforms and my Marines are moonlighting as servers. What's next, Hideo?"

"Let's be thankful they haven't taken away your Escalade, General. You remember how cramped you were in the Prius?"

The General's phone beeped again. Another text filled the screen.

Regiment of Swiss Guard captured by French. President wants to know what you plan to do about it.

"The President wants *me* to make the decision?" General Purpose threw back his head and laughed so hard that he spit. "What the hell is he doing? Another day on the tennis court? Searching for Internet porn that he hasn't already watched? And what the hell is the Pope's personal army doing in Switzerland?"

A second beep and more text.

Why are you not answering your secure phone?

The General shrugged. "Because it's in the car."

"Don't tell them that, sir." Corporal Tsunami got up from his seat. The chair breathed a sigh of relief. "I'll go get it." He reached down and scooped up the last of his fries, shoving a fistful of them into his mouth.

Pursing his lips, the General looked at his aide. "Do you want another burger and fries?"

"Sure. But no more onions and I'll take another shake. Thanks, Frank." Hideo twirled the keys and marched out the door.

.　.　.　.　.

Nearly five-thousand miles east of where General Purpose was ordering a blood-rare hamburger, three orders of French fries, and a vanilla shake with caramel sauce for his aide, eight members of the elite Swiss Guard were sitting in cow shit with their hands tied behind their backs. The balance of their regiment, which had crossed the Doubs River to buy Boulong's cheese before the meager supply ran out, had retreated with an irate mob of chefs at their heels.

Hours earlier, Boulong had arrived at the dock just downstream from a farmers market on the French side as the clock in a bank building flashed 8:00. With no one to help him carry the cheese and butter to his usual stall, Boulong decided to sell the French portion dockside.

He tied his skiff to the post closest to the beach and placed two milk crates upside down on the dock. On one he piled blocks of cheese and tubs of cheese spread. The second one was covered with one-pound sticks of his homemade butter. Boulong called out to a familiar chef who was walking to the market and told him that his products were available only at the dock this morning and to spread the word.

Within minutes, a crowd was hurrying down the street toward him.

One of the chefs who had a brother waiting on the opposite bank called his cellphone and passed on the word that Boulong was low on stock and should he get extra? The answer was a resounding "Yes!" and it wasn't more than a few minutes before boats on the Swiss side of the Doubs began crossing the river to get their portion of Boulong's bounty.

His wares disappeared before the first Swiss boat could dock. The French chefs weren't interested in sharing, especially with the Swiss. While they paid for their cheese and butter, their neighbors stood by and bemoaned the lack of Boulong's famous dairy products. Several folks from both sides of the river became annoyed and began shouting at those who'd secured the treasured goods that they should share them.

Boulong grabbed his now empty milk crates and tossed them into his skiff. He was untying the boat from the piling when a flaming arrow came from a nearby rooftop and jammed itself into the dock where moments before he'd been standing.

"What the hell?" Boulong scanned the building, looking for the shooter. "Did anyone see that?" He pointed in the general direction of the buildings. "Someone tried to kill me!"

"Serves you right," shouted a bystander. "You shorted us all today."

"It's not my fault," argued Boulong. "One of my sons broke his leg, and the other is..." He looked up at the sky and groaned. "Somewhere in Paris."

Deep in the crowd, someone began a chant of "We want cheese." Others picked up the cadence, louder and louder, some snatching rocks and slamming them together in rhythm to their words. A thrumming mass of humanity, they closed in on the dock. In a panic, Boulong jumped into his skiff and started the engine. He pulled his knife from his back pocket and slashed the rope tying him to the pier. Shoving the throttle to maximum, he tore across the river to the safety of his Paradise. Dozens of boats filled with angry cheese devotees set off from both shores after him.

The largest vessel in the armada came from the mountainous side of the Doubs and was painted in the official colors of the Swiss Guard from Rome. A unit of eight sentinels armed with halberds and swords had been dispatched by the Holy See to procure as much of Boulong's cheese as possible. They were told it was a mission from the Almighty and they would be put to death if they returned empty-handed.

The Guards were unaware that Boulong had already sold out and fled to his island when they landed at the boat dock on the French side. The mob, already at a fever pitch, captured the eight men without a sword being drawn and sank their boat. With no local jail available, they bound the eight and put them in a cattle holding pen by the pier.

. . . . .

Boulong's Paradise was surrounded by some of the trickiest rapids on that section of the Doubs. Boulders larger than a Prius hid just below the surface. When the mountain snows melted, the current raced so quickly that logs big enough to be telephone poles were nothing but a blur in the water. In order to reach the only beach on the tiny island, a boater had to go upstream for a hundred yards and fight a tough current around several of the largest boulders. The banks of Paradise were littered with debris from boats that had failed to negotiate the crossing.

Two small skiffs from the French side made it across, each with a single occupant. The pair, armed with swords, mounted a charge, running up to Boulong's barn while they shouted war cries. Mikey Boulong came out of the barn, leaning on a single crutch and Tasered the two men, but not before one of them had stabbed a nearby cow.

A Swiss boat crashed into the opposite side of the island with three teens waving knives. They jumped the fence that surrounded Boulong's pasture and pounced on a cow that was munching on the grass. In a fit of glee, they slit its throat and were trying to drag it over the fence when Boulong and Mikey came bouncing over the hill in the Gator. The boys ran for the river and jumped into their boat, but it was too badly damaged to float and it sank twenty yards out from shore.

Boulong and his son watched for the boys to surface, but they never did.

Chapter Three - Tenderloin, A British Fillet

To a chef, losing a single ingredient in a recipe can be disastrous. Sometimes, even the tiniest amount of a pungent spice such as cloves or nutmeg can have such a profound effect on the dish being prepared that the flavor profile is ruined by its omission. When that special ingredient is a component of a dish favored by a celebrity or perhaps someone of great importance, the chef will do anything to procure it in order to satisfy his customer.

In the tourist section of Liverpool, away from the football stadium and the factories, and one block west of the Beatles Museum, Chef Giuseppe Ronzoni (no relation to the famous and much wealthier pasta baron) got the news about Boulong's cheese at noon. He was walking to his one-star Michelin restaurant, twirling his cane, and quite pleased with seeing the sun for the first time in two weeks.

On the last Friday of the month for over five years, he'd been sending his sous chef to France to purchase ten pounds of Boulong's cheese spread. It was the basis for the sauce that finished his grilled boar tenderloin with pine nuts. The softened cheese was whipped together with freshly crushed Thai bird peppers, Himalayan sea salt, and ground lemongrass that had been soaked in rum and then sun-dried. This one entrée had been responsible for more than half the restaurant's dinners and the reason for the Michelin star.

Without Boulong's cheese spread, he might as well grind the tenderloin into burgers.

His sous chef, a dainty character who refused to wear a toque because it mussed his hair, had gotten close enough to the pier to see the last tub of cheese spread slip into a chef's apron pocket. He did his best to bargain with several Frenchmen, doubling and then tripling his offer against what they had already paid with no success. When he called to report the bad news, Chef Ronzoni was so enraged that the junior chef switched trains and headed south to Spain rather than face his boss's wrath.

. . . . .

Chef Ronzoni had prepared his famous boar tenderloin for the Queen on many important occasions. In fact, it was one of her favorite meals for a state dinner. She told the chef, in the strictest of confidence, that if she never ate another Beef Wellington again, she could live to a hundred and five. Without hesitation, he brought up her private cellphone number from his contacts and called Buckingham Palace.

The Queen had already heard of the attack by the Swiss Guards and was on the phone with the Pope. She asked Chef Ronzoni to wait on hold while she finished with His Holiness. Less than a minute later she returned to the line, laughing.

"He sent an entire regiment to get cheese. The nerve of that man. Did Mister Squeaky get enough for you?" The Queen had met the sous chef plenty of times and considered him a "poof." She'd tagged him with a nickname that was appropriate to the man's voice.

"Nothing." Chef Ronzoni sneezed and pulled a pocket square out of his jacket. "He texted me something about Barcelona, but it was mostly gibberish. Can you do anything about this? Have you spoken to Monsieur le President in Paris?"

"I was going to call him after I spoke to you." She paused, and the chef could hear several voices in the background. One of them said the words "white house," and then "idiot," but the rest was too soft to be heard. "Listen, Giuseppe, someone must have a substitute for Boulong's cheese. I'd hate to have to send in the military, but we've got guests coming for dinner next Saturday and I've already promised them your boar fillet."

The chef swept his auburn hair out of his eyes and stuffed the pocket square back into his jacket. He tapped the cane several times and nodded. "We'll give it a try, but I'm not hopeful, Your Majesty. My suggestion would be to not delay any longer than necessary. I'm not a military strategist, but I think the sooner you send in our boys to take control, the better."

"The Minister of Defense has you as an ally then, Giuseppe. I'll call Washington and speak to Baldy. I'll get back to you this evening. Ciao."

"Grazie, Lillibet." The chef ended the call and sighed. "You probably wouldn't know the difference if we used Cheese Whiz."

Shoving an empty beer bottle to the curb with his cane, Chef Ronzoni dug into his jacket pocket for the keys to the restaurant. He knew it, the Queen knew it, the whole goddamn world knew it: there was no substitute for Boulong's cheese.

. . . . .

Corporal Tsunami found the secure satellite phone on the floor under the front seat, passenger side...right where he'd shoved it before getting out of the Escalade. The National Security Agency controlled the data that flowed through the ether and into the special phone. According to NSA regulations, the phone was supposed to be carried by the owner twenty-four hours a day and never to be used for personal business. General Purpose only checked the phone before and after meals and while he was sitting on the toilet.

The screen was filled—seven pages in total—with call and text notifications that had come in while the two officers were eating lunch. He entered the General's security password—6969420—and scrolled through the phone calls first, dumping them into the trash as he read them.

The majority of the calls were wrong numbers and spam. At least Hideo thought they were. A dozen different gentleman's clubs, four health spas, and a gym that were all offering a free massage, free facial, or a way to better fitness. He deleted them all. The captain of the USS Enterprise, floating around in the Mediterranean, had called about dinner the following week. Hideo knew the General would want to tell him to go screw himself personally and left the voicemail intact.

As usual, most of the text messages were routine military traffic that didn't require a response from the commanding officer. Six others were from the pole dancer. She was pregnant. Hideo left those for the General to deal with. The last four were from the White House. Not the Office of the President, who didn't have the number for that phone, but from a Sergeant Zumba in the Situation Room.

Someone is still staffing the Sit Room? Hideo shook his head. The last time he'd been to the White House for a meeting, they'd been watching the SuperBowl downstairs in the secure military command center. The room had been packed with low-level cabinet aides, a bunch of White House reporters, and a janitor who was handling the bets. The President had wandered in at halftime in a bathrobe, shaving his scalp, and asked the score.

The first text read: "Switzerland invades France"

The next one was in all capital letters: "VATICON THREATENS ATTACK ON PARIS"

Hideo chuckled at the misspelling and then wondered why the NSA's spell-checker didn't correct it.

The third text was in lower case. *Calmed down a bit, Zumba? Someone should piss test you.* The message read: "mexico arming warheads"

The last of the four was brief, correctly spelled, and the only one with punctuation: "I quit."

Corporal Tsunami gave a few seconds thought to deleting the last message but decided to leave all them for the General to absorb. This was way above his pay grade.

He locked the car with the key fob and strolled back into the diner. Even after three burgers with onions and half a dozen orders of fries, the massive soldier was still hungry, and it would be hours before dinner.

. . . . .

Farmer Boulong finally got a text from his missing son—Mookie. The boy had met a strange woman in a bar and had spent the night at her flat in the Fifth Arrondissement.

Again.

When he awoke several hours after dawn, his wallet was there, but she'd taken all his money and credit cards.

Again.

The woman had left Mookie's clothes, except for his shoes.

Well, at least this one didn't steal his pants.

Boulong transferred a hundred Euros into his son's checking account and sent him a text, advising him of the cheese situation and to get his ass home on the next train.

His twin sons shared a birthdate and nothing else. They may have resembled each other as infants, but even as toddlers the differences were obvious. Mookie evolved into a young man with a magnetic attraction for women. He was movie star handsome with thick black hair that was combed into a pompadour and a chiseled, angular jaw line. Mookie outgrew his brother by several inches and took pleasure sneaking up behind Mikey and playing finger drums on his brother's bald head.

Born without a single strand of hair, Mikey's never arrived. Prominent doctors were consulted, and they concluded it was a rare condition that they claimed wouldn't last very long. He turned twenty-one and still had no need to shave. Mookie would kid his brother about the boy's lack of pubic hair when they hung out in the hot tub. In return, Mikey put red food dye in his brother's shampoo.

Mikey grew out instead of up. He compensated for his short stature with bodybuilding. As a young teen, he was carrying hundred-pound bales of hay as though they were feathers. When Boulong's skiff was damaged in a storm, Mikey lifted the boat over his head and carried it up to the barn where he repaired it. The boy had his father's strength and had accepted his destiny as a dairy farmer much more readily than his brother.

The spell of city life had locked its fingers onto Mookie's earlobes in the form of willing females, cheap booze, and wild nights. Finding him around the island farm on a weekend was rare, and lately, his weekends had been extended. He had no interest in cows, cheese, or butter unless it came to eating them. Having lost his virginity when most boys his age still belonged to a woman-haters club, Mookie considered sex to be as important as breathing. Boulong knew the boy would leave the island one day and never return.

. . . . .

With Mikey's help, they had loaded the dead cow into the six-wheeled Gator and hauled it back to the barn where the boy, standing with crutches, was butchering it and wrapping the meat. They stowed the fresh beef in the freezer, taking the tenderloin into the house for dinner. Mikey, an amateur chef, had been experimenting with a spicy cheese sauce and figured the tenderloins would be perfect for his first entrée.

They bound and gagged the two French teens who'd stabbed their cow, placing them in one of the skiffs they'd used to cross the river. Shoving the boat into the current, Boulong turned and walked back to the barn. The bovine's injuries didn't appear to be life-threatening, but the way it was cowering in pain, the farmer and son were unable to apply a bandage. They left it leaning against the side of a milking stall with a blanket shoved down its wounded side to absorb the blood.

From the west, several silver dots appeared in the sky, growing larger as they approached. Four jets passed low and slow over the island, circling once before heading back the way they came. Boulong strained to read the markings on their wings. "They're American!" he shouted to Mikey.

"What are they going to do? Drop rocks on us?" Mikey laughed and waved a retractable pitchfork at the jets. "Go eat your Kraft singles, you peasants!"

Melinda, Boulong's girlfriend, naked, called from the hot tub, "What's going on? Why are you home so early? Where's Mookie? Did you bring me the pregnancy test?"

"So many questions for a little girl." Boulong walked over and handed her a towel. "We'll deal with the test some other time. Right now, I think we're getting company. You might want to throw some clothes on."

She climbed out of the tub and stood dripping in the bright afternoon sunlight that filtered through the trees. "Are they staying for dinner? We should defrost some steaks."

Boulong looked down at his shoes, shaking his head slowly as her droplets formed a puddle that was leaking downhill toward him. "There's fresh meat in the freezer, but I don't think our guests will want any."

"Well, we can always just have a wine and cheese party." Melinda bubbled. "That would be fun. We never have any company and I'm getting tired of Netflix. Waddya say, Bouly?"

"Not without the cheese." Boulong reached over and wrapped the towel around the girl's quivering breasts. "Go inside and get dressed. There's a carton of bolts for the crossbow in the hall closet. Bring it out with you and a six-pack of cold beer from the fridge."

Melinda's eyes went wide with surprise. "Is there going to be trouble?"

He smiled. "Never in Paradise."

· · · · ·

Back in Orlando, General Purpose was reading the text from his girlfriend for the third time. He'd already sent a message to the White House Situation Room, but there hadn't been a reply in ten minutes.

"It's not my baby." The General looked across the table at Corporal Hideo and frowned. "My nuts were clipped twenty years ago. If that little pole climber is with child, she's going to have to find the real father and shake *him* down. I've been through this shit before."

"Do you want the MPs to move her out?" Hideo looked at his watch. "They can get her packed and off the base before your two-thirty massage."

General Purpose nodded but took his time to think about the woman...purposely. Finally, he slammed his hands on the table, upending his water glass. "Yeah. Dammit, I loved the way she sucked my toes. But a baby? Lock and load, Hideo, the enemy is at our shores and I know how you hate to get your feet wet."

Chapter Four - Nachos And Gangs

Mexicans eat their body weight in cheese every ten months. This little known fact is the result of careful experimentation by a Mexican scientist over a ten-month period in a recent year. Reportedly, the conditions weren't ideal for data collection. A spiral notebook was used to keep the tally, but it was also filled with his son's homework. He recorded his observations using four pencils without erasers, and some of the numbers were too indistinct, so he guessed when adding the columns.

To further muddy the results, some of his subjects crossed the border in the middle of the study and the researcher substituted his family members to fill in the columns. Despite the shortcomings of the man's research, the sheer volume of cheese that was eaten would have fed every rat in the New York City subway for a year.

So, when news of Boulong's cheese shortage reached Oaxaca late that summer evening, panic ensued.

"Will it affect cheddar?"

"What about pepper jack? Oh, God, we can't make nachos without pepper jack cheese."

"I heard that there's a chip shortage as well. We may have to eat the toppings with our fingers."

"It's the Americans. They're hoarding all the cheese."

"No, it's the Columbians."

"I heard it was the Chinese."

The wailing could be heard all the way from Tijuana in the north to the country's southern border with Guatemala. However, by the time word reached the most distant states of the cheese-obsessed country, the shortage included tequila, bell peppers, and avocados. The Mexican economy was faced with yet another monetary crisis in a year of poor crops, massive tropical storms, and an earthquake that had taken out the runways at Mexico City International Airport.

The Mexican President went on national television to quell the mounting fear but he was booed off the stage. A deputy minister told the press that the Mexican Air Force had an atomic bomb and they were ready to use it. He was reminded that the triggers had all been rendered useless because of their explosive components. The man shook his head and said they would ignite the bomb with disposable lighters and drop it on Washington D.C. unless the American President agreed to supply them with cheese spread.

In a public message that was re-broadcast on Mexican television with subtitles, the American President responded to the threat. He informed his Hispanic neighbors that a squadron of helicopters was hovering at the border and they were loaded with boulders big enough to wipe out his palace, fill the palatial swimming pool with gravel, and escape with his tequila collection before the Mexican Air Force could find rubber bands big enough to spin the engines of their Cessnas.

The Mexican head of state's response was translated, censored, and filtered. Two words were all that remained: "Up yours."

·　·　·　·　·

While few outside the Mexican borders believed that tequila would ever be rationed or worse–unavailable–the loss of Boulong's cheese had a profound effect on the Yucatan Peninsula and the fancy resorts crowded onto the beaches of Cancun. A cheese sauce appropriately named "Yuc" that was used on every entrée from fish to fowl was now in critically short supply.

Air freight had brought two dozen tubs of the special spread to the sandy playground once a month for years. A Mexican chef with a brother in Switzerland purchased Boulong's cheese, packed it in dry ice, and shipped it overnight. Tourists had come to expect the cheesy combinations along with cheap tequila and sunburns. A five-star resort tried making yuc with a mixture of cream cheese and lemongrass. According to one tourist interviewed on Mexican television the result was, "Yucky."

Tourists began packing their bags and heading home to more culinary friendly environments. Hotel operators offered free nights, then free weeks, and finally free nights with hookers in a desperate but unsuccessful attempt to staunch the hysteria of departures. Border patrol agents were overwhelmed by the rush to return to the

U.S. and shut the crossings. A heavy equipment operator from Denver who was vacationing with his wife and extended family commandeered a dump truck and crashed through the gates. Hundreds of cars, taxis, and trucks followed him through.

With this final death blow to the Mexican economy, the military took control of the government and declared war on the United States, France, Switzerland, and Afghanistan. No one was able to explain the last proclamation, but one Mexican general told CNN that there would be other countries named and they were going alphabetically from a list in a Rand McNally atlas.

The atomic bomb, which had been a gift from President Nixon just days before he resigned, was duct-taped between the landing gear of a crop duster. News media from around the world were invited to inspect the lethal cargo, and the NSA re-tasked a spy satellite to get the same photos that were already popping up on Facebook.

Generalissimo Newsenz, the commander of the Mexican forces, announced that the plane would be sent by barge across the Gulf of Mexico where it would attack Disney World from the air. Apparently he'd consulted a globe and decided that Washington D.C. was just too far away.

"The world will see that the Mexican aircraft carrier Dobby is a formidable enemy. Mexico will join the nuclear family and take control of North America." The Generalissimo leaned into the television cameras and sneered. "You thought a tin wall and paved highway would keep us out. Fine. Now we come by sea and you will pay the penalty for your foolishness. *Cabrones.*"

. . . . .

Several thousand miles away, deep within the bowels of the White House, a janitor was sweeping up the debris in the secure Situation Room and collecting the empty beer bottles. His family had crossed the Rio Grande in the middle of the night twenty-two years ago. He was a teenager then and watched his mother drown in the swift current. He'd never been to the Yucatan and had no memories at all of the place where he'd been born. Add to that the curse of lactose intolerance, and he couldn't understand what all the fuss was about cheese.

A red light on one of the phones lit up, and a bell rang. The janitor looked into the smaller rooms off the main conference area to see if someone was there to answer it. The ringing stopped after a few seconds and the man went about his tasks. Again the light blinked, and the phone rang. This time the janitor put down his broom and answered.

"Hello?"

"This is Colonel Mujalin with the Afghanistan Air Force, to whom am I speaking?"

The janitor looked over his shoulder and shook his head. A smile filled his face. "This is the President of the United States. What do you want?"

"Mr. President, war has been declared by your Mexican neighbors and we would like to know your intentions."

War? Shit, I better get outta here. "Listen, Colonel. If I were you, I'd surrender immediately. They have these gangs in Mexico City that will cut your nuts off just for fun and shove them up your ass with a two-by-four. Bandas, they call them. If they declared war on your ass, I'd say you best start shopping for a coffin and place to bury it, *pronto.*"

The janitor was about to hang up but several new voices joined the conversation speaking in some language that definitely wasn't in his repertoire. After a bit of what sounded as though a strong disagreement was being raised, the Colonel came back on the line.

"How many of these bombas do they have?"

Bombas? They're a brand of socks, right? "Bandas, Colonel, and they play for keeps. Boys got knives and crossbows and shit. For real, man. You don't wanna mess with them. They'll kill you, your momma, her momma, and every memory of all of you. Mexican bandas got long memories, too. You don't want no extended war with them. If they's demanding something, give it up and get it over with. You'll be thankful if you get away with your balls intact."

"You expect us to believe there is more than one bombas?"

"Yo, shit for brains." The janitor smacked the handset on the table twice. "Bandas, no 'o' an 'a' and no second 'b.' That's a 'd' like dog shit."

"Mr. President, are you saying that you gave the Mexicans another bomb?"

"I ain't giving the Mexicans shit, man. My mother died because she had to swim to freedom. I wouldn't go back to Mexico on a free first-class ticket with a hooker in the seat beside me."

More arguing and the Colonel muffled the phone. Lifting an empty pizza box from the nearest seat, the janitor dropped onto its padded leather cushions and put his feet up on the conference table. An unopened bottle of warm beer was laying on its side under a copy of *Sports Illustrated*. He pulled a screwdriver from his toolbelt and popped it open.

The Colonel unmuffled the phone. "If the Mexicans drop your atomic bomb on us, we will have no other option but to retaliate. Rest assured that we have the assets in place to turn your cities into radioactive wastelands."

The janitor looked at his watch. He was already working on his own time, thanks to the budget cutbacks Baldy had put in place. *Screw this shit.*

"Listen, Colonel. I'm not gonna say this again because I'm runnin' late for dinner and my wife will be pissed. Don't try to negotiate. Don't hesitate. Don't be a fool. Give the bandas what they want and run, don't walk, run the hell as far away as you can."

He dropped the receiver into the cradle and reached down for his broom. An empty condom wrapper was stuck to the bottom of the chair. The White House janitor jabbed it with the screwdriver and flipped it into the trash bag.

．　．　．　．　．

Back in Mexico City, the roving gangs had more serious problems than cheese. The tourists that were their favorite prey had left the country and weren't coming back while a war was going on. The border between their country and their customers was sealed tighter than a virgin's legs on her quinceañera. The gang members held an emergency meeting and a temporary truce agreed upon...at least until someone dropped the damn bomb and got this shit under control.

A chief from one of the largest bandas volunteered a pair of his lieutenants to fly the Cessna and manually ignite the fuse–a strip of white cotton that someone had tied around the nose of the weapon. (A scientist working at the university suggested it might be possible to get the nosecone hot enough to spark the atomic reaction.) Generalissimo Newsenz thanked the banda chief for his offer but told him the President himself would be handling the ignition of the atomic bomb. The President was unavailable for comment.

What little cheese was left in Mexico was being hoarded and occasionally defended with force. A chef from Guatemala crossed the border and attempted to purchase Boulong's cheese spread from a fellow chef who lived on the Mexican side. An angry group of the Mexican chef's neighbors surrounded the house and forced the Guatemalan cook to the sidewalk when he attempted to leave. One of the mob held a cleaver and threatened to cut off the man's fingers. Fortunately, the police were patrolling nearby and saved the cook from dismemberment.

A workers riot that began at one of the most exclusive resorts in Cancun was caused by a lack of funds to pay the kitchen and housekeeping staff. It seemed that many of the tourists departed without settling their accounts, and even those who had left credit cards on file were able to block further transactions due to the threat of war. (The U.S. banks shut down their Mexican links moments after the first newscast and word of the loading of the bomb-laden Cessna onto the Dobby.)

The military responded with teargas that had to be hand-sprayed at the demonstrators. A stiff offshore breeze blew most of the gas back onto the soldiers, and the cheering rioters rallied. With the Army in retreat, workers at all the resorts in the Yucatan went on strike, taking over the best rooms and depleting the tequila stock in a matter of hours.

· · · · ·

Generalissimo Newsenz came on the television at the start of the evening news to address his nation. He waved a sword while he spoke, standing in front of the Mexican flag, and pounded the lectern with his fist for emphasis. His address was carried live on the U.S. networks with subtitles.

"Those hotel workers who put down their bottles, leave the fluffy bath towels, and go home now will have jobs when this crisis is over. We will not stand for damage and destruction to our tourist revenue. Looting and rioting are crimes that we will not tolerate, especially as our nation prepares for war." He paused for a moment, narrowing his eyes and staring directly into the camera. "Those who continue to destroy valuable Mexican tourist attractions and damage our already struggling economy will lose their heads."

He reached down and held up a black-and-white photo of a guillotine. "This will be your fate." The picture was upside down and a medieval serf was holding the rope that released the blade. In one corner of the photo, the words "Fig. 17" were clearly visible if you tilted the screen. Generalissimo Newsenz grinned in a most evil fashion. "Even the bandas will fear us now."

· · · · ·

The White House janitor put down his can of Fresca, muted the television, and turned to his wife. "My Uncle Carlos was beheaded in an accident."

"I thought he died on a fishing trip, fell overboard or something?"

"No, that was my Uncle Jose." The janitor took another sip. "Uncle Carlos was a long-haul trucker. He was twenty minutes outside of Omaha when a tornado ripped across the interstate. The storm had just demolished a church, and the cross was airborne at over a hundred miles an hour. It smashed through the passenger window of his eighteen-wheeler and took his head clean off as it went out the other side."

"Jesus."

The janitor shook his head. "Nah, he wasn't attached, but Uncle Carlos' head ended up at the top of the cross."

His wife held her fork and knife in midair. "Oh, my God. Where did they find the cross?"

The janitor took a long sip of the soda and set the can down on the table. "It was embedded in the roof of a Jewish synagogue. The truck kept going after his head was sheared off. At the moment of death, they figured his body just froze in position. The truck was carrying hogs to be slaughtered and all of them survived the storm. Even after the truck ran out of gas and overturned into a ditch."

Finishing the last of the Fresca, the White House janitor pulled out his phone and showed his wife the photos he'd shot inside the Situation Room. It wasn't the first time, and he was sure it wouldn't be the last. He just hoped that the Colonel with the funny voice would heed his warning about the bandas.

Chapter Five - Take Me To The River

Boulong was on the Gator, coming back from fixing the fence where the three missing boys had broken through earlier. He'd cut his finger on the wire and slipped on a moss-covered rock. The farmer's patience was being tested, and he wasn't sure it was a test he'd pass today. Cows were gathering at the barn, waiting to be milked, and he was still short one son. Questioning his own sanity had become a regular event and today felt as though it was going to be worse than searching for a leak in the hot tub after a snowstorm.

He could see Melinda waving from the porch and leaned harder on the gas pedal. His girlfriend was shouting at him, but Boulong was too far away to hear her words over the roar of the two-stroke engine.

Pregnant. Jesus. How did that happen? He smacked his forehead. *Duh.*

Skidding to a halt, he parked the Gator alongside the house and ran up the stairs to the porch. Melinda was in the middle of a video chat with her parents and pulled her lover into the camera's eye. A woman who appeared to be even younger than his girlfriend was staring back at him. She put her hand to her mouth, but it was too late to hide the shock.

"Oh, Jesus! He's got gray hair and a beard. Mel, you told us he was a young man."

Smiling, Melinda tilted the camera away from Boulong and shrugged. "It's just his hair, mother. Don't get all righteous with me. My father was twenty years older than you and Valerian...is that really his name? Well, he's got you by at least fifteen."

"Sweetheart, you're only twenty-two and–"

"And I'll be twenty-three next month and you're going to be forty-one. So what?"

A man's face—rugged, deep-cut features, eyebrows so bushy they could probably hold a pencil stuck through them—squeezed into the frame. He smiled and the glare off his teeth was so bright that everything else in the picture was muted. When he spoke, the words were carefully crafted and delivered with perfect timing. Boulong thought he was a newscaster.

"Melinda, you do know that your mother and I only have your best interests at heart. You are old enough to make decisions for yourself but not worldly enough to foresee the consequences." He took a long breath and continued. "Every day we reach a crossroads. Every day we must make decisions that will affect our lives going forward. Making an avoidable mistake should never be an option and—"

"A mistake like my mother made twenty-four years ago?" He'd hit a nerve. "A mistake like me? Is that what you're trying to say? You asshole." Melinda handed the phone to Boulong. "You talk to him. I can't take anymore of his bullshit."

The farmer held the phone in front of him, inadvertently aiming it directly at his crotch. While he was out in the field, repairing the electric fence, Boulong had replayed last night's wild sex with his girlfriend in his mind. His manhood was still at attention and the bulge was obvious, especially at high def on her phone.

· · · · ·

His girlfriend had come out to the barn after midnight wearing nothing besides a smile while he was still filling tubs with cheese spread. At her suggestion, they'd gone down to the small, rocky beach to cool off in the Doubs. It was hot in the barn with all the equipment running, and Boulong was soaked in sweat.

Stripping off his clothes, he took Melinda's hand and led her into a small pool, deep enough to dunk into and wash away the barn grime. He went down and popped back up. She went under and latched her lips onto his flaccid tool. This was not unusual for the girl. In fact, it was her favorite way to pleasure the farmer. It was, however, the first time she'd done it underwater.

Boulong started counting seconds after she'd been down there for what seemed like forever. He got to thirty, and he felt her release. Surfacing, she took a huge gulp of air and went back down. This time, Boulong counted the moment her head dropped below the waterline. At ninety-five seconds her lips slipped off his shaft, and she came up and sucked in a breath.

He caught her by the shoulders before she could submerge again and led the girl up to the beach. Never having learned any life-saving techniques, the farmer wasn't going to take a chance on needing them tonight. One of the cows had wandered down for a drink, and Boulong lifted Melinda onto its back.

"Can she take the weight?"

Boulong nodded. "Both of us if we do this slowly."

Taking her hand, he climbed up and onto the cow, facing his naked girlfriend. The cow grunted and huffed several times, but made no attempt to toss the two lovers off its back. Melinda wondered if Boulong had trained this particular cow for just this purpose. It was one of the largest in the herd and significantly wider than your average bovine milk factory.

By spreading his legs, Boulong was able to pull his girlfriend forward and on top of him. She was ready. His erection slid inside her with less friction than an oiled mitten. Rocking back and forth, Melinda built up a head of steam and began mooing in rhythm. Her hands dug into his collarbone as she leaned forward to mash her sweet spot against his groin, and it made her moan with delight.

Boulong held her waist to keep the two of them on the cow's back. With each thrust, he locked his heels tightly against the beast and tried to focus on the mission at hand. But thoughts of his son, missing in action, and his other son with a broken leg, and the limited cheese production spoiled his concentration. The cow shuffled from side-to-side in response to Boulong's kicking and squeezing as though it could sense the farmer's urgency.

The fresh night air and the musky odor of the cow had brought Melinda to a frenzy. Her mooing was now bleats of pleasure in-between breaths that she sucked down at a pace that would rival an Olympic swimmer. The bliss she'd experienced in the hot tub paled in comparison.

She was moments from a screaming climax when the cow decided she'd had enough and needed a drink.

It was only a few feet to the rushing waters of the Doubs. The cow covered the distance before Boulong and Melinda could uncouple. Even if they'd had a few more seconds, the girl's vaginal muscles had a grip on the farmer's shaft that wasn't going to release until she finished. They slid off the cow as it sauntered into the water. Boulong shrunk instantly and Melinda was denied the grand finale just a few seconds short of the peak.

The cow took a drink, shook the water out of its ears, and strolled leisurely out of the river.

. . . . .

That was the previous night, when the world had yet to come unhinged. Melinda, already seated in the Gator after dropping the phone in his hands, shouted to Boulong, "Tell them both to go screw themselves silly. I'm not coming home...ever."

Ever? Boulong brought the phone up to eye level and smiled. "She's a wonderful girl. Loves the cows." He winked and ended the call.

They drove the Gator down to the small beach and parked on the dock. To the west, several large bonfires were burning. Blue and white flashes from police cars popped out from between distant buildings, the occasional streak of light across the water as one of them raced down the wharf.

"This is not going to last. We'll have plenty of cheese and butter once Mookie gets home." Boulong looked at his watch. *Should have been here by now. Dammit.*

"I can help." Melinda looked at the farmer and blinked her eyes.

Sighing, Boulong shook his head. "Sabrina said the same thing until the first time she handled a cow's udder."

"You said it feels just like a limp dick."

He laughed. "Not exactly, but close enough."

"I like–"

Her words were cut short by the sound of a large boulder that came whizzing down from above them. It crashed into the far end of the dock, not more than ten feet in front of them, and smashed through to the water. A second boulder and then a third followed it, missing the pier and thudding onto the rocky beach. They both searched the sky and strained to hear the sound of helicopter blades, but heard nothing except the wind and distant sirens from the French side.

Boulong started the Gator and gunned the engine, heading for the safety of the nearby forest. A second volley of rocks splintered the middle of the dock. One enormous chunk of gray basalt embedded itself in the wood where they had been parked. Roaring across the pebbles, the two-stroke engine screaming at full throttle, they bounced over a fallen log and narrowly missed a large evergreen. Boulong grabbed Melinda by the shoulders and pulled her down as they slipped under its huge branches for protection.

He cut the ignition and jumped from the seat, staring at the sky from below the tree. The moon was half full and what few clouds floated above them weren't enough to blot out the stars.

Something else did. Something large and black and completely silent. Boulong thought it was Satan himself, flying above his Paradise. But as quickly as it appeared, the darkness was gone and he could once again see the moon and stars. The farmer scratched the back of his head. He'd seen them disappear and come back again with his own eyes. It wasn't magic. Boulong didn't believe in magic, although he loved card tricks, but this wasn't one of those.

Whatever it was, it had destroyed the dock and nearly hit his skiff. Mookie would return, eventually, and he'd have to come by rowboat which could be beached. At least that part of the problem was solved. But there was no way to drag a skiff loaded with hundreds of pounds of dairy products off the beach and into the water.

The image of the wooden hot tub burbled into Boulong's head. He looked at Melinda and apologized with his eyes. She loved having sex in the tub at night. It was her favorite place for romance. He turned and stared at the ruined pier long enough for her to realize he was thinking.

"Can you fix it?"

He nodded. "We need a bunch of heavy oak timbers."

"What about the hot tub?"

Boulong held his breath.

"We can always get some wood to build another one." She turned and looked at the nearby trees.

"But I thought…"

Melinda took his hand. "I like the cow better."

. . . . .

The stealth bomber that dropped the boulders on Paradise had flown more than a thousand miles at the behest of the President of the United States. He'd ordered an attack on the tiny island following a phone call from the British Prime Minister who said an American tourist was being held against her will. Baldy, as the

President was referred to in private, consulted no one before ordering the silent attack. After all, he *was* the Commander-in-Chief.

He hoped that the bombing run wasn't going to have to be the precursor of an invasion. No other country had invaded another since Dud, although the online rhetoric hadn't slowed and those nations previously at odds with each other continued their battles with words. The President took a fresh pair of tennis sneakers out of their box and tried them on. He had nothing else to do until word of the bombing mission was received and his trainer was waiting.

. . . . .

It was pilot's choice for the target and she decided to eliminate the only structure visible from the air. Coming in as low and as slowly as the stealth bomber would allow without stalling, she ordered the bombardier to unload four of their boulders on the first pass. Not having the flash of an explosion to verify the demolition, she brought the huge black jet around for a second pass and unloaded the balance of her rocks at the same target.

Boulong was fortunate that his father had built the family house in the protection of the forest and that the generator was already off for the night. His luck held out even further as none of the boulders had struck his skiff. Fearing a third pass from whatever was dropping chunks of the Alps on his island, he grabbed Melinda's hand and raced the Gator up the path and through the forest to the safety of the house.

Mikey met them at the garage with two large, dry towels. He handed Melinda her telephone and hobbled over to sit down on the motorized cart.

"Some woman's been calling over and over again. I told her you guys went swimming, but she's been shouting about a lawyer and kidnapping since you left."

Melinda brought up the recent calls and blocked her mother's number. "Somebody bombed the dock. We're going to take apart the hot tub to repair it. Wanna help?"

Folding his arms over the top of his crutches, Mikey shook his head. "That's the only wood you can think of? I thought you guys loved the hot tub."

"Without the dock, we can't load the skiff. Without a skiff loaded with butter and cheese, we have nothing to sell and thus no money to buy gasoline for the generator. Without the generator, we have no way of heating the water in the hot tub. Thus, it would be a cold tub." He stood with hands on his hips and tilted his head to one side. "Does that sound appealing to you?"

"No, but what if they bomb it again? Are you going to take apart the house or the barn?" Pointing with a crutch, Mikey nodded slowly. "We just need to make enough cheese and butter over the next week and this madness will all come to an end."

Boulong looked up at the moon and sighed. "No, son, I think it's just beginning."

Chapter Six - Briefcases and Desert Sandals

Over the years following the 9-11 attacks, the Taliban and its offshoots infiltrated a large number of law firms in the major cities of the United States. The people they slipped into place were bona fide attorneys. Each one had a degree from a law school somewhere in Europe, and they had all marched through the educational system to gain their sheepskins.

But they were not in the U.S. to practice law or to fight for their beleaguered countrymen who were still battling American armies around the globe. Terrorism hadn't gone off somewhere to hibernate. It just found a better way to achieve its goals. What better place for a criminal to hide than in the midst of a bunch of lawyers? These legal landmines worked diligently to win their cases, but in reality, they were simply waiting for the message to attack.

Before they left Afghanistan, each of the attorneys was given a red leather briefcase loaded with a cheap nuclear device. It was what the NSA and its cohorts named a "briefcase bomb." It was designed to ruin lots of peoples' days, pollute the neighborhood where it was detonated, and generally make a statement about right and wrong, albeit with a self-aggrandizing punch.

Fifty identical red lawyer's bags were purchased wholesale from a distributor in Brooklyn and shipped to Kabul via London, Jerusalem, and Cairo. Enough nuclear material to contaminate ten square miles was packed into a false bottom of each bag along with a trigger mechanism. The bombs could have been designed with remote firing mechanisms, but the trend in religious fanaticism at the time was suicide. In order to explode, the lawyers would have to detonate them by hand.

They entered the United States through a variety of international airports during the holiday season when Homeland Security was already overworked. Fifty well-dressed gentlemen with the exception of their desert sandals slipped through security and into the heartland of America. It was a religious thing, and they weren't going full-American just yet. No one thought to look at their feet.

The lawyers moved into townhouses and apartments that were prepaid by the Taliban through offshore banks. None of them lived in penthouses, but not a single lawyer suffered the shame of a basement. Opulence would be handed out at the gates of Heaven. Storing their briefcase bombs in coat closets and garages, they waited patiently for the sign to take revenge and accept their reward.

. . . . .

The problem with the devices was that they were constructed before Dud and relied on the same explosive trigger as their big brothers that were dropped from planes or delivered by intercontinental ballistic missiles. The terrorist lawyers were stuck with a radioactive nuisance that wouldn't explode, even if it was smashed with a hammer. When they questioned their superiors about the triggers, the reply was, "Allah has kept them intact."

So when the signal was sent out from the motherland and these would-be-terrorists kicked off their wingtips and slipped into their sandals to deliver their deadly packages, none of them were aware that they were only endangering themselves. They took their red leather briefcases to their designated explosion points and squeezed the triggers...over and over again.

When none of them exploded, the temptation to poke around the device became too much to resist, and most of them received a radioactive dose many thousands of times stronger than a dental x-ray. Whether they glowed in the dark or not was never recorded, but the only casualties of their briefcase attacks were the terrorists themselves who would eventually succumb to radiation poisoning.

Several of these would-be mass murderers were captured in the act. A bus driver in Houston, Texas watched a man in worn leather sandals and gray socks as he got off at a major intersection. What struck him as odd was the red leather bag. An upside-down U.S. flag sticker was attached on both sides–the universal distress signal. Not knowing how they were supposed to be displayed, the man had put them on incorrectly in an attempt at faux patriotism.

Making it even more ominous, the driver, a *true* patriot, was certain the man was muttering in Arabic (it was French) when he stepped down from the bus. Fearing an attack, he pulled the bus to the curb a short distance past where the man was standing. While the driver radioed for assistance, the man took a seat at an outdoor café and opened the bag where it sat under the table.

Now realizing that the man *must* have a bomb in the bag, the driver reached into his lunch pail and took out a slingshot he'd been practicing with in his backyard. The man was quite a bit larger than the birds he'd been plinking which made him a much easier target. Stepping out of the bus, the driver let a marble fly from the cast aluminum slingshot and hit the man squarely between the eyes, briefly knocking him out.

Police who arrived on the scene moments later had already been warned about well-dressed men in sandals carrying a certain red leather briefcase. They cleared the area and found someone to drive the bomb squad truck over to the location. Using a pair of mop handles, two officers lifted the bag into the massive truck and slammed the door closed. The semi-conscious terrorist was taken into custody, insisting in French that he had no idea whose bag it was and that he wanted to press assault charges against the bus driver.

The driver was awarded a medal by the city later that evening, but lost his job when the other passengers on the bus complained about being late. He received a phone call from the terrorist he'd taken out with the slingshot who was watching the news in his holding cell. Despite his situation, the man was offering his legal services to help the driver get his job back in exchange for a reduced sentence. The driver thanked the terrorist lawyer but declined. He'd decided to go to culinary school and seek employment as a sous chef rather than risk his life in a city bus again.

. . . . .

Two terrorists walked into Macy's Herald Square at the same time the bus driver was shooting their friend and tried to explode their devices with lighters normally used to ignite backyard charcoal grills. Other than burnt fingers and a broken nose, the explosive triggers failed to work. A brief closing of the perfume counter was the only outcome of the attack.

Hundreds of shoppers witnessed the attempted bombing and the brave security guard who wrestled the two men to the ground. (They were already sitting on the floor and tried to get up when he walked over.) The Internet was flooded with video, some of it live-streamed, of the drama taking place in one of New York's busiest department stores. Close-ups of the guard punching one of the terrorists in the nose was so vivid that viewers could see drops of blood flying from the man's nostrils with the second and third punches.

The security guard who confronted and subdued the pair was later interviewed on the afternoon network news. He took full advantage of his fifteen minutes of fame.

Television host: "Did you know they had atom bombs in those bags?"

Kevlin (the security guard): "Hell no. You crazy? I'd been six blocks from the damn store afore they could say word one had I known that shit."

Host: "There's a photo circulating on the Internet of you holding the two briefcases in the air and howling."

Kevlin: "Yeah, my girlfriend seen that shit and now she wants me to get a chest x-ray to make sure I ain't glowin' inside."

Host: "Did the police tell you the bombs were inert?"

Kevlin: "Yeah, as they was loading them into that big ass truck that says 'Warning, big ass bombs inside. Keep your ass way the hell back.' Shit."

Host: "I understand the Mayor is going to give you the keys to the city tomorrow."

Kevlin: "Screw that shit. Dude should give me the keys to his Lexus."

Host: "There's a rumor the President is flying in to award you the Medal of Honor."

Kevlin: "I didn't vote for that bald ass, tennis freak. Screw him. Let him cover my mortgage for the balance of the year. Shit. Medal of Honor? I hope it's solid gold. My cousin got a pawn shop up on 137th Street. Turn that gold shit into cash. Bet there's five large in that trinket."

Host: "You realize it's illegal to sell it?"

Kevlin: "Shit, my cousin don't give a damn about that. Once it's melted down, no one gonna know where that shit come from. Hey, I could show you a real good time with five large in my wallet. You single?"

Host: "Thanks, but I'm in a relationship."

Kevlin: "He got five large and the keys to the Mayor's Lexus?"

Host: "No, but–"

Kevlin: "But what, bitch? You don't like neegros?"

Host: "We've got to take a commercial break."

Kevlin: "What's up with that? You ain't gonna answer the question?"

Host: "We'll be right back."

Kevlin (yanking the microphone off his collar): "And I'm in the wind."

General Purpose muted the television screen built into the passenger seat of his Escalade and rolled down the window. The sweet fragrance of the nearby citrus groves filled the car and made him smile. Citrus was a manly odor. His shampoo was lemon-lime. Orange juice was liquid citrus. It gave him strength and kept his bladder cancer at bay. He insisted that the pole dancer bathe in citrus water before they had sex. The addition of six drops of concentrated citrus oil let him think he was screwing her in an orchard. It made her sneeze.

"Do you smell that?" he asked Corporal Tsunami.

"What?"

"Citrus, son." The General pointed out the window. "Nothing else in the world smells like that. I love the smell of citrus in the morning."

Hideo glanced at the dashboard clock. "It's two-fifteen in the afternoon."

"One morning in Baghdad, we had a mission to clear a village that was surrounded by an orange grove. We went in after they firebombed the place." General Purpose closed his eyes and sighed. "We didn't find one single Iraqi body. But that smell...the smell of roasted oranges and burnt flesh..." He leaned forward and whispered in the Corporal's ear, "It was the smell of–"

"Fried dead people with an orange glaze would be my guess, General."

"Orange glaze smells burnt to you?"

"The restaurant in Pirates Cove has a frozen dessert with orange glaze on top. They toast it with a little torch. I think it ruins a ball of good ice cream, but Cassandra loves it."

The General sat back in his seat and rolled up the window. "When is she coming over to hook up my new television?"

Staring out the windshield at the line of traffic in front of them, Hideo shrugged. "She's been working double shifts since the vaccine. You wouldn't believe how far behind these construction projects got with the shutdown. I'm getting a little tired of eating dinner alone."

"Army Corps of Engineers could finish one of those big hotels in a week."

"If they weren't busy paving the desert along our southern border."

"It wasn't my decision." General Purpose shook his head. "I told the President it was a stupid idea to put a half-mile of asphalt on our side of the border. Mexico wasn't going to pay for his wall. What made him think they'd pay for a paved killing field?"

"They weren't going to tell the Mexican President about the gun towers until it was finished, were they?" Corporal Tsunami put the Escalade in park as they came up to a railroad crossing and turned to face the General. "Did the President really think the Mexicans would buy his story about a new interstate?"

"The Mexican Department of Transportation offered to paint the lines and build the tollbooths."

"Jesus."

The General nodded. "Yes, and a church at both ends."

"Well, Dud put an end to that plan." Straining to see the last of the railcars, Hideo lowered the passenger side window. "Damn train goes all the way to Georgia."

"They could still turn the thing into a highway."

"All eleven miles of it?"

"A local highway, then." The General dropped his window and joined his aide in the search.

"There's no town for twenty miles in any direction." The caboose came into view and Corporal Tsunami rolled up his window. "What do you think about the security guard at Macy's yesterday?"

General Purpose folded his hands in his lap and closed his eyes. "I'd promote him if he was under my command."

"The President is giving him the Medal of Honor this evening at a ceremony at the Mayor's mansion in New York City." The crossing gates went up and Hideo put the car in gear. "You should be there."

"Bullshit. You go."

"I'm not the commanding officer of the United States Armed Forces."

The General took off his hat and put it on his aide's head. "I hereby promote you. Now, get me home. I wanna make sure that lying midget has been packed, processed, and shipped off base."

Chapter Seven - Dirty Sex, No Tennis

When the Boulong estate was built, several generations of the family were living on the island. Father Boulong, in his desire for privacy and a good night's sleep, constructed the master bedroom in the basement of the house. It was a brilliant idea as the room was always cool in the summer and well-insulated against the snow and ice of the winter.

The original bedroom was large enough for a king-size bed and a pair of dressers. Over the years, Boulong had enlarged the room to include an office where he kept track of the dairy business. He was sitting at his desk when Melinda came bouncing down the stairs. She was singing an old Rolling Stones hit titled *Satisfaction* and clapped her hands every time she sang, "I can't get no...satisfaction...hey, hey, hey."

"You have a problem?"

"I'm horny."

Boulong closed his ledger and turned around in his chair. "You're always horny."

"Are you complaining?"

"No, but..."

"But what?"

The farmer got up from his seat and walked over to his girlfriend. "I'm trying to wrap my head around the possibility that you really are pregnant."

"I told you to get the test while you were in town yesterday." Melinda kicked off her flip-flops. "It's the only way we'll know for sure."

"I thought you were taking the pill."

She shrugged. "It doesn't always work."

"That's not what you told me when we had sex the first time."

"I said I used them with all my previous boyfriends and never got pregnant." Taking his hands in hers, Melinda squeezed them lightly. "You must have very powerful sperm."

Boulong let out a nervous laugh. "We should go into town right now and get the test kit."

"It's dark outside. Do you really want to risk crossing the Doubs at night?"

"Dark?" Boulong checked his watch. "Wow, I didn't realize it had gotten this late."

"You work in a cave." She frowned. "It's always dark down here. I'm amazed you aren't growing mushrooms behind your ears."

"Any sign of Mookie?"

Melinda shook her head. "Nothing. A couple of boats passed south of the island while I was hanging out by the beach. How is he getting back here?"

"The train will drop him off about twenty miles upriver. There's a public dock in a town not far from the station. Mookie leaves the small rowboat with the outboard motor tied up there when he goes to Paris. He'll float downstream and then use the motor to power around the boulders. I sent him a text about the dock so he'll just beach the boat and pull it ashore."

"Have you checked the train schedule lately?" Melinda pointed at the laptop sitting on the floor next to Boulong's desk. "With all the craziness going on outside, maybe the trains aren't running."

Boulong smiled. "Sweetheart, this is Europe. The trains always run. It's the schedules that need fixing."

He started toward the stairway, but Melinda held him back. "Where are you going?"

"To see if Mikey needs a hand with the cheese."

Unzipping the light jacket she was wearing, Melinda stood and let the garment fall to the dirt floor of the bedroom. She wiggled out of her hot pants and tossed the Mets baseball cap behind her.

"Mikey doesn't need a hand. But I do."

Boulong unbuttoned his shirt and took a few steps toward the bed. Melinda shook her head.

"Uh, uh. Let's get down and dirty tonight." She pushed the chair out of the way and lay down on the hard-packed soil floor. "You're not going upstairs until you make me moo like a cow, squeal like a pig, and soar like an eagle."

Turning to look up the stairs, Boulong took off his shirt and tossed it onto his desk chair. "Did you lock the door?"

. . . . .

It was still dark when the farmer walked outside to the porch. Melinda was snoring so loudly that he could hear her, and Boulong kicked the door closed for some quiet. He'd used a condom this time. Until she was tested, he wasn't taking any more chances. Being a dairy farmer, a pregnant cow was a reason for celebration. A pregnant girlfriend, especially one with strings still tied to home, was a disaster.

It's bad enough living with a grown baby that still needs me to wet nurse him. I can't possibly imagine starting with another one. Maybe I should call her mother back and insist she fly her daughter home. Boulong turned around toward the door. *But I do need another hand right now.* He reversed and walked down the steps into the forest. Moving slowly by the minimal amount of moonlight, he came within twenty yards of the beach and stopped to gaze at the skiff, bobbing in the current. *Where the hell is Mookie? God dammit, I'm gonna have to teach that girl how to run the milking machine, pregnant or not. Just as long as she keeps her hands off the milk.*

Picking up a small stone, Boulong sidearmed it over the rough ground. The rock bounced off a tree, scaring a bird that was watching from a low branch. He grabbed another slightly larger stone and threw it at the bird. It missed. Strolling over to the tree, he found the first rock and threw it again. The stone hit a larger one at the edge of the beach and bounced back into the forest.

Boulong ran over and got the stone while it was still rocking and threw it with all his strength into the Doubs.

And now we're going to lose the hot tub as well. Shit. Look at the dock. Why the hell did someone bomb my dock?

Most of the pilings were intact, but the only boards still horizontal were the two closest to the shore and the very last one over the deep water. A boulder as big as the Gator was wedged next to the third piling, and another one almost as large was sticking out of the water halfway to the end of the dock.

If I frame out the two rocks, I can make enough of a walkway to get to the skiff. We'll have to hand carry the butter and cheese around it, but at least we can get a full load.

Boulong made a finger frame and outlined the project around the obstructions. Turning back toward the house, he pulled a dead limb from a tree and swung it over his head. If he'd had a flag to tie to the stick, it would have definitely displayed a skull and crossbones. He had no idea who attacked his home last night, but he was now a pirate and this was his treasure island. No one was going to steal his Paradise away.

The bird that had been chased off the branch swooped in low and crapped on Boulong's shoulder. He looked up at the winged bomber and laughed. "You'll have to do better than that, my friend." The bird chirped, dove again, and unloaded dead center on the farmer's head.

. . . . .

The President plucked the strings on his new racket. They were much tighter than the old one. He tapped the tennis racket on his knee several times and was pleased with the action. Snatching a fresh ball from the tennis bag embroidered with the Presidential seal, he took a step toward the court.

His phone erupted with "*Hail to the Chief*" and he stopped, turning to look at it. The lock screen displayed the wrinkled face and glimmering crown of his least favorite monarch. The President took another step toward the court, hoping that voicemail would solve the problem.

On the fifth ring, he shoved the ball into the pocket of his sweatpants and answered the phone.

"Lizzy, what's up?"

"Are you mad, Mr. President?"

"Only according to Fox News."

"You bombed Boulong's island?"

The President looked at the phone and squinted. "Who's Boulong?"

"Oh, good Lord." The exasperation in the Queen's voice grew deeper. "Why do you do these things without consulting us, Joseph? You have the political sense of a newt and the patience of a two-year-old."

Yeah? Well you wear a crown, you old fart. "I was told that an American citizen was being held captive."

"Did you affect a rescue, Joseph?"

"The Marines are on their way." The President checked the time. "They should be on the ground in four hours."

A sliver of panic slipped into the Queen's dialog. "You sent the Marines? How many?"

"Just a single platoon."

He could hear keystrokes in the background. The Queen must have been typing on her laptop.

"A platoon, Joseph? You sent an entire platoon of more than forty armed Marines to invade a dairy farmer? Are you out of your mind?" She was shouting now. "Do you know what will happen if they put Boulong out of business? You moron!"

The President scratched his back with the tennis racket. "Who's going to rescue our citizen? Is James Bond available, Lizzy?"

"Abort the mission, Joseph." She blew a long breath into the phone. "Abort it right now or you're not going to play Wimbledon this year."

Oh, shit. "Fine. I'll take care of it."

"Right now, Joseph. I'm not kidding."

"Right now. I promise." The President threw the racket out onto the court. "See you in a few weeks."

"I look forward to it, Mr. President." The Queen ended the call and immediately made another much more important one.

**

At the Marine base in the U.S. Protectorate of Jerusalem, Sergeant Gregory Zumba, newly transferred from Washington, read the secure transmission for the fifth time. Despite the spelling, the message was clear: "Operashun Flintstoned new targit." It was followed by a latitude and longitude that the Sergeant logged into his war computer.

"Paris?" He entered the numbers a second time. "The President wants us to attack the Eiffel Tower?"

Sergeant Zumba had worked for the United States Government long enough to know that you never questioned an order. He corrected the spelling and sent the message, along with the coordinates to Marine platoon Flintstone, airborne over the Med. It took less than ten seconds before he was asked for confirmation.

"Target one is the Eiffel Tower." He typed the reply and hit send.

An unusual second confirmation request hit his screen moments later: "In Paris?"

The Sergeant recalled seeing a smaller version of the famed tourist attraction while he was on leave in Las Vegas. He replied, "Yes. The one in France."

. . . . .

What the Sergeant didn't know was that the President was not a man to back down once he'd made a decision. Regardless of what he'd promised the Queen, the President had decided to flex some of his military muscle. Oh yes, there would be an attack on something. He just had to decide what.

Never having had much success beating French tennis players, the President figured this was a good excuse for revenge. He'd thrown up on his last trip to Paris when the French President insisted they hike instead of taking the elevator to the top of the Eiffel Tower. They were five steps from the end of the forced march when the President's vertigo kicked in. He'd blown chow all over the French President's Air Jordans and twisted his ankle in the expelled goop.

If the Marine platoon was as good as they claimed, they'd topple the Eiffel Tower and he'd never have to climb it again.

Chapter Eight - Take the Tower

Captain Aloysius Crunch had been waiting eighteen months for a promotion. He'd taken enough ribbing about his name for a lifetime. When he discovered boxing as a teen, his last name was a bonus. Back then, the kidding about "Captain Crunch" was done with respect. Even as he moved up through the military ranks and boxing justified his name, junior officers knew better than to mention the breakfast cereal in his presence.

The weight he'd added to his frame was all muscle. Rumors of his ability to punch through a sheet of plywood were verified by dozens of witnesses. But that was so far in the past that no one could remember the thickness of the wood. These days, any new pounds attached themselves to the Captain's expanding waist.

The last few years had been a struggle as new recruits snickered and some of the more weather-beaten soldiers joined in. The leap to Major would put an end to the annoyance and Captain Crunch was willing to do just about anything to make it happen. Dud had done more than just break down gunpowder into dust. Military discipline was also becoming ragged, and it infuriated him.

He read the text again and turned to his aide, slapping the Muskratbox on his knee. "You're sure about these coordinates? That's the freaking Eiffel Tower according to Google Maps."

"Captain, I checked it, the corporal checked it, and we both verified with Jerusalem." Master Sergeant Spinwacker shook his head. "The President of the United States, our Commander-in-Chief, has ordered us to attack the Eiffel Tower."

"I don't get it." Captain Crunch sat back in the webbed seat of the V-22 Osprey and looked out the window. "What are we supposed to do? Attack the tower and bring it down? Does the President want us to capture it intact? Christ on a cracker, am I the only sane person left in the Corps?"

The Master Sergeant stifled his laughter. "Maybe they want to bring it to Arizona and put it next to the London Bridge."

"Do we have torches? Bolt cutters?" The captain turned back to his aide. "How big is the goddamn thing?"

A private sitting across from the Captain leaned in. "What if we just surround it and raise the flag, sir? We can claim it as the property of the United States like we did with Jerusalem."

Captain Crunch pinched the bridge of his nose. "That would be an act of war. Are you ready to go to war, soldier?"

She nodded vigorously. "Yes, sir. Very much so, sir." The other thirty-seven soldiers in the chopper shouted, "Boo rah, Captain!"

"Well, I'm not. So get your shit in order, Marines. We're not going to start World War Three over a tourist attraction." Captain Crunch flipped the cap off his waterproof watch and checked the time. "We should be on the ground at oh-four-twenty. That's less than an hour from now." He handed the satellite phone back to Spinwacker. "Get the Sit Room on the line. I want additional confirmation and clarification of the objective. Have someone drag that hairless tennis player out of bed and confirm if they have to, but I'm not attacking Paris or dismantling the goddamn Eiffel Tower on my own."

·　·　·　·　·

The janitor leaned on his broom and watched the flashing lights on the telephone for a few moments. He'd already taken a couple of calls while he was watching *Family Feud* on the big screen. Only one of the two dozen secure workstations was littered, and it took the janitor less than a minute to tidy up. The nameplate on the back of the padded leather chair said "Zumba" but a black "X" had been drawn through it with a Sharpie that was lying on the seat.

The rest of the White House Situation Room was as clean as it had been when he left the other day. He turned his attention back to the flashing lights, trying to decide which one to answer. Lifting the handset, he closed his eyes and tapped one of the buttons.

"Yo, Situation Room. Who's this?"

"This is Master Sergeant Spinwacker, 3rd Battalion, 7th Marine Regiment, Flintstone Platoon."

Flintstone? "For real?"

"Yes, sir. We request clarification on our mission instructions."

"You're on a mission? Star Fleet send you orders? Where's Captain Kirk?" The janitor covered the phone and laughed out loud.

"Sir?"

"Just screwin' with you, *ese*. Whaddya need?"

"Sir, we've received orders to land in Paris and advance on the Eiffel Tower. Captain Crunch would like to know what we should do when we get there."

Eat breakfast? Who is this guy? "I'd say go up and check out the view. My wife's been bugging me to take her on vacation and she says that Paris is at the top of her bucket list."

"Sir? Who is this?"

"The freakin' President of Mexico, fool."

The janitor could hear yelling and anxious voices over the phone. He put the receiver down on the conference table and changed the channel on the one-hundred-inch flat screen. *Family Feud* was in commercial. ESPN was on the next channel and he brought up the volume to hear their take on the baseball season.

. . . . .

On board the Osprey, Captain Crunch had listened to the conversation and decided that an unknown terrorist or perhaps an army of unknown terrorists, possibly Hispanic, had taken control of the White House and the secure command center. The logic of a first strike on Europe suddenly made sense.

"But why Paris?" Master Sergeant Spinwacker shook his head. "Why not Madrid or Lisbon?"

"Maybe the Spanish have already taken Paris?" Captain Crunch blew out a breath. "We're the first wave." He turned to his platoon. "We may already be at war. Communications have been compromised. The President is ordering a first strike and we are the spearhead."

"Boo rah!" the soldiers shouted.

"The Eiffel Tower is a communications beacon for most of France. If it's been captured by enemy forces, then all messages, even the secure ones, are suspect." Turning to the Master Sergeant, Captain Crunch's face hardened. "We are only a single platoon against the entire French, perhaps a combined European Army. But we are Marines and Marines don't count live bodies, we count dead ones."

"Boo rah, Captain!" the soldiers screamed.

Captain Crunch stood, smacking his head on the ceiling of the helicopter, and folded his arms across his chest. "Our mission is to destroy a valuable military target that's fallen into the enemy's hands. We shall not fail!"

Master Sergeant Spinwacker joined the Captain. "Lock and load, ladies. This one's for the Corps!"

· · · · ·

The janitor took another call from an irate politician who kept saying he was a close ally of the President and the senior Representative on the Arms Committee. The janitor told the politician that he was the senior broom pusher and the man could kiss his ass.

He answered one more call, hoping it would be that Colonel with the weird accent. The janitor wanted to know how things were going with the Mexican banda gangs. But it was a wrong number. At least that's what the woman on the other end of the line said before she hung up.

ESPN went to commercial break, so the janitor switched back to *Family Feud*. His television at home was on the fritz again, and the Mets were playing the Nationals at three o'clock. He punched a free telephone line and ordered a pizza. Maybe he'd call his wife and ask her to come down there to watch with him. The janitor shook his head. He decided to call his girlfriend instead. At least she understood the difference between a ball and a strike.

· · · · ·

The Osprey loaded with battle-hungry Marines set down in the middle of the Avenue Gustave Eiffel, the tower's namesake. It would be dawn in another hour and they used the cover of darkness to surround the structure. While it was on the ground, the Marines loaded the chopper with paving stones from the roadway. The blocks were small, but they were solid granite and would be useful to keep attackers at bay. Two of the Marines went aloft with the helicopter to act as bombardiers.

Resistance was light. The Marines captured four street sweepers, a newspaper delivery van, and a Paris cop who was on his way home from his shift and stopped to take a piss in the bushes. Repairs to the avenue had closed it to traffic. Collecting orange safety cones from the construction site, the Marines widened the detour to include all the adjacent streets.

The structure itself was sealed for the night and all the entrances padlocked. One of the soldiers broke into a parked Citroen and found the tire jack. They used it to snap two of the locks and pry open the metal doors. A private with some electrical knowledge found the panel that controlled the elevators and activated them. Unfortunately, as she was flipping breakers, the private accidentally turned on the spotlights for a few seconds.

In less than a minute, Parisian police had converged on the Eiffel Tower. They approached the monument with crossbows drawn, but were pummeled with paving stones from the helicopter that had been hovering just out of sight. As the police retreated, the Marines squeezed into the elevators and rode to the upper observation deck.

Captain Crunch was the first off, swinging his crossbow left and right in search of a target. Of course, the deck was empty, and the Marines rushed from the elevator to take up strategic positions.

"Hell of a view from up here." Master Sergeant Spinwacker pulled his binoculars from his rucksack and surveyed the city. "I don't see any enemy activity."

A private standing next to him shrugged. "Maybe they're all still asleep, sir."

"No sentries? No armored vehicles?" The Master Sergeant shook his head. "I don't like this."

Taking the field glasses from his hand, Captain Crunch walked around the observation platform, checking in all directions.

"Nothing." He handed the binoculars to Spinwacker. "There are lots of blue flashing lights heading toward us, but nothing else."

Two privates marched over and saluted. They had the four street sweepers in tie-wrap restraints and blindfolds. Their brooms and spiked litter poles had been tossed over the side, leaving them without weapons. They'd bound the peeing police officer to a girder at the base of the tower and sent the newspaper delivery man on his way. The Marines had no interest in unarmed civilians.

"We questioned them in English, but they only speak French, Captain."

Captain Crunch smacked his forehead. "What did you expect? Cajun? He shouted to the other soldiers. "Anyone here speak French?"

A corporal stepped forward and saluted. "I had a few years of it in high school, sir."

"Good." The Captain grabbed the woman by the wrist. "Come over and talk to these people. Ask where the invading army is billeted."

The private twisted her lips and looked up at the sky. "I don't know any of those words, sir."

Captain Crunch put his hands on his hips and shook his head slowly. "What can you ask them?"

Walking over to the captives, the private folded her arms across her chest. *"Voulez-vous coucher avec moi ce soir?"*

The four men chuckled. One of them said, *"Oui."*

"What did you ask them?" the Captain whispered.

"I don't know. It's the only full sentence I remember." She blushed. "I think it has something to do with sleeping, though."

Master Sergeant Spinwacker laughed. "I'm not sure what you asked him, but he said, 'yes' in response."

"Yes?" Captain Crunch leaned close to his prisoner. "Yes, what?"

The man said nothing and so the Captain asked again.

"What are you agreeing to? Surrender?"

Just then the lights came back on. The Eiffel Tower was lit up as though it was Christmas Eve and Santa was homing in on Paris. The Marines all ducked for cover. Several of them fired bolts into the nearest lights, shrouding the observation deck in darkness. Silently, the elevator doors slid shut and the empty lifts began their descent to street level.

Captain Crunch looked down at the growing mass of police cars and grabbed his cellphone from his belt. His first call was to the Situation Room. He let the phone ring ten times without an answer before he tried the number again. Next, he sent a text to the Marine Command Center in Jerusalem, telling them that his platoon was under attack and he needed reinforcements.

Sergeant Zumba, the only officer on duty at the time, was in the men's room trying to figure out which of the snacks he'd consumed over the past day had given him cramps. He'd left his secure phone on the console and wouldn't see the Captain's text for almost an hour.

Walking around to a private location on the observation deck, the Captain's last call was to his mother's house. He told her that he loved her and that he might not be coming home. It was the middle of the night in Los Angeles and his mother was asleep. His call went to voicemail along with all the others the eighty-one-year-old woman had never heard.

With the necessary communications completed, Captain Crunch put his cellphone on the metal deck of the observation platform and pierced it with his sword. They might take him alive, but they'd never get any secret information from his telephone.

Chapter Nine - Production

Sliding off the metal bench, Mookie rubbed the knot in the back of his head. The hooker who'd conked him with a pipe had taken his wallet, his cellphone, and his shoes. Fragrances of urine and sweat overwhelmed his cologne, and he tried to remember what had transpired the previous evening after he'd fallen down the stairs from her second-floor apartment.

Reeking from sex and cheap wine, Mookie had stumbled barefoot into a liquor store and begged the shopkeeper in French to call the police. The wary storeowner pulled a baseball bat from under the counter and chased what he thought was a bum out to the street.

Mookie grabbed the bat from the man's hand just as he reached the sidewalk and came around with a home-run swing that knocked the man out. Going back into the liquor store, he ran for the cooler in the back and popped the top of a forty-ounce malt liquor. He was going to take the cash from the register, but a passing bus driver saw the assault and called the police. Mookie was arrested as he stepped over the unconscious shopkeeper on the sidewalk.

With no means of identification and no phone to call for help, the boy spent the night in the local jail and was scheduled to appear before a magistrate on Monday. He stuck his head under the faucet in his cell and washed the grime of the Parisian streets from his face. It wasn't his first visit to the lockup, and it probably wouldn't be his last.

. . . . .

Back in Paradise, the sun had long since risen, and Boulong was in the barn milking cows. Melinda came in with a tray of peanut butter and jelly sandwiches and placed it on the workbench.

"Mikey just called. He's on his way back in the skiff and said that Mookie's boat is still tied up where he left it."

"Shit." Boulong yanked the tubes off the cow's udder a bit too quickly and the beast let out an anguished "Moo."

"I can help you, Bouly." She bit her lip and raised her eyebrows. "I'm not as stupid as you think."

"No one ever said you were stupid, Melinda."

"Then why haven't you showed me how to use this stuff and make your job easier?"

Boulong led the cow over to the indoor pen and pushed it in. "Bad luck."

"What?"

"It's bad luck to let a woman handle the cow's milk."

"That's bullshit." Melinda walked over and petted the cow. "Who told you that?"

"My father, who heard it from my grandfather, who was told in no uncertain terms by my great-grandfather that if a woman touches fresh cow's milk it will curdle."

"And you believed him?"

Nodding, Boulong opened the valve that would send the fresh milk into the processor. He set a temperature control and flipped four switches. "My ex-wife came into the barn once while I was in the bathroom. We'd just finished milking ten cows, and the vat was filled to overflowing. She climbed up the ladder over there and stuck her finger in to have a taste."

"She'd never had fresh cow's milk before?"

"Uh, uh."

"I thought you said she grew up on a farm." Melinda cocked her head to one side. "How can you grow up on a farm and never have fresh milk?"

"When the farm grows only wheat and corn." Stepping between Melinda and the milk vat, Boulong reached up and snapped the cover closed. "I came out of the bathroom while she was still on the ladder. I asked Sabrina if she'd touched the milk and she smiled and then wiped her mouth with the back of her hand."

"She did it?"

"Yep. And the entire vat was spoiled. The butter wouldn't congeal. The cheese spread was hard and flaky. And the blocks of cheese went moldy, almost overnight."

Melinda frowned. "And you think it was because she stuck a finger in there? Oh, Bouly, you really have shit for brains. Look, pour off some milk from that vat into a bucket and let me touch it. If it curdles like you said, I'll believe you. But if nothing happens, then I think you should let me help with the production...at least until Mookie returns."

"You're asking a lot of me."

"Hey, you knocked me up. It's the least you can do."

Boulong shook his head. "Possibly knocked you up, sweetheart."

"Well, possibly or not, you should trust science and not some family bullshit."

"If it's bullshit, how do you explain what happened with Sabrina?"

Melinda winked at him. "Maybe she was a witch."

. . . . .

Word of the capture of his Swiss Guards was given to the Pope on Sunday morning just before Mass. From behind his sealed chamber doors, several bishops were able to make out phrases in German that should never have been used by His Holiness. When the Pope opened the doors and waved them in, he was breathing heavily and his face was flushed. A broken shotglass lay on the floor by the Papal desk.

"Trained by the Israeli Mossad. Hardened in the Iraqi desert. The most able swordsmen in the world." The Pope wrung his hands. "How in God's name were they captured?" He spun on his heel and glared at the bishops. "And by the French, of all people? *Gott in himmel.*"

The eldest of the bishops stepped forward. "Shall we send reinforcements, your Grace?"

The Bishop of Rome, the head of the Catholic Church, the only German in the room, looked at the man and shook his head once. "No. I will call someone after Mass." He looked at his watch. "Perhaps Mass will be a few minutes late this morning. Go tell the organist to play a bit longer."

Without another word, the Pope turned and walked over to his balcony. The group of bishops filed out, closing the heavy doors behind them. Hearing the thud and latch, Pope Victor snatched his cellphone from beneath his robes and pulled up his Contacts.

Christ, I hope she's up this early.

. . . . .

Queen Elizabeth answered the phone on the second ring. She looked at the digital clock on her nightstand before checking the caller ID on the phone.

"For the love of God, Victor, it's not yet seven o'clock in the morning."

"Liz, you know I would never call you this early on a Sunday if it wasn't of the greatest importance."

"To me, you, the Church, or all of us?"

"Let's start with peace on earth."

The Queen reached over and tapped the button to open the massive embroidered curtains across the room. "Did a war start overnight?"

"No, but tensions are high in France."

"Boulong?"

"Yes."

"Relax. I sent someone to handle it."

The Pope opened his mouth to speak but covered it with his free hand. He tiptoed over to the doors and leaned against them to make sure he was not being overheard. Quickly, he crossed to the opposite side of the room and whispered, "She's back?"

"Yes. Fully recovered."

"The leg?"

"A new knee and lots of rehab. Her doctors tell me that she ran a five-minute mile the other day." Reaching for the nearest lamp, the Queen of England lit up her room and slid from under the light summer blanket. "Your boys are sitting in some serious shit up there, Victor. I don't know why you sent them without calling me first. I'm going to solve this problem for all of us. But you're going to owe me, Victor."

"The Good Lord shall provide."

"No, Victor. This one's on you."

"Christ, Liz, I'm already into you for a Ferrari. What else could you want?"

The Queen smiled. "Give me the morning to come up with something, your Holiness. You know I don't blackmail so well before breakfast." She ended the call and rang the bell for her lady-in-waiting. It was way too early for solid food. At this hour, she needed gin.

. . . . .

Inez Trusk stood on the balcony of her room and focused the high-powered binoculars on the tiny island. The bed-and-breakfast on the side of Mount Racine in Switzerland would have been a perfect sniper's perch if not for Dud. Even the compound bow she'd restrung that morning was useless beyond a thousand yards.

If she was going to be successful, the hired killer was going to have to get up close and personal with her targets.

Bending down, Inez smoothed the Velcro knee brace and pulled her ski pants down to cover it. They were baggy, but they hid the bulge. She shot a few pictures through the binoculars before folding them and stuffing them into her backpack. Closing and locking the patio doors behind her, Inez slid the bow into its silk sheath and pulled the string to close the end.

Grabbing an extra bottle of water from the mini fridge in the room, she left the six-room inn and headed down the mountain on foot.

· · · · ·

It had been early morning when Boulong had filled a bucket with one gallon of fresh cow's milk and handed it to Melinda. She'd dunked her hand into it, up to her wrist, and then filled a red Solo cup to the brim.

"It's warm." Was her first comment. "But more creamy than I've ever tasted." She finished the cup and filled it again.

"You probably don't remember the taste of being breastfed."

Melinda thought about her mother and laughed. "Her boyfriend is the only one sucking on those tits."

· · · · ·

Nothing happened to the bucket of milk. It was almost lunchtime, and the liquid looked exactly the same as when he'd filled the container. Out of an abundance of caution, Boulong put the milk in the large refrigerator and labeled it "Melinda's" to make sure it wasn't used for their production. He tried Mookie's cellphone several times while they worked, the span between attempts growing longer.

Between Mikey, Melinda, and himself, they processed three-quarters of what would normally be handled by Boulong and his boys. It was too late to cook a proper Sunday dinner, so they decided to have a cookout down by the beach. Mikey got a small fire going. Boulong carried a tray with hot dogs, buns, mustard, and ketchup. Slicing a head of lettuce into three chunks, Melinda followed behind with her "salad" and every bottle of dressing she could find in the kitchen.

They were sliding the hot dogs onto improvised skewers when the first arrow slammed into the package in Boulong's hand.

. . . . .

Inez had hiked the three miles only to find that the river was impassable. Even with a speedboat, the current was too fast and there were too many boulders. She turned and hiked back up the mountain until she could see the fire on the far side. According to her scope, it was nine-hundred yards away.

Slipping the high-powered bow out of its silk condom, she unlocked the mechanism and set the pulleys. The arrows she pulled out of the sack were designed to be accurate to within one-inch at a thousand yards. Inez mounted the scope and adjusted for the distance and slight wind coming from her left. She braced herself against a granite boulder and let the arrow fly.

. . . . .

"Get down!" Boulong dropped the hot dogs, package and all, into the fire and grabbed Melinda.

The second arrow splintered one of Mikey's crutches and embedded itself in his calf. He screamed and pulled the arrow out, falling to the ground in worse pain than his last root canal.

Boulong pushed Melinda to the ground behind a large evergreen and crawled over to his injured son. "Who the hell is shooting at us?" He locked his hand around Mikey's elbow and dragged him to the safety of the forest next to his girlfriend.

"Someone who doesn't like ketchup on a hot dog?" Mikey held the two largest pieces of his crutch up in the air. "Someone who doesn't like wooden crutches?"

. . . . .

Inez looked up at the sky again. *What the hell is that?*

She wouldn't live long enough to ask again as a boulder of magnificent pink granite the size of a side-by-side refrigerator smashed into her skull and ended a most successful career.

. . . . .

Boulong looked up at the sky and pointed. "Do you see that?"

"See what?" Melinda and Mikey asked in unison.

"That black thing. Like a moving darkness." Boulong followed the black image with his finger until it disappeared over the horizon.

Melinda shook her head. "I saw something, or maybe I saw nothing. Maybe it's where the arrows came from."

"No. The arrows came from the Swiss side. Had to be shot from the western slope of Mount Racine." Boulong slid up the trunk of the evergreen and peeked around it. "I don't see anyone, but they have bows that shoot an arrow over a thousand yards."

"So what do we do? Sit here and wait until whoever is shooting at us tries again?" Melinda wrapped her sweater tightly around her shoulders. "It's getting cold."

Mikey stood up and nodded. "Let's give the shooter a target and see what happens."

"Get the hell down here." Boulong grabbed his son's arm and pulled him to safety. "Let's just sit here for a few minutes and see what happens. There's no way for the shooter to get across the Doubs. If nothing happens, we can make our way through the forest to the house. I have a compound bow in my office with a laser sight on it. It's accurate to eight-hundred yards. If the shooter comes close enough, I can hit him."

"What about Mookie?" Looking out at the river, Mikey tried to see across in the dark. "What if he comes floating in and the shooter is still out there?"

Boulong put his hand under his chin and sighed. "Let's hope I can shoot first."

Chapter Ten - Something Smells

Sadly for Inez Trusk, she was not trying to kill Boulong and his cohorts. Her orders were to scare them off the island so that a peaceful invasion could take over the land and control the dairy production. Her first shot—into the package of hot dogs—was perfect. She had aimed for the package away from Boulong's hand and was dead center on the middle hot dog. The second arrow was supposed to flip the crutch out of Mikey's hands but he must have had all his weight on it, so the arrow simply split it in two and then embedded itself in his thigh.

The pilot of the stealth bomber had returned on a surveillance mission and caught a glint of moonlight off the metal pulleys of the assassin's compound bow. Using her infrared radar, she watched as the image fired two arrows at the island and decided to eliminate the threat. She sent video of the mission back to the NSA and noted that the infrared went dark after the boulder had been launched. The pilot messaged that she would mark it up as a kill.

Boulong, Melinda, and Mikey waited for over an hour in the cold to see if the attack would continue. When nothing happened, Mikey got up first, covering the wound on his thigh with his hand, and hobbled to the house. He waved from the porch and went inside. Boulong and Melinda followed him. They held hands at the start and then Boulong sprinted away, yelling, "Serpentine!"

"What?" Melinda stopped next to a tree and shrugged. "What did you say?"

"Serpentine. Run in a zigzag pattern. It makes it harder for someone to shoot you."

"You're really crazy, Bouly." Nonetheless, Melinda sprinted from side-to-side until she crashed into a bush.

Once inside the house, the trio ran around locking windows and moving the heaviest furniture in front of the two doors. It was after midnight when they all slipped downstairs, locking the door behind them.

Mikey went to sleep on the couch in his father's office. Boulong and his girlfriend got into bed fully dressed. Each of them slid a hunting knife under their pillow, and Boulong had stood his loaded crossbow next to the bed.

. . . . .

Hundreds of miles away in Paris, Mookie finally convinced a fellow inmate that he was indeed the son of the famous Boulong, the dairy farmer. The chap, who worked as a sous chef, had been arrested as he attempted to break into a neighbor's house under the influence of seven pints of ale. He'd spent most of the day in a bar after finding out his wife was leaving him for a position in the London Zoo...and the head zookeeper.

Not having the faculties to select the correct residence or find his keys, he'd smashed a window in the rear door and assaulted the homeowner with a broom. His luck was running downhill at an increasing pace. The homeowner was an off-duty security guard armed with a Taser and shocked the man into unconsciousness.

Lucky enough to have a brother who was a lawyer that orchestrated his immediate release, the now-sober fellow told his attorney about the famous cheese spread and said they should help the kid get home. Mookie gave the lawyer Boulong's private cell number and waited while he placed the call.

Unfortunately, Boulong's phone was upstairs in the kitchen being charged. With the heavy cellar door closed and Melinda snoring louder than a pen of farting bulls, no one besides a mouse who lived behind the refrigerator heard it ring.

. . . . .

Not more than three miles from where Mookie sat cursing his father, his brother, the stench in the cell, and the woman who'd seemed so friendly just hours prior, the Marines were searching for food. They'd broken into the concession stands and ransacked their dry storage. Piles of candy bars, bags of granola, and tubes of breath mints were sorted and distributed to the platoon.

A group of soldiers were huddled over a trash can that they'd inverted to use as a cooker. They'd made a tiny fire in the concave base and were mashing jelly beans into their military-issued mac and cheese MREs when the elevator doors began to rumble.

"They're coming back up!" shouted one of the Marines.

Captain Crunch ran over and kicked their improvised kitchen out of the way. He put his hand on the door and turned to the platoon. "Take cover and make every shot count. This is not a goddamn practice field, ladies."

The elevators on the opposite side of the observation deck showed signs of life, and the Marines on that section of the platform spread the alert. Master Sergeant Spinwacker split the platoon into two fire teams arranged in semi-circles in front of the approaching elevators.

The soldiers released the safeties on their crossbows and opened the Velcro wrist pouches that held spare bolts. All four of the archers took positions on the upper platform where they could shoot directly down on the enemy. Captain Crunch pulled his sword from its scabbard and held it above his head, Andrew Jackson style.

Silently counting the digital numbers as the elevators approached, the Marines focused on their mission and the pending attack. The sounds of the city waking up were muted. Sirens from the phalanx of Parisian Police still rushing to the Tower were silenced in their ears. All eyes were on the eight gleaming metal doors.

Motors stopped.

Chimes jingled.

The eight doors opened simultaneously.

Trigger fingers tightened and the Marines let out the breaths they'd been holding. Expert marksmen one and all, they would have decimated their targets if they hadn't been aiming too high.

Hundreds of skunks poured out of the elevators. It was a river of black and white fur that scurried and chittered over the polished metal floor of the observation deck. Many of the animals had already sprayed the elevators with their hideous cologne. The rest of them unleashed a gas attack that would gag a maggot.

Captain Crunch looked down at the floor and screamed, "Fire!" Three dozen of the tiny attackers fell dead. The bolts pinned them to the floor where, in their last "up yours" to humans, they dumped the balance of their malodorous scent glands. Sensing that trouble was upon them, the rest of the skunks increased their spraying as well, and within seconds, the observation deck was awash in a stench that would choke an outhouse cleaner.

No one thought to put gas masks into their packs for this mission. After all, they were invading Paris, not some third-world country. The Marines scrambled to cover their mouths and noses, but the odor was far too pungent. They ran for the stairs to the upper deck, but the skunks followed them. Being smaller and not overcome by the smell, the little creatures beat the Marines up the stairs, unloading their natural protection behind them as they ran.

Blindness hit first, followed by nausea that brought up all the candy bars, granola, and breath mints the Marines had taken from the concessionaires. (Strangely, the MREs mixed with the mashed jelly beans stayed down.) Falling to the deck, the soldiers gasped for air but only sucked in more skunk cologne as the liquid excreted from the animals formed puddles on the metal deck.

· · · · ·

None of the Marines noticed the elevator doors close. Those who were still conscious were more concerned with breathing and getting away from the horrible smell. They were the only ones who saw the helicopters float up to their level and tilt sideways to clear the air, blowing the skunk scum over the side.

The elevators returned moments after the helicopters departed. Fifty Parisian police protected by gas masks and armed with Tasers, crossbows, and clubs pounded onto the observation deck. The cops placed the 3rd Battalion, 7th Marine Regiment, Flintstone Platoon under arrest without a fight.

At least for now, the Eiffel Tower was safe.

· · · · ·

Mookie and his fellow inmates had been moved to a holding area just before the aromatic assault on the Marines. When word came down that all hands were needed to defend the Eiffel Tower, the three prisoners were shackled together and left alone.

"They're gone?" a one-armed taxi driver asked. He'd run a red light and smashed into a police car. Drunk when he'd been arrested, the taxi driver had sobered up and was sporting a large knot in his forehead where he'd hit the steering wheel.

Mookie leaned around the corner. "Yeah. No one's here. What the hell is going on?"

"Dem say, Eiffel Tower under attack." The Jamaican kid was a week short of nineteen and still pissed off about the shit with his girlfriend. She could have left his stuff in her apartment until he had a chance to get it out. But no, his shit went out the window as he was leaving for work. He'd broken down the door to her apartment but forgot that her neighbor was a cop. His knuckles still hurt where he'd gotten in one good shot to the cop's jaw.

"We need the key for these padlocks." Standing up from their bench, Mookie dragged his companions with him.

"Mon, slow down." Jamaica's foot was caught under the bench. He pulled it free and stuck a finger in Mookie's face. "I comin'. Ain't no race, white bread."

The trio shuffled over to a desk on the other side of the room and dug through the drawers with no luck. They made their way to a coat rack and riffled the pockets. Cigarettes, lighters, car keys, and condoms were all they found.

"I hear sirens!" Taxi driver pointed toward the door. "They're coming back."

"They don't use the siren to return to headquarters, you idiot." Mookie rubbed his lower back with his knuckles. He couldn't wait to get back to Paradise and soak in the hot tub.

The taxi driver grabbed the ring of car keys. "Let's go. I'll drive."

"Drive what?" asked Mookie.

"Whatever this key fob unlocks." He dragged his foot toward the door. "Let's go, before they come back."

· · · · ·

Squished into the two-person front seat of a Mini Cooper with the taxi driver at the wheel, Mookie and his companions were crossing the Seine and headed east when the front tire blew out. Still shackled together at their ankles, they got out of the overpriced clown car on the passenger side and were trying to wrestle the donut tire out from its mount when a plumber in his work truck pulled in behind them.

"You gentlemen seem to have a very unique problem."

Mookie smiled, pointing at the Jamaican kid. "We're on our way home from a costume party and shithead over here lost the key to these shackles."

The plumber laughed and walked back to his truck. He returned with a bolt cutter and in seconds had separated the three men. "Whose Mini?"

"His." Mookie nodded toward the taxi driver. "My son here isn't old enough to drive."

"Your son?" The plumber squinted at the boy.

"Adopted, mon." Putting his arm around Mookie's shoulder, the kid pulled him close and grinned. "For real."

"You guys know how to change the tire on a Mini Cooper?"

The taxi driver shrugged. "Same as any other car."

"Uh, uh." Walking over to the driver's side, the plumber opened the door. Bending down, he lifted a small lever tucked alongside the driver's seat. "This releases the donut." The fake tire dropped from its perch, clattering onto the Belgian block roadway.

Mookie grabbed the tire and walked around to the flat. "Bring the jack, someone."

The Jamaican teen looked at the taxi driver, who turned with an upraised palm toward the plumber.

"Open the hatch and lift the ring on the floor. It's underneath." Walking over to the one-armed taxi driver, the plumber scratched the back of his neck. "How long have you had this car?"

"Oh, it's brand new." Leaning against the car, the one-armed taxi driver pulled a cigarette out of the pack he'd found in the police station. He slipped it between his lips and lit it with a stolen disposable.

"It's a model from five years ago." The plumber took a step back and shook his head. "Six years ago. It's not brand new."

"Brand new used. I just got it last weekend from a dealer. It's brand new to me, okay?" Taking a deep drag on the cigarette, the taxi driver blew the smoke over the plumber's head.

"Well, looks like this brand new used car needs some brand new tires." Kneeling, the plumber stuck his fingernail in the grooves of the closest tire. "I'd say before the cold weather gets here, especially if you're heading toward the mountains."

A helicopter passed overhead, flying toward the Eiffel Tower. More sirens in the distance and behind them, the dawn was arriving.

"I'd help you with changing the tire, but I'm on my way to a flooded toilet emergency." A gust of wind hit and the plumber stuck his nose in the air. "Skunk. Phew. Smells like we're standing on its back."

Mookie picked up the odor. "Jesus. I'll bet one of those cop cars ran it over."

The plumber walked back to his truck. "Good luck, gentlemen." He hopped inside, rolled up the window, and left.

Yanking the tire jack from the back of the Mini Cooper, the Jamaican boy set it up and cranked the dead tire off the ground. In less time than it took to steal the car, he'd switched tires and thrown the flat over the side of the bridge into the

Seine. He took the backseat of the car to himself and stretched out with his hands behind his head.

"Where we goin', mon?"

"East toward Switzerland." Mookie got in on the driver's side and pushed open the passenger door for the taxi driver with his foot. "Get in. I know the way."

Chapter Eleven - Tikopango

Corporal Tsunami pulled into the General's driveway and cut the engine. The usual group of news media was much larger than normal. He considered driving the Escalade into the garage, but it was too big to fit.

"What the hell is going on?" General Purpose slinked down in the seat. "Did the President lose a match?"

"I think it's worse than that, sir."

A reporter walked over and tapped on the rear window. The General lowered it several inches.

"The White House is saying you've declared war on Mexico. Would you care to comment, General?"

War against Mexico? Is he kidding? "I don't have the power to declare war on anyone. That's the responsibility of the Congress."

Another reporter shoved a microphone into the General's face. "Did you personally deliver an atomic bomb to the Mexican President?"

A bomb? The Mexicans have an atom bomb? "No. And I have no knowledge of such an exchange."

The first reporter picked up the line of questioning. "There's a report out of Washington that scientists have figured out a way to trigger an atomic weapon without using explosives. Would you care to comment on that, sir?"

"I don't believe it." *Am I supposed to believe it?* "Dud destroyed all the nuclear triggers. We saw that yesterday in New York when terrorists tried to explode their devices inside Macy's and failed."

Just then, Tanya came running out of the house. She was wearing a bikini that covered very little and red cowboy boots. She had a crossbow in one hand and a hunting knife in the other. The reporters scattered, thinking that it was an attack.

The diminutive pole dancer climbed onto the running board of the Escalade and shouted to the General through the crack of the open window.

"They tried to chase me out of the house!"

"Who?" General Purpose slid over in the seat but kept the door closed and locked.

"Soldiers." She dropped the crossbow and tried to stick the knife into the door lock. "They came about an hour ago and said I had to leave."

"Hmmm." He lowered the window and reached for the knife. "Give me that. You're going to scratch the paint."

"Let me in." Tanya reached inside with her free hand and groped for the door handle.

"First, tell me you're not pregnant."

"You want me to lie to you?"

"No. I want the truth." The General grabbed the knife out of her hand. "Yes or no. Are you pregnant?"

"Yes, but it's not your baby."

. . . . .

Tikopango is an island in the South Pacific Ocean in-between the "E" and the "A" of OCEAN on a standard sixteen-inch, Rand McNally globe. It's seventeen miles long and eleven miles wide in the middle of the oval-shaped atoll. Originally part of a chain of volcanoes, the caldera has become a fresh-water lake that's fed by an underground spring.

Coconut palms and Ironwood trees taller than a house ring the lake and passing frigate birds drink from its crystal clear water. The leeward side of the atoll has a beach that would rival any stretch in Cancun. It's protected by a coral reef, impassible by most vessels. High cliffs on the windward side drop into the ocean and protect the island from storms.

At last count, sixty-two Tikos lived together in a community of very large huts on the island. The humans shared the water and the land with over a thousand head of cattle, hundreds of goats, and a family of blue macaws that moved from hut to hut with the phases of the moon. Friendly birds, they would sit by the doorway and beg for table scraps, never entering a hut or pooping on the doorstep when they were done.

A large statue of a woman, naked except for aviator's goggles, stood next to the Tiko's common meeting hall. It had been hand-carved out of a dead Ironwood tree and colored with berries from a local bush. Special attention had been paid to the areolas and nipples. They were the only part of the idol that appeared to have constant maintenance. The natives worshipped their goddess and called her "Aheart." It was rumored that the artist and the image were one and the same.

. . . . .

Dutch sailors discovered the island in the 1600s and traded cows for fresh water. The original six cows and one bull were seen as deities by the Tikos. The beasts wore headdresses made from palm fronds and collars with seashells that tinkled as they walked. The Dutch instructed the Tikos in milking techniques but never said a word about butter or cheese.

Several years later, a British Man-of-War chased a Dutch trading vessel from Jakarta, across the South China Sea, and sunk it within sight of Tikopango. The British sailors traded their dress uniforms for fresh water and milk. A dairy farmer who'd been conscripted into service showed the Tikos how to churn the cream into butter and the curds into cheese.

. . . . .

Passing centuries brought more visitors to the island, even though it never made its way onto a map. With the advent of transpacific yachts, the atoll became a fashionable stopping point on the way across the ocean. The Tikos were always well-dressed in their red and white military uniforms when they catered to their wealthy guests. Clothing optional was the only dress code on Tikopango when the islanders were alone, and they stripped off the silly garments moments after their visitors departed.

A large thatched concession stand was erected on the beach, and the CEO of a solar cell company gave power to the Tikos at his expense. The neon "OPEN" sign was a gift from the owner of a novelty shop in Hong Kong who sailed across the Pacific twice a year. His first mate was also an electrician and wired the sign to a switch that the Tikos could flip on or off as they saw fit. He replaced the device every time the yacht docked at the island.

The Tikos kept the flags of more than a dozen nations flying from palm trees, but only the Jolly Roger flew above their beachfront store. It was a gift from Walt Disney, who visited the island in the 1960s just prior to his death. Most of the manmade landscape used in Pirates of the Caribbean was inspired by drawings he'd made of the lush tropical atoll. The flag flew upside down for decades until a Hollywood movie producer insisted they right it for a short film he was shooting.

Cruise ships bypassed the atoll due to its lack of a t-shirt shop and duty-free liquor store. The British Man-of-War was the last military vessel to anchor there. Battles between the Japanese and the Allies missed the area by hundreds of miles. If not for wealthy yacht owners and word-of-mouth, the Tikos would never have known the outside world existed.

When it rained on the island, the people would sit in the beachside store and read newspapers and magazines that were dropped off by their visitors. It wasn't unusual to find the latest issue of *Architectural Digest, The Robb Report,* or the *Sydney Times* in a Tiko's hands. English was spoken as often as Dutch, and several of the locals had learned French. They read *Le Monde* and only answered *oui* or *non* to simple questions.

The Tikos had a well-balanced diet of beef, fish, fresh vegetables, and a lifestyle that pulled the rich and famous to their shores.

They also had some of the finest cheese spread south of the equator.

The Dutch had brought Gouda, which none of the Tikos favored. It was hard. It had a sharp taste that didn't work at all with coconut. After the Dutch ship departed, they cut the cheese into bite-size pieces and fed it to the macaws.

So, when the British dairy farmer first mentioned cheese, the Tikos turned him down, thinking it was the same crap (yes, they used the word "crap") cheese they'd already tried. But the farmer's recipe yielded a soft, spreadable product that was perfect on the biscuits the Tikos baked from coconut flour. Aheart was pleased.

The volcanic soil was rich in the same minerals that enhanced the grass on Boulong's island on the opposite side of the globe. Giant pterodactyls, a frigate bird's great-ancestor, had fished in the caldera's lake and crapped on its shores. The effect, over the millennia, was happy cows and gourmet cheese spread.

Tikos perfected the soft cheese spread and discovered that the deep waters of the lake were cold enough to keep it fresh. They wrapped coconut shells filled with the cheese in palm fronds and dunked them in the water inside nets. At any given time, the Tikos had several hundred pounds on hand to sell to their visitors.

The cheese was sold on the condition of secrecy. Even an uneducated South Pacific islander knew when it was best to keep something that tasty under wraps. Cooks who made it to the island were sold no more than six shells of cheese, regardless of price. New visitors to Tikopango had to name a prior customer in order to even taste the Tiko's cheese spread.

However, once they began operating the Tiko Hut with its orange neon OPEN sign that could be seen from a mile offshore, the secret of the Tiko's delicious spreadable cheese melted faster than a pound of butter on a hot sidewalk.

. . . . .

When the culinary world loses out on a delicacy, chefs will scour the planet looking for a replacement. Three days after Boulong ran out of cheese, a yacht staffed by a crew of sixteen, with a helicopter and four jet skis mounted on an upper deck, dropped anchor off the beach at Tikopango. The captain came ashore in a rubber Zodiac with the ship's owner—a Wall Street investor from California who loved to cook.

The owner spent half an hour inside the Tiko Hut while the neon sign was turned off in the middle of the day. He walked out and whistled to the captain, who was waiting with an ice-filled cooler. Together, the investor and the captain carried the sixty pounds of cheese spread back to the rubber boat and left.

The investor's satellite phone call to a fellow cook in San Diego began the invasion of the tiny island forty-eight hours later. Knowing that his money would only buy the six-shell limit, the investor had brought something of much greater value to the Tikos: a case of twenty-four dozen propane-filled, heavy-duty charcoal fire igniters. Their days of flicking tiny Bics, rubbing sticks, or waiting for lightning were over. A reliable source of instant fire was now in their hands.

. . . . .

The seaplane came over the mountains from the windward side of Tikopango. It panicked the cows and brought every Tiko to their knees. None of them had been alive when the last aircraft had landed on the island, but they'd heard the legends.

Dipping its wings left and then right, the plane banked hard and buzzed the Tiko Hut. It flew away from the atoll and the Tikos stood staring at its shrinking image. Then it turned and began an approach, closing in on the surf beyond the coral reef.

The aircraft's only color other than the glass windshield was black, and even that was deeply tinted. It cleared the reef with inches to spare and touched down less than twenty yards off the beach. The Tikos ran for cover, thinking that it was going to crash, but at the last moment, the pilot spun the plane around in a half-circle and cut the engine.

Older members of the clan chanted, "Aheart, Aheart" and urged their neighbors to join in. A teenage girl ran naked to the shoreline and held her arms in the air. At the urging of King President Vatu, a pair of men sprinted to the lake and returned with their arms full of coconut shells, dripping and still wrapped in palm fronds.

The seaplane's door opened upward and locked in position. Ducking his head so as not to smack into it again, the pilot stepped onto the pontoon and shielded his eyes against the sun.

"Is this really Tikopango?"

· · · · ·

The General opened the door and grabbed Tanya by the wrist. "Get in here, quick."

Scurrying into the backseat of the Escalade, the pole dancer ended up face down in the General's lap. He pulled the door closed and told Corporal Tsunami to get the hell out of there.

"Where to, sir?"

"Your place for now." General Purpose lifted the girl's head out of his crotch. "You can get up now."

Tanya slid off and fixed her hair. One of the extensions was loose, and she yanked it off, tossing it onto the floor.

"Who's the father?" Sitting back against the opposite door, General Purpose crossed his arms over his chest and waited for an answer.

"A pilot." Tanya shoved her tongue into her cheek.

"What airline?"

She shrugged and let a sly smile fill her face. "None. He's freelance. He owns a seaplane."

"A seaplane?" The General shook his head. "A single seaplane? You know I have control over the entire United States Air Force?"

"Big deal. Kamikazes and rock throwers."

"Where is he now?"

Tanya looked out the window. "I don't know. He was supposed to pick me up this morning, but there's no answer on his cellphone and his house is locked up tight. We were supposed to fly to Cancun. I left you a note."

General Purpose lifted the secure NSA telephone from its charger. "What's his name? We'll find him."

Chapter Twelve –
Kings, Presidents, And Cows

King President Vatu had celebrated his twenty-first birthday several months earlier. Thus, it was his turn to rule the island. When the British man-of-war visited the island in the late 1600s, the captain of the ship asked to meet with the island's chief. Never having needed someone to tell them what to do, the Tikos got along just fine with each other. Decisions about which cow to slaughter, who should repair a leaky roof, and whether or not the paths to and from the beach needed widening were done by unanimous agreement.

"Well," asked the British captain, "what happens if someone disagrees?"

"Why would they?" asked a little boy, munching on a chunk of coconut.

The Captain had been a politician before he set to sea. "It's human nature. People will disagree just for the sake of an argument."

"What's an argument?" asked the boy.

"Well..." The Captain thought for a moment and then pointed at the coconut. "Suppose I said that I wanted that coconut."

The boy held it out in his hand. "Take it. I'll get another."

"And what if I said I wanted all the coconuts?"

The boy laughed. "How many do you think you can eat?"

Shaking his head, the Captain knelt so that he was eye level with the child. "It doesn't matter. I just want to have all the coconuts."

"The trees will grow more. Do you want to have all the trees, too?"

"Since you've mentioned it, yes."

"Then what will the rest of us eat?" Taking a step back from the Captain, the boy held his coconut close to his chest.

"I will decide that."

"But what if it's not enough?" The boy squeezed the coconut so tightly that his fingers blanched. "What if we are hungry?"

"I won't let you go hungry, but I will make sure that everyone gets their fair share. I will see to it that the roofs get repaired and that the paths are kept clear." Standing, the Captain held his hand out to the child. "I will bring order to chaos."

An elder, leaning against an Ironwood tree, shook his head. "You will bring order where none is needed."

The Captain smiled and walked over to the man. "No one realizes how disorganized their life is until someone in authority gives them clarity of purpose."

. . . . .

It all came across as frigate bird poop to the islanders, but the Tikos were open to new ideas. With the British warship shrinking in the horizon, they gathered on the beach and discussed the possibility of selecting a leader. Unanimously, they rejected the idea and went for a swim.

Four hundred years later, however, the arrival of wealthy tourists brought the disease of government with them and the islanders no longer had a choice. Someone had to wear the British Sea Captain's uniform to greet the senior officer of a large yacht. Someone had to don the Captain's hat and shake hands with the billionaire and his wife when they stepped off the ship's landing craft and onto Tikopango for the first time. And that same someone had to toast their guests with shells filled with coconut liquor as they entered the Tiko Hut with gold coins at the ready.

It was a simple solution. Their first ruler would be someone who had just turned twenty-one. The Tikos had no idea why that number was so important to the rest of the world, but it seemed relevant, so they agreed on it. Their first King, since that was what the British called him, would be in charge for a minimum of one year. The next person to reach the magical age would then take over as the new King.

No King would be in charge for less than a year. Since the plan had been enacted, several had ruled for more than three years before the next person turned twenty-one. It didn't matter whether the monarch was male or female; they were still referred to as King.

In the early 1950s, American yacht owners discovered Tikopango and introduced the word "President" with a capital "P" to the Tikos. They explained the difference between a King and a President to the islanders, but it failed to make much of an impact. The Tikos agreed that the terms were synonymous and that "King President" had a nice ring to it. They decided unanimously to change the name of their ruler to use both words in order to please visitors from a variety of countries.

. . . . .

King President Vatu strode over to the pilot and held out his hand. "I am KP Vatu. Welcome to Tikopango."

"Well, KP, glad to meet you." The pilot shook Vatu's hand, dropping a gold Krugerrand into the King President's palm. "My name's Nixon. Xavier Milhous Nixon. Folks call me 'XM' for short."

"XM?" The leader of the Tikos cocked his head to one side.

The pilot nodded. "Seriously."

Tossing the heavy coin back and forth, the King President smiled. "And this?"

"His brothers are in a sack behind me." Stepping off to the side, Xavier nodded toward the sandy brown burlap sack just inside the open door of the seaplane. "I'm here to buy cheese."

Vatu shielded his eyes and stared into the plane. "How much cheese do you want?"

Xavier smiled. "All you got, brother."

. . . . .

The NSA found a flight plan filed by XM Nixon and forwarded it to General Purpose's secure phone. Nixon had outlined a round-trip journey from Miami International Airport, through Houston to Los Angeles, and then on to a set of coordinates somewhere in the South Pacific. The General walked over to the lighted globe on his aide's desk and traced the longitude and latitude lines to where they crossed.

"There must be an island between the 'a' and the 'e' in ocean."

"It's all blue on the globe." Corporal Tsunami walked over to his bookcase and pulled out the Rand McNally atlas. "Tikopango. It's a tiny atoll in the Pacific about two thousand miles east of New Zealand."

"What's there?" Spinning the globe once, General Purpose walked over to the patio doors and slid them open. He sniffed the air and then shoved the doors closed, marching over to the couch.

Tanya came out of the kitchen carrying a tray filled with beer cans and empty glasses. "Cheese. XM is trying out for a slot on the *Iron Chef*. He heard about this cheese thing in France and then someone told him about Tikopango." She placed the tray on Hideo's coffee table and sunk into the leather couch next to the General.

"They have cheese on an island in the South Pacific?" General Purpose shook his head. "What's next? Single malt scotch?"

Hideo laughed and reached for a beer. "Hopefully, they have a good sushi bar."

"I dated this yacht captain for a while. He said that the owners planned two trips a year across the Pacific from San Diego to Sydney. They always stopped at Tikopango to buy cheese and get fresh water. He tasted the cheese a bunch of times and said the only thing better was sex." Opening a beer and emptying the can into a glass, Tanya took a sip and wrinkled her nose. "It's warm."

"So, your ex-boyfriend, who knocked you up, has flown off to the South Pacific in search of cheese?" General Purpose rolled his eyes. "When is he coming back?"

Tanya shrugged. "I don't know if he's ever coming back. I don't think he wants to get married and have kids."

"You know that abortion is legal in this country, right?"

"If it was your baby would you kill it, General? Is that how the military solves its problems these days?" She moved to the opposite side of the couch. "I already spoke to my priest."

Corporal Tsunami pulled the ring off the beer can and chugged the warm brew down in one gulp. He opened another and pointed the can at the pole dancer. "Do you expect the General to marry you and raise someone else's baby?"

"No." Tanya shook her head and looked down at the floor for a moment. "I want him to fly me to Tikopango."

. . . . .

Xavier Milhous Nixon, named by his mother after a distant relative, could fly everything from a Cessna to Boeing's new 787 Dreamliner. He was certified to operate helicopters, fighter jets, and seaplanes, but had failed his driver's license test in three states because he couldn't parallel park.

With friends in high places, the pilot was able to refuel over the Pacific from an Air Force KC46A flying tanker. It would meet him again halfway back. The Krugerrands were from a woman who he'd never met but had run errands for over the years. She'd called him three days prior and told Xavier where he could pick up the coins in Miami and how to spend them.

The mysterious woman had explained to Xavier that the cheese was worth far more than the value of the coins. If he could bring her at least a thousand pounds of the Tiko's cheese she had clients that would pay a hundred times what the pilot would spend for it and Xavier would earn enough to finally pay off the loan on his seaplane.

King President Vatu bit into the gold coin to see if it was real, a technique that had been passed down through the ages. Trading fresh water for cows or military uniforms had long since been replaced with the need for currency in any form. The Tikos learned that currency could be traded for anything the people on the yacht brought with them. They kept a waterproof box filled with dollar bills, Euros, and yen. Gold was something they hadn't seen in many years and the King President wasn't sure if it really had value.

"You don't have paper?"

Xavier looked confused. "What kind of paper? Toilet paper? Copy paper?"

"Money paper." Vatu handed the coin back to the pilot. "Visitors to our island trade money paper for our cheese and water."

"This is better than paper." The pilot flipped the coin in the air and caught it behind his back. "This is solid gold. It's what paper money relies on for its value."

The King President wasn't convinced. "We know how many papers we sell the cheese for. How many of your gold coins are equal to a coconut husk filled with our cheese?"

Hefting a couple of filled husks, one in each hand, Xavier figured they weighed around two pounds a piece. The sack held ten-thousand Krugerrands. Smiling, he pointed at the bag. "I will give you ten gold coins for every coconut husk you have to sell." It wouldn't be possible for the seaplane to take off with a thousand containers of cheese if he still had all the weight of the gold. *Best to just get rid of it here.*

"Ten?" The King President's eyes shot up in surprise. "We have hundreds of husks in the lake, maybe more than a thousand. Do you want them all?"

Xavier nodded. "You bet, and I'll even give you five coins for that funky hat."

. . . . .

It took the Tikos most of the early afternoon to bring all the cheese spread to the surface of the lake and pack it into the refrigerated cases on the seaplane. The sack of Krugerrands took two strong men to carry it safely from the plane to the waterproof vault built into the floor of the Tiko Hut.

Xavier radioed his sponsor as the seaplane rose above five-thousand feet, heading for the open sky.

"I counted eleven hundred and twenty-two coconut husks filled with cheese."

"That was every one of them?"

"Yes, ma'am. They'll need at least a month to process more cheese but there's a wicked storm heading toward the island. I think that will delay them for a least a week just to get enough cows milked."

"You'll be met in San Diego by a British chef named Ronzoni. Give him fifty husks and not one more. He's already paid for them."

"Ronzoni? Like the pasta?"

"Yes. How soon will you be in New York?"

Xavier pushed the throttle to full. "Wednesday, the latest. I have to fly to Orlando and take care of some unfinished business."

"The pole dancer?"

"Yeah."

"What are you going to do about her?"

Placing the antique British sea captain's hat on his head, Xavier Milhous Nixon banked the seaplane to the east. "Not sure yet, but I might just let the military take care of her problem."

Chapter Thirteen - When Royalty Calls

A fog as dense as whey had crept in overnight. Boulong sat on the porch swing and sharpened another bolt. He'd turned on the hot tub heater an hour before, figuring one last dunk before they unscrewed the hoops and knocked the staves apart. Job number one today would be the restoration of the dock.

Mikey was already moving cows into the barn. Boulong could hear their grunts from where he sat. Having accepted that his fear of a woman's touch on the raw milk was unfounded, the farmer was planning to awaken his girlfriend to give Mikey a hand.

Kicking the screen door open, Melinda walked out naked with two cups of coffee.

"Is it hot yet?"

Boulong checked the remote sensor on his hip. "Ninety-four. Give it another twenty minutes and I'll go in with you."

"Any word from Mookie?"

He shook his head. "No. I'm going to wait another hour and call the police."

"We can skip the tub and go help Mikey with the cheese if you want."

"Nah. It'll be a long time before I can build another one." Boulong looked into Melinda's eyes and grinned. "Plus, we have plenty of cows."

She bent over to kiss him, accidentally spilling both coffees on Boulong's slippers. "Shit."

Stepping out of the slip-ons, he stood and put his arms around her waist. "Relax, they're waterproof."

Melinda kissed him quickly and spun out of her boyfriend's grasp. "I'm gonna go brush my teeth and grab some towels for the hot tub." Snatching the now empty coffee cups, the girl disappeared into the house.

Boulong finished sharpening the last bolt and dropped it into the shoebox with the others. Getting up to stretch, he was about to go inside and hang up his clothes when his cellphone jingled. The call was from central London. He had a cousin who lived in Chelsea and recognized the area code and exchange.

But my cousin never makes voice calls. It's always a text. Who's this?

Tapping the green button to accept the call, Boulong leaned against a post and undid his belt. The voice was male, British, and quite formal: "Please hold for Her Majesty, the Queen."

Boulong froze with the belt in his hand. *What?*

"Mr. Boulong? Good morning. I'd like to speak to you about your cheese."

"I...I'm sorry. Who is this?" A grin formed in one corner of Boulong's mouth. *It was his cousin, and he'd put some bimbo up to this shit.*

"This is Queen Elizabeth. I'm calling from Buckingham Palace. Is this not Boulong the farmer who sells the award-winning cheese spread?"

"Did Theodore put you up to this, sweetheart? The accent's good, but who was the guy? It didn't sound like my cousin."

A muffled sound came from the other end of the conversation before the Queen returned to the line. "Mr. Boulong and I know that's to whom I'm speaking as we've just verified the number, you are indeed on the phone this morning with the Queen of England and I'd like to discuss the cheese situation."

Boulong laughed. "Okay. This is good. Can you do Facetime? I'd love to see if you're wearing costumes. And where's Theo?"

A bit of exasperation tinged the Queen's voice. "This is quite unusual, Mr. Boulong. I know that telephone calls from the Monarchy are not on your daily schedule, but I can assure you that I regularly converse with world leaders who would never question the sound of my voice."

"So, that's a no to Facetime?"

He could hear her ask, "What's Facetime?" to someone in the background and the words, "video conference" was the reply.

"No. Video conferencing is not available to me on this telephone, Mr. Boulong."

"Fine." Boulong put the phone on the porch rail and unbuckled his pants. "I've got your number on the caller ID. Tell my cousin this was quite interesting. I'm not sure what he was trying to accomplish with this little skit, but tell him I'm going in the hot tub now and if he really wants to talk, he should call me himself."

Boulong ended the call and stepped out of his jeans.

· · · · ·

The Mini Cooper that Mookie and his fellow prisoners had stolen ran out of gas six miles west of Chaumont on the A5. They were only half a mile past a service plaza, but none of the three had any money or credit cards. A quick search of the seat cushions produced a collection of stale potato chips, a pop-top ring, and one-Euro-fifty in coins.

"We're over a hundred and twenty miles from my home." Mookie kicked the front tire and put his head down on the roof of the car.

The taxi driver who'd fled the Parisian jail with Mookie and the Jamaican kid tried to flag down a passing van with no success. "I don't care where we are as long as we're out of Paris." He spit. "That's the last time I get arrested for some bullshit."

"You were drunk." Mookie shook his head. "Don't blame the cops."

"Screw the cops. Screw the taxi business." Waving his arm in the air, the man spit again, narrowly missing Mookie's shoes. "My brother has a farm ten miles outside of Lisbon. The weather is always warm, even in the winter. He says it's a microclimate. Whatever the hell that means. I will drive his tractor and plow his fields."

The Jamaican boy pointed at the driver's stump. "You best hope him got de automatic, mon. Not gone be easy drivin' tracta wit one arm."

"How are you going to get to Lisbon?" Mookie opened the driver's door and sat down sideways on the bucket seat, his feet kicking the gravel.

"We can sell the car." Walking around to the hood, the taxi driver shined the ornament with his sleeve.

Mookie bit the tip of his tongue and looked up at the sky. "Good idea. Let's make a cardboard sign and stand on the side of road. 'Stolen Mini Cooper. No reasonable offer will be refused.' How's that sound?"

Opening the hatchback, the Jamaican kid found a bottle of water and a small tattered blanket. "Everyting mi own is back in Paris, mon." He shoved the bottle in his front pocket and stuffed the blanket under his arm. "Mi gone back. Whole world crazy. No one gone look for one boy."

"What about the cop whose jaw you broke?"

The kid laughed. "Him be de last one on eart gone mess wit me again." He slammed the hatch closed and jogged across the highway without looking back.

"Yeah? That cop is gonna spend the rest of his life looking for you, junior." Turning toward Mookie, the taxi driver cocked his head to one side. "What about you, Paul Newman, you going back to Paris or to somewhere safe?"

"My dad needs me." Mookie gazed east down the A5. "I'm going home." He closed his eyes for a moment and then spun around and nodded at the one-armed taxi driver. "We could always use another hand on the farm."

The taxi driver kicked a pebble onto the highway. "Nah, I'm not one for cows. Corn? Wheat? Sure, they don't crap and they don't smell. I'm gonna hike back up to that service plaza and try my luck playing the sympathy card. It's always worked in the past." He held out his hand. "Good luck, kiddo. Squeeze an udder for me when you get home."

. . . . .

Melinda was already in the hot tub when Boulong came around the side of the house. He'd checked his phone before plugging it into a charger in the kitchen. Two calls had come in from that same number in London, but there were no voicemails. He was going to call the Paris Police Department to make a missing persons report on Mookie, but Melinda shouted that the water was hot enough and he decided to wait.

"Mikey was just here in the Gator."

"Is there a problem?" Boulong paused with one foot in the tub.

"One of the cows is having a calf."

Boulong pulled his foot out of the tub. "In the barn?"

"No. Out in the far corner of the pasture." Melinda's face was covered in concern. "Should we go help?"

"Help a cow give birth?" He shook his head. "No, but it's like show time for the other cows. They'll all want to stand around in a circle to protect the one giving birth. Mikey will have a hell of a time getting them into the barn to be milked."

Melinda followed Boulong out of the tub. "I've never seen a cow give birth."

"Good. Let's watch. Maybe it will help you decide whether *you* want to go through it some day." Boulong handed her a towel and then walked around to the side of the tub where he opened the drain valve. Slipping back into his jeans and workshirt, the farmer unhooked Melinda's bathrobe from the nail where she'd hung it and gave it to the girl. Naked in the tub was one thing. Running around the farm without clothes was too dangerous.

His phone was ringing. Boulong could hear it through the open kitchen window. Mikey was at the top of the hill, waving. Boulong shouted, "We're coming" and then grabbed his girlfriend by the wrist. "Let's go. Reality is waiting in the far pasture."

· · · · ·

The Queen handed the cellphone to the Prime Minister. "I can speak to the Pope, the President of the United States, even the palace janitor, but I can't get a dairy farmer to take my call? What do you make of this, Freddy?"

"He's French, your Majesty, one must make allowances."

"We've done what we can to frighten him off the island, to no avail. It's Tuesday morning and we must get his cheese to Chef Ronzoni before Saturday at the latest for the dinner." The Queen put her hand on her crown to hold it in place and shook her head. "I've never liked the military option, but I see no other way."

"Are you going to order the Royal Air Force paratroopers to take the island, your Majesty?"

"Not without first alerting the French." Reaching for the official phone on her desk, the Queen dialed nine and told the operator to get the French President on the line. She checked her watch as the call was going through and sighed. "Freddy, it's after noon. I hope he's sober."

Chapter Fourteen - Cheese and Crackers

Chef Ronzoni waited in the British Airways lounge with an open bottle of twenty-one-year-old Balvenie Portwood single malt scotch. Sixteen hours prior, he'd been sitting in the kitchen of his one-star Michelin restaurant testing cheese spreads. Then *she'd* called. Ronzoni hadn't heard the woman's voice in years, but the way she rolled her Rs and called him "Rizzo," he had no doubt as to who was on the other end of the line.

His instructions were to retrieve a round-trip ticket at Heathrow for a non-stop flight to San Diego, California. He would be met at the airport by a man wearing an antique British sea captain's hat. The man would give the chef fifty coconut shells filled with a cheese spread that was rumored to be better than Boulong's.

Chef Ronzoni, who disliked mysteries and secret agent crap, bit his tongue and told the woman he would leave immediately. She was not a person one refused.

. . . . .

Xavier watched the flying gas station accelerate away from him. Even at full throttle, the seaplane had a hard time keeping up with the KC46A tanker. The three grand he'd laid out to have a refueling jig installed in the nose of the seaplane was worth every penny. Having friends in the Air Force made it all work.

At ten-thousand feet, Xavier locked the autopilot and went back to check his cargo. He'd brought along a box of Ritz crackers and opened the nearest cooler to sample the ridiculously expensive cheese spread. Each of the coconut shells held a bit over one-and-three-quarter pounds of cheese. Based on the current market price for a Krugerrand, Xavier had paid close to one-hundred-and-fifty dollars per pound. He was certain they'd be resold for over a thousand dollars per husk.

He'd never tasted Boulong's cheese, and the only other spread that he'd ever used was Cheese Whiz. Xavier had no way of knowing if the Tiko's cheese would be a suitable substitute for the exotic concoction that was bringing the world closer to war every day. Not being much of a gourmet, the pilot's favorite dairy product was the half-and-half that he used with his coffee in the morning. His refrigerator held Kraft Singles and a moldy package of Muenster cheese.

It smells like a grilled cheese sandwich. Xavier dug a Ritz into the soft spread and scooped out a dollop that he sucked off the cracker as though it was a spoon. *Mmmm. Much better than Kraft. Tastes like cream cheese with honey and butter.* He took a second sample, this time eating the cracker along with the cheese. *Hot damn, tamale. This is some really good shit.*

The seaplane hit some turbulence, forcing the pilot to grab the nearest handhold. Losing his grip on the coconut husk, the shell rolled under a seat, jelly side down.

Shit! Letting go of the leather strap, Xavier grabbed the seat with one hand and reached under to retrieve the fallen container with the other. Sliding and tilting the shell at the same time, he managed to save most of its precious contents, but a layer of cheese slime remained behind on the cabin floor.

Fifty dollars' worth down the drain. Using a piece of palm frond, he wiped the grit off the top of the cheese still in the husk and resealed it. *Can't sell this one.* He shrugged. *I'll buy it. What the hell.*

· · · · ·

Chef Ronzoni refilled the rocks glass and shoved the cork back into the bottle of scotch. The plane was supposed to have landed an hour ago, and the whisky was almost gone. Boarding would begin on his return flight in ninety minutes. Folding his copy of *Le Monde*, the chef shoved it into his armpit. With the nearly empty bottle in one hand and his glass in the other, he backed out of the first-class lounge in search of a duty-free shop.

XM Nixon, rolling a pair of coolers, came off the escalator and was walking toward the British Airways lounge when three masked bandits jumped from a motorized cart in front of him. They were holding spearguns and shouted at the pilot in Spanish (translated loosely here for those who don't speak the language.)

"Drop the suitcases, you monkey. Twice if I speak, you will be holy."

Xavier, who spoke fluent English, French, and one of the three most common Hindu dialects, didn't understand a single word but recognized a threat when it was pointed at him. He put the two coolers on the ground and raised his hands.

"You guys are making a big mistake. If you knew who paid for these boxes, you'd leave immediately and go rob a bank. It would be much safer in the long run."

The largest of the three nodded at his cohorts and they ran over and snatched the coolers, holding their spearguns by the shaft. One of them dropped his weapon as he backed away from Xavier, and the pilot shifted his bodyweight as though he was about to grab it.

The tall man covering his companions took a step forward and aimed at Xavier's chest. Smiling, he narrowed his gaze and said, (again, translated for your convenience) "Do not tickle it, mister. I go kill at you."

Xavier took a step back and raised his hands as high as he could.

. . . . .

Still standing in the open doorway of the British Airways lounge, Chef Ronzoni watched the robbery in silence. Several air travelers videoed the action with their phones and posted the crime on social media. Ever since Dud, there had been little need for security in the terminal. Weapons were easily detected by the scanners and bombs were no longer a threat. Those TSA officers still on the job never left the initial checkpoints, and local police had been reassigned.

No one came to the aid of the man with his hands in the air. No one tried to stop the three masked men as they sped away on the motorized cart.

Chef Ronzoni tilted the bottle to his mouth and swallowed the last dram in a single gulp. Letting the liquor handle the talking, he marched over to the man he'd now realized was his contact and chastised him for his tardiness.

. . . . .

The two men sat in a bar several blocks from the airport in the booth furthest from the entrance. The chef, quite drunk and nursing his jaw where Xavier had punched him, waved at the bartender with his free hand. For his effort, the bartender flipped him the bird and went back to watching the baseball game.

"He's not going to serve us, XM. What the hell? Does he know who I am?"

Xavier finished his beer and slammed the empty can on the table. "We're in deep shit, pasta breath. I knew I should have locked up the plane." He spun the can around with two fingers. "Twenty-two-thousand and it would have been paid off. I still would have had three-grand left over. Goddamn Mexicans. Shit."

"Goddamn Mexicans." The Chef echoed his companion and tried to slap the table. He missed. "Shit."

"You have to call her."

"Bullshit."

Xavier held his fist up to the chef's nose. "I'll beat you so silly that you'll start speaking Spanish."

"Go ahead. We're both dead men, anyway." A moment of clarity poked through Ronzoni's alcoholic haze. "It's all over the Internet. She knows by now. I just can't figure out why we're still breathing."

"What was I supposed to do against three Mexicans with spearguns?"

"Duck?"

"And to steal my seaplane? Over some goddamn cheese? What the hell?" Xavier slammed his fist on the table so hard that the empty can bounced. "They hot-wired it. Can you believe that shit? Steal an Escalade, steal a seaplane, it's all the same if you can jury-rig the ignition. Goddamn punks."

Chef Ronzoni shouted, "Hey!" at the bartender. The man dropped his rag on the bar and leaned over toward the two drunks. The chef smiled and held up his empty glass. "A refill, kind sir, and another cold brew for my friend."

"How do you think she'll kill us?" Xavier stood the empty beer can upside down and slid it back and forth in front of him.

"Slowly and in some grand fashion." Sitting back in the booth, the Chef pursed his lips. "I would like to be roasted like a suckling pig with an apple in my mouth."

"Alive?"

"No, you idiot. Once I'm dead. That's how I'd like to be cremated."

"I want my asses dropped from five-thousand feet."

"How many asses do you have?" The chef snorted. "Asses!"

"Ashes, you asshole." With a shove, Xavier launched the can across the table. It landed in the chef's lap.

The bartender sauntered over to their table, carrying a can of beer and a scotch on the rocks. He put them on the table and then crossed his arms over his chest. "It's almost midnight, gentlemen. Last call is on the table. Don't bother to ask for another round and if either of you has car keys, I'd like them right now."

XM Nixon reached into his pocket and pulled out the keys to the seaplane. "It's probably parked in Mexico City by now, but you're welcome to the keys."

. . . . .

The city lights poked through her silk shades, making star patterns on the marble floor. She'd been watching the baseball game, deep into extra innings, on a television screen that was actually painted onto the wall. Several friends had stopped by. One of them bringing her favorite caviar, another with two bottles of Dom.

All the women wore white bathrobes that they'd changed into after arriving at the penthouse. Hers was lavender, and it had the initials "LD" over the pocket. Everyone was barefoot. No one needed a pedicure.

The woman with the beluga had also brought along a friend who styled hair at a Broadway theater. She let the stylist take an inch of split ends off her black ponytail and even out her bangs. It wasn't as professional a job as her regular hairdresser, but she'd been too busy with the cheese problem to bring the man over to get it done.

When the alert came over her cellphone, one of her friends had just placed a mirror with lines of cocaine and a rolled up hundred-dollar bill in front of her. She pushed the mirror away with her toe, ruining the perfect lines.

Xavier, how could you be so stupid? And Giuseppe? You couldn't distract them long enough for him to run? You two are such a disappointment.

She looked up at the television as a fly ball went deep into the left field stands. The game was tied again. Fourteen innings, but it made nice wallpaper while the girls got high and played Mah Jong.

I should hang these two out to dry as an example. But the chef is Lizzie's friend, and expert pilots are getting harder to find. Reaching, she pulled the mirror closer and snorted a line. Another fly ball, but this one was caught for the third out. Top of the fifteenth, right after a few words from our sponsors. She rubbed a few white crystals on her gums and dragged her cellphone over with her toe.

Cheese? What's next?

. . . . .

Landing the stolen seaplane at Mexico City's International Airport was rough. The rogue pilot had never flown a seaplane before. He had trouble lowering the landing gear past the pontoons and had to go around twice before attempting a touchdown.

Only one of the runways had been partially repaired since the earthquake and he ran out of flat concrete, smashing the right wing into a light pole and spinning the plane around.

Generalissimo Newsenz watched the crash from the airport tower and ordered his men to ride out with the fire trucks. He radioed the firefighters to hurry before the cheese melted and all was lost.

What little fuel that was left in the wing tanks was not enough for an explosion, and the pilot stood waving at the approaching rescue armada from an unbroken wing strut. His cellphone rang just before the first fire truck roared up and he stared at the strange number. It was from the United States. That much he was sure of. His brother lived in the Bronx and his phone had the same area code.

He accepted the call and said, "*Hola*."

A woman's voice on the other end of the phone replied, "*Adiós*" and an arrow fired from a compound bow almost a thousand yards away blew through his chest.

Chapter Fifteen - Choppers

The calf had been born without a hitch. Melinda, overcome by the smell, had watched from a distance but ran over when the tiny calf struggled to its feet. With the show over, the cows had sauntered off to find fresh grass to chew. Boulong led two cows into the barn and connected them to milking jigs.

"I'm going to get started on the hot tub. It should be drained by now."

Mikey watched as Melinda walked a cow over to an empty stall. "You're okay with her touching the milk?"

Boulong nodded. "She's not Sabrina."

"Do you need help with the tub?"

"Nah. I'd much rather be here making cheese, but we've got to get the dock repaired." The farmer double-checked the tubes on both cows and started for the barn door. "Have you been calling your Uncle Theodore in London?"

Mikey shook his head. "No. Does he need money again?"

"I don't know." Boulong pulled his phone out of his pocket. "Somebody in London does."

• • • • •

The Queen listened to the mysterious woman's report without saying a word. LD never repeated herself and it was best to just let her speak. When she was finished, Her Royal Highness simply said, "Thank you" and hung up the phone. She had spoken with the French President before midnight and informed him of her plan to take over Boulong's island in the interests of culinary peace.

He offered the assistance of the French Artillery, which he claimed now had seven trebuchets mounted on flatbed carriers. The military could have them in position before daybreak if she wanted.

"No," the Queen told him, certain that Monsieur le President was lying. Her intelligence chief had reported that the French had pulled the three ancient trebuchets out of the Musee de l'Armee in Paris and were able to make one working catapult out of the lot. It had been bolted onto a flatbed wrecker donated by a Parisian towing company, and its only test had resulted in a broken windshield on the truck when the rock failed to release from the basket.

With the loss of the Tiko's cheese and the proximity of the weekend, she had no other choice. The Queen picked up the phone and told the operator to find the Minister of Defense and the Commandant of the Royal Air Force. It was time to plan the C-Day invasion.

· · · · ·

The rusted nuts binding the ends of the hot tub's metal hoops took an hour each to spin free. Boulong poured motor oil on the threads, heated the nuts, cooled them down, and finally slipped an iron pipe over the end of his wrench to get enough leverage. He unseized the top three hoops and was working on the bottom one when he lost his grip and smacked himself between his thighs with the heavy wrench.

Both Melinda and Mikey came running down the hill, hearing his screams. His girlfriend, not having to use crutches, got there first and offered to, "Kiss it and make it feel better." Seeing his son hurrying down the gravel path, Boulong shook his head and reached for Melinda's hand to pull himself to his feet.

Mikey picked up the wrench and broke the nut free with a single tug. He spun it off the threaded end of the hoop and tossed it to his father. "You should call me for stuff like this rather than risking your manhood."

"Listen to him." Melinda put her arm around her boyfriend's shoulder and squeezed him close. "I'm gonna need you in one piece for a long time, Bouly."

"Bouly?" Mikey laughed. "That's perfect."

Boulong shooed his girlfriend and his son back up to the barn to continue the processing. Using a small mallet and a chisel, he began breaking the seals on the wooden staves of the tub. Most of them broke free with little effort. Those that stuck and splintered annoyed the farmer. Hardwood was a precious commodity in Paradise. However, realizing that the oak boards would never be used again to hold water, he worked with less consideration for quality. Within an hour, all of the staves had been separated and loaded into the Gator.

The midday sun had baked the planks dry by the time he finished and headed toward the beach. Dust blew off the dirt roadway and into his eyes. The farmer shielded them with his arm and squinted at the path ahead. Picking up the pace, clouds of fine silt spun out from the six wheels of the small carrier as Boulong rolled over to the remains of his dock. Finally clear of the manmade dust storm, he parked the Gator at the water's edge and unloaded the timbers.

Several rowboats floated past with naked sunbathers who stood and waved. Boulong smiled and nodded at them. He was about to pee into the river when another boat came into view. It was white with the British flag painted on the prow, and it had two women in white jumpsuits onboard. One was operating the outboard motor while the other held a cellphone in midair.

Boulong was going to wave at them but realized that the standing woman wasn't talking on her phone. She was filming his island as they passed. He might have chalked it up to work on a promotional video for the British Tourist Agency, but the woman also wore a utility belt with a dart gun holster on either side.

Maybe it's for a British hunting journal? He shrugged and started the Gator. Waiting until they were around the bend and out of sight, Boulong drove up to the barn and left the cart running next to the tool shed.

"Mikey!" he yelled to his son. "Give me a hand with the generator."

Wiping his hands on his jeans and using only one of the crutches as a cane, the boy came out of the garage with tears streaming down his face.

Unaware as to whether they were from joy or pain, Boulong rushed over to his son. "What happened?"

Mikey doubled over with laughter and pointed back into the barn. "Melinda bent down to connect the tubes to one of the cows and it let loose. Must have squirted a gallon of milk in her face."

"Is she okay?"

"Soaked, but smiling."

Together they loaded the generator, both of the longest extension cords, and the electric saw with an extra blade into the Gator. Boulong followed his son into the barn and stood in the middle of the building with his hands on his hips. Melinda was topless. Her blouse was hung on a hook by the door and she was wearing her sunglasses.

"That's a look." Boulong walked over and kissed her. "I'm sure that the cows don't mind looking at your udders."

"That's what you call them? Udders?" The girl shook her head and pointed at the nearest cow. "They should have valves on them. Look at my hair."

Boulong ran his fingers through her jet black locks. "Milk is a great conditioner. You should do this more often."

"And you should get the dock built instead of standing here giving orders." Melinda slipped the halter off the cow's head and turned toward the door. The smell of the cow and her memory of the other night gave her pause. "Wanna hike out to the pasture with me and ride the back of a cow before you go back to work?"

. . . . .

The Commandant of the Royal Air Force had spent thirty-one years taking orders from the Queen. Never had he questioned one before, but this was about as strange as the time he was ordered to attack and destroy a pod of sperm whales that had drifted into the English Channel.

The massive beasts were interfering with a cross-Channel swim that was scheduled for the coming weekend. It was a showdown between the Brits, the Americans and a team from Egypt that had learned to swim in the Red Sea. In a moment of brilliance, the Commandant had instructed his sailors to raid a fresh seafood stand on the French side and hook the fish to lines strung from a helicopter. They led the whales out of the Channel and back into the North Sea without firing a shot.

He turned to his aide after reading the orders for the third time. "An island in the middle of the Doubs River?" Scanning the surveillance photos and video that had been sent earlier that day, the Commandant shook his head. "There's only one place to land a helicopter and there's no cover for a thousand yards in any direction once they put down."

"What's the objective?"

"It says take control of the island and secure the cheese."

"Cheese?"

The commandant nodded. "Must be a code word for something."

. . . . .

Boulong pushed the electric start on the generator and smiled. It hadn't been run in over a year, but he'd put additives in the carburetor that were guaranteed to protect the engine. Plugging in the saw, he tapped the switch twice to make sure it was working and began cutting the oak staves of the former hot tub into deck planks.

Fortunately, all of the upright piers and the vertical crossbeams of the deck had survived the aerial avalanche. Boulong was able to rebuild the first eight feet of the dock in under an hour.

The middle section still had an enormous boulder protruding from the water, and there was no way the farmer was going to move it without heavy equipment. It took him more than two hours to cut planks into smaller pieces and build a walkway around the rock on one side.

Late afternoon clouds were gathering by the time Boulong finished cutting the boards for the furthest end of the twenty-five-foot dock. He nailed the final planks in place, stomping on them as a test to see if they'd come loose. Powering down the generator, he was wrapping the extension cord around his arm when he heard the sound of helicopters coming from the west.

He threw the extension cord in the Gator and jumped in. The engine kicked over on the first try and Boulong threw the cart in gear, shoving the throttle to the top. The steering wheel was equipped with a horn that sounded exactly the same as a dying goose. Boulong leaned on it as he sped up the path toward the barn.

Melinda heard the horn first and was running toward him, her breasts flopping up and down with each stride. Slowing, Boulong reached for her hand and pulled his girlfriend into the passenger seat.

"What's going on?"

"Choppers."

"Motorcycles?"

"Huh?" Boulong turned and squinted at the girl. "What the hell are you talking about?"

"Choppers. Big motorcycles with ape hangers."

"Ape what?"

"High handlebars. You ride the chopper with your arms up like this." Melinda demonstrated with her arms up and fingers wrapped around an imaginary grip.

"I have no idea what you're talking about." Boulong looked over as Mikey hobbled quickly to the Gator. "Choppers. Lots of them and they're getting close."

"Is it an invasion?" Wiping his hands, Mikey looked up at the sky.

"I think so." Boulong cut the engine of the Gator. "I checked the Internet last night. There's a lot of crazy shit going on in Paris and something happened in Mexico, but I got distracted before I had a chance to read the article on my phone." He winked at Melinda. "And you know how easily I'm distracted these days."

· · · · ·

The lead pilot radioed his team, "One mile. Lock and load."

Pointing at the radar, his copilot tapped his microphone button. "Something large coming in from one-o'clock. No. Wait. It just disappeared."

"Radar glitch?"

"No. There was definitely something there a second ago." The copilot tapped the screen. "Nope. Nothing now."

The pilot called the other two choppers and asked if they'd seen anything. Both replied, "Negative."

"Okay. We'll come in from the French side with the setting sun behind us. Bovine Two, you'll hover to the west. Bovine Three, I want you ten feet off the ground and ready to provide cover." The pilot turned and nodded at the Marines. "Get ready, gentlemen. This LZ is hot."

Forty-two cows were grazing on the large pasture when the three RAF helicopters descended. The largest cow had just given birth that morning and took the threat personally. She pawed at the ground and charged the chopper from the side. It took a few long strides for her to get her fifteen-hundred pounds up to full speed, but when she did, the only thing that was going to stop her was a very thick brick wall.

The side of the helicopter collapsed as she hit it. The force of the collision tilting the spinning blades just enough to catch in the soft earth on the opposite side. Boulong and company heard the explosion from inside the barn where they had closed and latched the doors.

Seeing Bovine One explode into a mushroom cloud, the other two helicopters began a retreat. Neither pilot noticed the stealth bomber coming up from behind.

The bomber passed over the slow-moving helicopters at the speed of sound. Its wake was too much for the pilots to handle, and its powerful gust flipped the choppers on their sides. Crashing into the rapids on the French side of Boulong's island, all aboard were able to escape before the helicopters sank into the rushing water.

Sixteen British commandos floated down the Doubs with their life vests inflated. They were caught in the rapids for almost five miles before they could swim to shore and report the mission as a total failure.

Chapter Sixteen - Invasion?

On orders from the President of the United States, the stealth pilot was protecting Boulong's island against invasion. She was in orbit at forty-five-thousand feet with the stealth's radar jamming equipment in standby mode when she saw the trio of helicopters cross the English Channel.

The President had been given a cheese briefing by a deputy from the NSA in-between sets where he was beating the pants off the senior Senator from Illinois. Not having much interest in the cheese aspect but having a deep-seated disdain for the French, he saw Boulong's island as another chess piece in the game of world domination. Adding to that, the British Queen seemed to be dipping her toes in the puddle of power once again.

The two monarchs (the President also had a crown that was left behind by his predecessor but he kept it under the bed and only wore it when he was having sex or won a match) had been at odds since his election. While the Queen was happy to finally have some calm in the world, the new President was an opportunistic egomaniac who loved to flex his muscles and parade his troops. A wonderful plan if Dud hadn't rendered his armies powerless to mount a major offensive.

However, the President still found ways to piss off heads of state who disagreed with his policies. His ban on Spanish rice in favor of the Chinese crop had done nothing besides raise the wholesale cost of the grain. When the President stood behind the White House podium and claimed that no Canadian would ever be allowed to play in the National Hockey League again, he never considered their neighbors to the north would finance the Alaskan secession movement and then claim the territory as their own.

To the President, Boulong was a Cracker Jack prize. He'd open every box in the store to find it, whether or not it upset the shopkeeper. Baldy wanted the island because everyone else wanted it. What he'd do with Boulong's Paradise wasn't even in the back of his mind.

. . . . .

The Queen of England took off her crown and scratched the top of her head.

"What just happened, Lord Fitzpatrick?"

The British Minister of Defense turned to the radar operator. "What just happened, lieutenant?"

Taking off his headphones so that he could hear the Minister, the officer shrugged. "I'm not sure, sir. But we've lost radar contact with all three helicopters."

"Were they attacked on the ground?" Lord Fitzpatrick adjusted his tie. "Could you tell?"

The operator tapped several keys and clicked the Replay button on his monitor. The entire forty-five seconds of the landing and unexplained disappearance of the first helicopter was repeated. He reset and played it again at half speed, then at one-quarter speed, then so slowly that the Queen cleared her throat and began tapping her fingernails on the armrest of her chair.

"It could have hit something on the ground, but it was coming in at a normal rate of descent." The lieutenant sat up a bit straighter in his seat. "We weren't able to re-task the satellite, so there's no video, Your Majesty."

The Queen nodded. "What about the other two helicopters?"

"They went down in the Doubs." Advancing the playback, the officer slowed it to normal speed as the blips passed over the outline of the river. They shuddered on the screen and then disappeared into blue.

"And no other aircraft were in the area?" Finally locating the itch, the Queen placed her crown carefully in the center of her gray hair and sat back in her chair. "Nothing else came up on radar before or after our helicopters were attacked?"

"We don't know that they were attacked, Your Majesty." Locking his hands behind his back, the Minister of Defense walked over to the computer monitor and bent down, gazing as though the answer was there and he just couldn't see it.

"Do you think they all had a malfunction and simply stopped flying, Lord Fitzpatrick? Perhaps the Americans found a way to make them crash by remote control. You've been spouting fear of a U.S. takeover of the British Isles for years. Is this the onset of an invasion, Lord Fitzpatrick?"

The Minister shook his head, most emphatically. "No, Your Highness. The American President is crazy, but he's not insane." He stood and closed his eyes for a few moments. Taking a deep breath, Lord Fitzpatrick laced his fingers and whispered, "It's possible that Boulong has built a trebuchet."

· · · · ·

The farmer hadn't built the medieval weapon in his backyard...his grandfather was the architect and his grandmother was the carpenter. At the start of the First World War, the Boulong family found itself in-between a neutral country and one that an attacking army had already overrun. Grandfather Boulong knew the defense of Isle de Boeuf was in their hands and it required heavy artillery.

He drew the plans from the memory of a picture he'd seen during his university days and presented them to Boulong's grandmother. The child of a long line of carpenters (her mother was a traveling prostitute who only serviced home builders and only at the job site) she never knew her father but had been born with a splinter in her thumb and a tape measure as her first birthday gift.

Together, Boulong's grandparents constructed a working trebuchet and a variety of missiles. Fortunately, the war never reached the Doubs and other than several test flings, it wasn't used again for more than sixty years.

The weapon had been resting under oilskin cloths behind the house since Boulong was a teen. For his thirteenth birthday, Boulong's parents rolled the trebuchet down to the beach and fired balls of flaming grass into the river. Father Boulong, who was an ordained minister in his spare time, baptized the boy, read from the Jewish scripture since it was the priest's favorite version of Creation, and sacrificed a goat right there on the beach while Boulong watched.

It was Boulong's last contact with religion.

· · · · ·

The force of the explosion shook the barn so violently that the three occupants were thrown to the floor. Mikey was the first to lift his head. "What the hell was that?"

"A bomb." Melinda spoke the word into the dirt floor, still afraid to look.

"There are no more bombs, sweetheart. Something exploded, though. My guess is that one of those helicopters misjudged its landing and hit a tree." Standing up, Boulong crept to the door and put his ear against it. "Nothing."

Reaching down, Mikey tapped the girl on her shoulder. Melinda rolled over and took his hand. They joined the farmer at the door, all three of them leaning against it with an ear on the wood.

"I can hear cows walking around and some birds, but nothing else." Boulong took a step back and opened the latch.

Mikey pushed one of the heavy doors open wide enough to stick his head out. "Smoke! In the far pasture!"

Boulong shoved the other door open and ran for the Gator. Mikey, hopping without his crutches, jumped into the passenger seat and yanked Melinda onto his lap. Boulong shoved the throttle to full as clouds of gravel spun out from the drive wheels.

They could see the wreckage from the crest of the hill. Black clouds of smoke billowed from the twisted frame of the helicopter. The broken blades had formed a cross over the top of the canopy: one vertical, the other perfectly level across it with the tips bent up toward the sky.

Closing the distance, several charred corpses were visible in the open doorway. The canopy had cracked but held its shape, although the interior was coated with black soot. Boulong parked the Gator twenty yards away from the wreck and walked up to inspect it with a crossbow in his hands.

Melinda slid off Mikey's lap and started to follow her boyfriend. Boulong turned back and shook his head. "No. Wait there. You don't need to see this."

She paused and looked back at the farmer's son, who nodded and held his hand out. "Come on back. Let him do this."

. . . . .

No one had survived the crash. Boulong choked but stuck his head inside the crumpled coffin. He counted four dead in the cabin and could see the remains of the pilot but the copilot's seat was empty. Boulong found the body on the other side of the chopper. It had been thrown clear in the crash and wasn't burnt, but he could see the agony of death frozen in the man's face.

Mikey walked up to join his father. "We'll have to bury them."

"Where's Melinda?" Spinning quickly on his heel, Boulong shielded his eyes from the sun and stared back toward the Gator.

"Walking back to the house." Taking a deep breath, Mikey turned away from the corpse. "Crying. She broke down when the wind changed and we could smell the burnt flesh."

Boulong walked back to the helicopter and shook his head. "We don't have the equipment to take this apart and dispose of the trash." He spit on the British flag decal that had somehow survived the heat. "Goddamn foreigners."

. . . . .

The Queen was furious. "Do you mean to tell me that a farmer with a catapult as old as Buckingham Palace has just destroyed three RAF attack helicopters worth thirty-five-million Pounds a piece?"

Lord Fitzpatrick looked at the radar operator, who leaned closer to his keyboard and began tapping random keys. The British Minister of Defense, second in command only to Her Majesty, furrowed his brow and tried to find a suitable answer. None came to mind.

"Well?" The Queen raised her left eyebrow. "Anyone?"

Silence filled the room until the radar operator burped. "Sorry."

"That's the most intelligent thing I've heard since this whole operation started." Pushing herself up from the thickly padded chair, the Queen pointed at her Minister of Defense. "You'll find out what happened and apprise me within the hour or your next command will be on a submarine that patrols the English Channel looking for whales."

Chapter Seventeen - Mongolian Baking

Ulaanbaatar is a quiet outpost in the plains of central Mongolia. It's one of the primary stations on the Trans-Mongolian Railway, an extension of the more famous Trans-Siberian Railway, and a hub for the export of Mongolian dairy products. Nearby farmers claimed the fierce warriors of their past as descendants and often staged mock attacks on the trains as they arrived loaded with Chinese tourists on their way to Moscow. In reality, they had more in common with shepherds than soldiers.

While horses outnumbered the cattle, those cows that flourished in the often frigid conditions dined on a grass equally as potent as the plants on Boulong's island and much more nutritious than the foliage found on Tikopango. The farmers processed bovine milk together with ox and goat's milk to create a creamy cheese spread they called "otgon byaslag" (which is a literal translation) or "slag" for short.

The Internet was a stranger in Ulaanbaatar. Telephone communication still required a wire, and the stationmaster was fluent in Morse code. Television sets received two channels: one in Russian and the other in Chinese. The news was the same, just spoken in whichever was your favorite language.

. . . . .

Yan Ling Po was a first-generation British dairy farmer. His parents were both renowned professors at Oxford. His father taught physics with a concentration on advanced string theory. His mother was an English professor who also taught Mandarin Chinese and Tongan, the official language of Tonga, where she had been born.

They lived on a small farm not far from the university where Yan learned about dairy production and animal husbandry from the farmer and his wife who owned the farm and rented its four-bedroom cottage to the Po family. The boy had few friends other than the animals and spent most of his free time buried in his books.

Having been raised in such a stodgy environment, Yan desired fresh air and open spaces. Originally, he was headed to the United States, but got onto the wrong plane and ended up in Beijing three weeks prior. The adventurous boy joined a westbound caravan that got as far as Ulaanbaatar before it ran out of money and the participants abandoned their plan to reach Paris by crossing the entire Asian continent on camels.

Average height and just a bit malnourished, Yan had been forced to learn cooking at an early age due to his parents' extended teaching schedules. He was six-years-old when he made his first grilled cheese sandwich and was baking soufflés when he was ten. When his camel finally gave up the march and collapsed several blocks from the Ulaanbaatar train station, it hit the pavement with a thud in front of a bakery.

Knowing his basic baking skills were probably more than adequate in this sleepy, backwoods community, Yan marched into the bakery and demanded a job.

The owner, an overly plump woman who wore a red gingham patch over her missing right eye, leaned across the counter and laughed at the boy.

"You look too skinny to be a baker. What do you eat for dinner? Crackers and water?"

Yan shook his head and pulled his shirt out of his pants in an attempt to hide his emaciated frame. "I can bake cakes and cookies." He smiled and winked at the baker. "I know how to measure and I'm an expert when it comes to cleaning up."

The baker's face showed a combination of surprise and disbelief. Nonetheless, she was only a year away from retirement and had considered selling her shop if she couldn't find an apprentice before winter.

"That's all well and good but can you bake slag buns?"

"Slag buns?" Yan squinted at the baker. "What are those?"

She reached into the display case and pulled out what appeared to be your standard hot cross bun. Splitting the pastry in half with her hands, she gave a piece to Yan. "Taste it first and then I'll tell you about it."

Shoving the entire piece in his mouth, Yan's tongue hit the cheese spread and curled. "Wow, that's sweet." He chewed the bun, savoring the sugary flavors and soft, gooey sponge. Sipping some water from the canteen he'd unhooked from his belt, the boy smiled. "Can I have another?"

. . . . .

Mongolian bakers discovered the soft cheese after a chef passed through on the train heading to China. Intrigued with the barren landscape and simple life, the chef ended up staying for over three months to educate the Mongolians in the culinary arts. Prior to his visit, they had been letting the cheese harden and age so that it would last through the long winters when milk production from all the aforementioned mammals was at its lowest. The chef had arrived just before the farmers were going to wrap the fresh cheese and bury it until spring.

Revealing the technique for making cheese spread, the chef spent his time in Ulaanbaatar helping the Mongolian dairy farmers perfect their product. When it was ready, he decided to experiment with the spread to see if there was something unique he could bake with it to showcase their efforts.

He bought a gallon of soft cheese and begged some time in the bakery where Yan was currently standing. Using the same bun recipe that he'd baked in London, the chef produced a tray of slag-filled buns that he handed out for free. The Mongolians fell in love with the pastries and began baking them daily to eat in the morning with their vodka.

Word of the tasty buns and the amazing cheese that filled them spread slowly. The nearest town was an hour away from Ulaanbaatar, and the train only came through once a week. Chinese who lived close to the train station in Beijing were the first outsiders to try the slag buns. They thought the cheese tasted worse than three-day-old stir-fried tofu.

Going in the opposite direction, the Russian dairy farmers were stunned that a bunch of former raiders and rapists could produce a cheese that fine. They did their best to replicate the slag but failed at every attempt. Bakeries from Moscow to St. Petersburg sent representatives east to Mongolia, where they did their best to purchase all the available slag.

The Mongolians laughed at their feeble attempt to control the slag production. They were pumping out the soft cheese spread by the ton every twenty-two days, which was all the time they gave it to age. All the rubles in Chernobyl weren't enough to buy every ounce of slag in Mongolia.

·　·　·　·　·

Yan's cellphone had been out of contact with the real world for the last ten days and he had no idea what a treasure he'd just swallowed. With the westbound train due that afternoon, and his wallet nearly empty except for his prepaid rail pass, Yan had stumbled on one of those forks in the road that either saves your life or screws it up beyond your worst nightmare. He could use the rail pass and take the shorter trip back to Beijing, simply retracing his steps, or continue his adventure and bring the slag buns home via Moscow.

"Can I borrow a coin?" He squeezed his most pathetic look onto his face. His eyes were almost melting and if he'd hung his head any lower, he might have snapped his neck. "Just for a moment. I'll give it back. I promise."

The baker picked at something on her neck and squinted at the boy with a look of distrust. "Are you're staying right there with the coin or running off somewhere so that I'll have to worry if you're coming back with my money?"

"Right here." Yan stomped his foot.

She dug a ruble out of her apron and dropped it into his open palm. Yan flipped the coin in the air, caught it, and slapped it down on the counter. It showed a head facing west. He smiled.

"I have seventeen dollars, twenty Euros, and what I think is about four dollars and change in Chinese money." Peering down into the glass display case, Yan counted the slag buns. "I'd like to buy all three dozen of them."

The baker picked up a calculator and tapped furiously for a few seconds. She shook her head and rechecked the answer. Finally, she shrugged and looked over at Yan. "You can keep the Chinese money and the U.S. dollars. Both of them are worthless here. For twenty Euros, I can give you sixteen slag buns."

"I can throw in a camel." Yan turned and pointed toward the street.

"The dead one?"

Yan ran over to the door and stared at the beast for a moment. "It's still breathing."

"I don't need a half-dead camel." The baker laughed. "What else do you have?"

· · · · ·

The conductor slid the rail pass through his machine a third time. It finally blinked green, and he handed it back to Yan who was seated in the last row in the economy class car. Sliding the door open, the man moved on to the next railcar, letting the door bang closed behind him.

Thirty-five slag buns were in four bags on the wire luggage shelf above where Yan sat. One was in his hand and as yet, unbitten. He'd managed to save a couple of joints and the disposable lighter, but the baker took the twenty Euros, his entire baggie of cannabis *and* his rolling papers. She wanted his Manchester United cap, which Yan refused to give up, but she agreed to dispose of the camel in exchange for his Swiss Army knife.

He put the pastry on the folding tray in front of him and took a series of photos with his cellphone. Digging in his rucksack, the boy retrieved his mess kit and, using the short camping knife, cut the bun in half.

Yan took another half-dozen pictures of the bun, squeezing it several times to show the interior in more detail. The train was several hours from the Internet, so he queued them in an email to his mother and loaded them to his Facebook page in a holding pattern.

The sun was way ahead of the train, rushing toward the horizon as the moon came up from behind. Yan unhooked his airplane pillow from the clip on the rucksack and wrapped it around his neck. It was the most comfortable he'd been since leaving Beijing.

· · · · ·

The National Security Agency had been tasked with spying on the world for decades. They monitored everything. When Yan's Facebook post, sent from a Russian railcar in the middle of the night, was detected because of the keywords "cheese spread," alarm bells rang from one end of the NSA's basement watchtower to the other.

Within sixty minutes, an unmarked white van was parked in front of Yan's parents' cottage on the farm, and two new students had been enrolled in their lectures at Oxford. It was after midnight, but Lord Fitzpatrick was awakened. He read the dispatch once, crumpled it, and shoved the paper into a pocket of his robe.

Placing his glasses carefully on the nightstand, the Minister of Defense sighed. "Someone will have to wake the Queen."

The aide who'd brought the missive shook his head. "Not me again."

Lord Fitzpatrick pursed his lips. "Do you have a coin?"

· · · · ·

He'd never seen Her Royal Highness so happy to be awakened from a deep sleep. She read the note, not even bothering to ask why it was so crumpled.

"How soon can we get someone to Mongolia?" She asked the question but held her hand up, not waiting for an answer from Lord Fitzpatrick. "No. Don't bother. I know who to call." The Queen squinted to read the digits on the clock. "Let's hope he's still alive."

. . . . .

Xavier Nixon was alive. At least he was breathing and had a feeble pulse. He'd been in Mexico City since early morning and had eaten a taco without cheese, drank half a bottle of cheap rum (there really was a tequila shortage,) and had been beaten senseless by a roving Mexican banda gang.

The rental car was mounted on cinderblocks with the keys still in the ignition. If he had remembered to fill it with gas, XM would never have been stranded in that part of town. They'd taken his wallet. No loss since the credit card had less than fifty bucks available and his motor club membership was expired.

But his cellphone had flown out of his hand when the kid hit him with the bat. Xavier found it under some trash and was about to call for help when help reached out and called him.

Chapter Eighteen - DEFCON 3

General Purpose tossed the secure phone to his aide. "Put this goddamn thing in the vegetable drawer and lock the refrigerator." Walking over to the patio, he opened the doors and let Tanya back in. The tiny pole dancer had been wailing about being cooped up without Netflix while the General was on the phone with the President.

The trio had been sequestered in Corporal Tsunami's townhouse for two days. Cassandra, his live-in girlfriend had been off working in Miami Beach on a forty-seven-story condominium tower. She would be coming home on Saturday and had threatened to move out unless they were gone. Hideo wanted his boss and the whiny, half-size woman gone just as much as Cassandra, but the news media were still holding court at the General's house.

Grabbing a handful of nuts from the bowl on the coffee table, General Purpose dug through them for the macadamias that he put back. He selected several cashews from the pile in his palm and popped them into his mouth. "The insanity continues. The President, who I didn't vote for but still accept as the Commander-in-Chief, is so obsessed with this little skirmish in France that he's re-tasked a satellite and put one of our stealth bombers in orbit over the fighting."

"Without telling you?" Corporal Tsunami opened a two-liter bottle of Mountain Dew and chugged half of it. He belched and then asked, "Doesn't the President want your opinion before doing anything?"

"That was four days ago. The U.S. Open Tennis Championships got underway that afternoon." Clicking the TV remote, the General surfed up to ESPN. "Semi-finals are still in rain delay. He must have had some spare time with the pause in the action and decided to see if the rest of the world was doing anything important."

Tanya went digging in the nut bowl and came away with a fist full of macadamia nuts, her favorite. She'd been wearing one of Cassandra's t-shirts as a cover-up to and from the pool. It was obvious that she'd taken off the wet bathing suit. "I need to do a wash. You rushed me out of the house so fast that I didn't have time to get enough clean clothes."

"We're leaving." General Purpose buttoned his shirt and adjusted his tie.

"Oh, thank God." Stripping off the t-shirt, the woman tossed it to Hideo. "Thanks." She ran into the bedroom and slammed the door.

Corporal Tsunami opened the laundry closet and dropped the shirt in the clothes washer. Reaching for the keys to the General's Escalade, he wrinkled his forehead and asked where they were going.

"First, we're dropping tiny Tanya at the bus station." The General pulled out his wallet and laid a hundred dollars on the coffee table. "Then we're going to the base and deal with this situation in Europe."

"Deal with it?"

"We can't let a lone stealth bomber fight this battle. That pilot needs ground support. We need intel and analysis." Flipping his hat from hand-to-hand, the General's face was as serious as Hideo had ever seen it. "If there's going to be a war in Europe, we sure as hell don't want to be the last ones to the battle."

· · · · ·

Sitting across from each other in the White House Situation Room, the President and Vice-President were playing backgammon. The rain had stopped in Flushing Meadows, New York, and play was about to resume at the U.S. Open Tennis Championship with the first round of semi-finals. The janitor who'd let the two men into the room (neither could remember the secret password) was mixing Bloody Marys while smoking a joint.

The phone, halfway between the two men, buzzed and a red light in the corner of the unit flashed. The Vice-President, holding the dice in his hand, looked over at the President. "You gonna get it?"

The President looked over at the janitor. "No olives in mine." Turning back to the Veep, he shook his head. "Nah. The last time I took a call down here, it was some idiot farmer in Wyoming who claimed the Canadian Army had crossed the border."

"There is no Canadian Army."

"Precisely." The President nodded toward the board. "Roll. You need a six or a five to come in."

Walking over with the drinks, the janitor set them down where the two men could reach them. "I'm going down to the Mess. Can I get you anything, sir? Chips? Salsa? The chef makes some killer guacamole."

The phone continued buzzing, the light blinking furiously. "Do me a favor, son, and answer that. If anyone's looking for me, tell them you haven't seen me or the Veep."

The janitor flipped the handset in the air with his pinkie and caught it before it hit the table. He tapped the flashing button and winked at the President.

"Situation Room. Place your bet."

. . . . .

Twelve hundred miles to the south, General Purpose held the secure phone at arm's length and looked at it with one eye closed. *Place your bet?* "Hideo, are you sure you dialed correctly?"

Corporal Tsunami nodded. "1, 2, 3, P for President."

The General shrugged. "This is General Purpose. I need to speak to the President."

The janitor couldn't stop laughing. "General Purpose? Are you shitting me? Where's your brother, Nuisance? And what about your uncle in the appliance business, General Electric?" He doubled over, smacking the receiver against the oak conference table again and again. "No shit, bro. You just made my day." The janitor dropped the handset back into the cradle and relit his joint. "Damn, Mr. President, this place gets some funny ass calls."

. . . . .

With his screen showing that the call had been disconnected, General Purpose stared at the phone as if it farted. "He hung up on me. Can you believe this craziness?" Looking up at the wall of monitors, he highlighted Western Europe and zoomed in on the Franco-Swiss border. "I want the 1st Armored Division to pack up and move south from Berlin." He paused and shook his head. "No, that's not a good idea." The General switched screens. "We can mobilize the 3rd Marine Division instead."

"From Okinawa?" Corporal Tsunami cocked his head and squinted at the General. "Are you sure?"

"No." General Purpose locked his hands behind his back and marched around in a circle. "We've got to provide some ground support for the pilot of the stealth bomber."

"What about–" With his finger in the air, Hideo was about to suggest the Marine platoon that was holding the Eiffel Tower.

"Aren't the Marines in Paris somewhere?" Straining to read the labels on the various monitors, the General tried to figure out which dot was Paris.

A sergeant manning the console to his left shook his head. "We haven't heard from them since they were attacked, General."

"Attacked? No one told me there was an attack." Turning to his aide, General Purpose shrugged. "Did you know our troops were under attack in Paris?"

Corporal Tsunami shook his head. "No, sir. The last I heard, the situation was under control and they'd taken the high ground."

The wheels in the General's brain picked up speed. "We're under attack from two fronts and the President won't take my call? Screw that." He reached down and grabbed the microphone. His voice would be heard throughout the command center and the General paused to clear his throat before pushing the talk button.

"As commanding officer of the United States military forces, I am declaring a need for an increased level of readiness." He looked down at the sergeant and nodded once. "Sergeant, take us to DEFCON 2."

The sergeant paused with his finger on the red button that would indicate the United States was one rung down the ladder from war. "General, we're at DEFCON 5. Do you really want to skip two levels?"

General Purpose scratched his head. "Really? We're at five?" He shrugged. "Okay, let's go to DEFCON 3 instead. I like odd numbers."

Not wishing to confuse the General further, Corporal Tsunami bent down and whispered in the Sergeant's ear, "Just do it. We can change it later when he's having his massage."

· · · · ·

In the U.S. protectorate of Jerusalem, Sergeant Gregory Zumba watched the threat board change from blue to yellow without stopping at green. He knew the President wouldn't know how to do it and correctly assumed that the commanding General of the Armed Forces was behind the increased level of readiness.

Sergeant Zumba also knew that it was his job to put the Mediterranean fleet on high alert and put the strategic bombers in the air. They were still two steps away from war, but those were baby steps compared to DEFCON 5. He sent a coded transmission to the captain of the USS Enterprise and forwarded the coordinates of the current front lines.

On board the mighty aircraft carrier and namesake of the most famous starship in the Federation, a new type of missile was being attached to the wings of the fighter jets. Thousands of small chunks of recycled tin cans and broken glass bottles had been packed into the inert bombs. Compressed air was pumped into the deadly projectiles so that when they hit the ground, the bombs would explode and send shrapnel flying for hundreds of feet in all directions.

The new missiles had been tested first in the desert with plywood targets, then in a pasture filled with cows. The results were devastating. Bits of cola cans punctured the beasts. Slivers of glass tore through their hides, unfortunately ruining their use in handbags and boots. Those cows closest to the explosion were ripped into steaks, rib roasts, and tenderloins. The meat, delivered to several Air Force bases in the northwest, was cleaned with metal detectors and magnifiers and served as a special Sunday dinner.

An Army regiment stationed outside Stuttgart mobilized, and within four hours, fifteen-hundred soldiers were in trucks moving south toward the French border. Armed with crossbows, high-powered slingshots, and flatbed-mounted catapults, the men could be heard singing "*I can't get no...Satisfaction*" as the troop carriers rumbled through the gates of the military base.

．　．　．　．　．

In the throne room of Buckingham Palace, the Queen was eating lox and bagels for lunch. She'd just remarked that the bagels were nowhere near as good as the ones she'd had in Brooklyn several months prior when she spoke at the United Nations. Lord Fitzpatrick nodded his head in agreement, just as he did whenever the Queen voiced an opinion. A guillotine in the Tower of London was still in operational condition and he had no desire to lose his head over a pastry, cheese-filled or not.

A soldier in full dress uniform marched into the dining room, bowing to Her Majesty and saluting the Minister of Defense. "We've just gotten word that the Americans have declared war on France."

The Minister couldn't control himself. "Bollocks!" His face reddened. "Pardon me, Your Royal Highness."

"That's okay, Freddy. Nothing the Duke hasn't uttered before." She turned to the soldier and raised her left eyebrow. "This has been confirmed?"

"Yes, Your Majesty."

The Queen sighed and dropped the last of the bagel on her plate. "I thought the previous President was dangerous. This one lacks common sense, patience, and every leadership characteristic necessary for the job."

"His re-election is eighteen months away. Do you want to call the Kremlin?" Lord Fitzpatrick reached for his cellphone.

"And speak to that Cossack?" The Queen shook her head. "No. We've all learned what happens when outsiders tinker with the U.S. election system. We don't want a repeat of the previous debacle."

The Minister of Defense sat back in his chair. "So, do we help the French or the Americans?"

Closing her eyes, the Queen of England weighed the options in her mind. On one side of the pond, the American tourists were responsible for the bulk of their revenue during the busy vacation season. On the other, the French had Boulong's cheese. She smiled and opened her eyes, staring hard in the face of Lord Fitzpatrick.

"Put the RAF on standby. If the Americans make any attempt to land on the farmer's island, I want them driven back into the river." The Queen picked up the telephone and dialed the operator. She closed her eyes and lowered her head to her chest as she spoke. "Get the U.S. President on the phone."

Chapter Nineteen - Hostage

It took Mookie over an hour, but eventually, he was able to hitch a ride. The woman who picked him up in her Jaguar was headed south and could take him as far as Tavaux. Mookie had a friend who lived just outside of town who would drive him the rest of the way home if she could drop him off at his friend's house.

She had the top down and in a flannel shirt and ripped jeans, looked a bit too casual for the auto. The radio, tuned to a rock station, was muted when Mookie first got into the car, but the woman cranked up the volume, singing along and letting her blond hair float back in the wind.

Reaching inside the loose flannel shirt, she took out a joint and handed it to the boy.

"Light this, will ya? There's a disposable in the armrest."

Mookie found the lighter and was able to ignite the joint by bending low enough to get out of the wind. He took a few hits and handed it to the woman. She puffed quickly and exhaled, handing it back to him.

"Go ahead and smoke it. I only need one hit."

Smiling, Mookie sucked harder, burning it halfway down. He joined her singing, but only the chorus. She seemed to know every word and could easily carry the tune. Mookie held his hand out in the slipstream and pretended he could fly.

. . . . .

A mile north of Dijon, the woman suggested they stop for a quick dinner, her treat. It was getting late, and she'd been driving since dawn without stopping.

"I don't have any money." Mookie turned his pockets inside out. "But my friend can pay you back when you drop me off."

She pulled off the highway at a rest stop and parked as far away from the road as she could. "I don't need your money, Mookie."

"How do you know my name?" He sat against the door and tried to focus on her face. It was a blur and her cheeks appeared to be caving in on themselves.

The woman smiled and pulled a pneumatic syringe from her purse. Without another word, she leaned over and discharged the device into Mookie's neck.

· · · · ·

When he awoke, the boy was strapped into a seat onboard a small jet. His hands were shackled to his waist and ankle cuffs bound his legs. The woman who'd been driving the Jaguar sat opposite him, drinking Mountain Dew from a bottle. Her hair had changed from blonde to black, and the jeans and red flannel shirt had been replaced by a lavender jumpsuit with the initials "LD" embroidered over the pocket.

Mookie looked out the window and saw nothing but clouds. "Where are we? Where are we going?" He shook his head. "You looked better as a blonde."

"So many questions for a little boy."

"Six-two is little? And I've got your 'little boy'." Mookie nodded at his crotch. "Cut me loose and this little boy will bring your education up to date."

She laughed. "Here I am with a degree and you're still in kindergarten."

Mookie opened his mouth to retort, and she shoved a lace handkerchief in before he could speak.

"Now, listen to me very carefully because I never repeat myself. You're in a very expensive jet that's on its way to Rome. There's a nice old German fellow who needs you to convince your father that his cheese spread belongs in the Vatican's kitchen before Sunday Mass. He's not as patient as I am and certainly not having as much fun. But he pays well and absolves me of all the sins I'm prone to commit, so we have a very amicable working relationship between a Catholic and a Jew."

The jet bounced through some turbulence and the woman paused while the captain came over the intercom and apologized. He also let his two passengers know that they were forty-five minutes from landing. She pulled the handkerchief from his mouth and dropped it on the cabin floor.

"Did you get all that?"

"You're holding me hostage for my father's cheese?" Mookie's eyebrows shot up and he laughed. "Are you shitting me?"

. . . . .

In the rain, Boulong and Mikey dug six graves on the east side of the island facing the Alps. It was a rocky area where the cows never grazed. The farmer was loath to build a pyre and finish the cremation of the already well-done bodies. His family's ashes were the only ones that were going to rest on his island. Mixing them with strangers was never going to happen. The final resting place of these warriors would give them a marvelous view of the mountains and isolated them from Paradise.

Father and son completed the repairs to the dock just before sunset. Thunder and lightning surrounded them as Boulong drove the Gator up to the tool shed.

Melinda was downstairs in the bedroom, splayed out on the king-size bed with an empty wine bottle in one hand. From the depth of her snoring, Boulong knew she would sleep until she got up to pee before dawn. He eased the bottle from her fingers and went upstairs to make dinner.

. . . . .

Mikey was hobbling around the house, closing windows and wiping up rain with a roll of paper towels.

"I filled the tank on the generator. We're good until morning."

"I'm going to check the Internet." Boulong walked into the kitchen and took the laptop down from the shelf by the bathroom.

Just across the Doubs, on the Swiss side, a retired taxidermist had put up a Wi-Fi repeater and given Boulong the password. In exchange, Boulong let the man come over to his barn every few months and butcher a cow that they all shared. The murdered bovine that Mikey had put in the freezer the other day would mean the old stuffer would have to wait until autumn, but Boulong would make it up to him with a goat as a bonus next time.

While the laptop awakened, Boulong put on a pot of water to boil and pulled the wrapped tenderloin from the fridge.

"Do you want to make that spicy cheese sauce you've been talking about?"

Mikey shook his head. "Nah. Not tonight." He nodded toward the stairs. "Is she okay?"

"Drunk." Boulong shrugged. "Out until her bladder calls."

"Not the kind of shit you expect to see in Paradise."

"Not the sort of thing that's ever happened here before, and I want to know what the hell is going on in the world to cause it."

The laptop beeped and the login screen came up. Boulong sat down and entered his password. He gave the computer a few minutes to load whatever it was loading that made the little blue circle spin so frantically and checked the pot of water on the stove.

Boulong received email on his cellphone but the tiny screen was useless when it came to getting the news on a web browser. He tapped the icon and began scrolling through the articles. The skunk problem in Paris was the lead. It was followed by news that the U.S. State of Hawaii was now an independent nation and an article about falling cannabis prices.

·   ·   ·   ·   ·

When a man sees his name in the news for the first time, he immediately wonders if it's someone else with the same name. Maybe he's won the lottery and doesn't know it. Perhaps he's a wanted criminal and the police are announcing a lead. Perhaps it's something much worse. Boulong read the headline twice to himself before turning the screen toward his son.

"I can't read it from here." Mikey squinted. "What does it say?"

Boulong didn't need to see it again. "War over Boulong's cheese imminent."

·   ·   ·   ·   ·

The runway was still wet as the jet landed at the private airstrip. Mookie expected to see a black stretch limousine and was a bit disappointed when he was shoved into the backseat of an old Chevy Blazer. The woman got in from the opposite side and took out a compact to touch up her face. Having switched to jeans, a black t-shirt, and a Mets baseball cap, the pilot who'd flown them to Rome took the wheel.

"When we get to the Vatican, we will go in through a delivery entrance. I am going to remove your shackles. If you attempt to escape or to alert anyone of your situation, you will suffer terribly." She took his chin in her hand. "You have such a pretty face. It would be a shame to ruin it because of some cheese."

Mookie pursed his lips. "Look, as much as I love my face, sitting me down with the Pope isn't going to help you get my father's cheese. The guy who gives him free Wi-Fi can't get him to give up a pound of that shit." He shrugged. "And my father groups God together with Santa Claus, the Easter bunny, and free cannabis."

Squeezing his chin hard enough to cause the boy pain, the woman pulled him closer to her face. "You don't have the mental capacity to understand the gravity of this situation." She reached into her pocket and pulled out Mookie's cellphone and wallet. "You don't realize just how far my arms reach."

He gulped and tried to pull his head away, but her grip was too strong.

"I am not a killer. You don't have to worry about me pulling a knife and gutting you or shooting a bolt into the back of your head." She sighed. "That was a long time ago. Now, I pay a very obedient fellow to handle those affairs. I'd be glad to introduce you to him, but it's better for you that you two never meet."

The pilot called from the front seat, "Next left, two blocks, and then we're there."

She took the key from her purse and unlocked the ankle shackles first. "Are we communicating?"

Mookie nodded. "Yeah. I hear you."

. . . . .

It was Mookie calling. Boulong, still in shock from the newsfeed, tried to make himself pissed off at his missing son and failed.

"Where are you? Are you okay?"

"Dad, listen to me very carefully. First, I'm totally sober. Second, I'm not in jail. I was, but I got out, and, well, I'll tell you about that some other time."

Boulong's temper took control. "Where the hell are you?"

"Look, I'm in Rome, okay? It's not my fault and I've been trying to get home to help with the cheese."

"What are you doing in Rome?" Boulong dropped his hand with the phone to his side. He looked over at Mikey and furrowed his brow. "Your brother is in Rome. I thought he was in Paris?"

Mikey shrugged. "How did he get to Rome and when is he coming back?"

Boulong failed to see the importance of either of those questions and posed his own instead. Tapping the speaker button, he asked in his most neutral voice, "Have you heard about the war?"

A few seconds of silence were all that they heard, and the farmer was about to repeat his question when Mookie answered.

"That's what I'm calling about, dad."

Chapter Twenty - Grapple This

Yan Ling Po wasn't surprised to see Russian soldiers lined up on the platform as the train pulled into the station. He'd been to Moscow before, where the military and police still outnumbered regular citizens. Of course, anyone could be a member of the Secret Police. And then there was the Top Secret Police and an even more mysterious So Secret that even they didn't know they were Police. Yan squinted through the window. These guys were regular Army.

Tying his boots, the boy swallowed the last chunk of a slag bun. It was the best breakfast, just as it had been the best dinner the previous night. He washed it down with the last of the water from his canteen and wiped his hands on his jeans.

The soldiers poured into the train car, rushing toward him with their crossbows and dart guns pointed at his heart. An officer worked his way around the men and came to a stop in front of Yan.

"You are Yan Ling Po?" he asked, which seemed to the boy to be obvious by the British flag on his baseball cap.

"Yes." Yan held out his hand. "And you are?"

The officer pointed at the bag of slag buns on the seat. "You bought those in Ulaanbaatar?"

"Most of them." Sliding the paper sack closer to him, Yan burped. "I ate a few of them on the way here."

"They are contraband." Bending over, the officer grabbed the paper sack before Yan could stop him. "You are under arrest for bringing contraband across the border and into Russia."

"What? Wait." Yan held his backpack tightly, but the soldiers were too strong. They yanked the pack out of his hands and pulled the boy from his seat, throwing him to the floor of the railcar.

The officer reached for the radio clipped to this collar. "We've got him."

. . . . .

Xavier read the text a third time and checked the coordinates again. "Mongolia?"

He sent the woman a reply: "What's in Mongolia?"

Her reply was one word: "Cheese."

Blowing out a long breath, the pilot shrugged and stuffed his cellphone into his back pocket. A limo was on its way to pick him up and take him to an airport. According to her instructions, he was to fly her jet to Hong Kong, where he'd be refueled. From there, Xavier was to fly to an airport on the outskirts of Ulaanbaatar where he'd be met by a baker.

A baker? XM looked out the window of the San Diego Hilton and smiled. The weather was perfect, as it always was in Southern California. He loved to fly, especially if it was someone else's jet. Her Gulfstream was one of his favorites.

Having bid farewell to Chef Ronzoni, Xavier drove to Mexico City in a failed attempt to retrieve his seaplane. Thankfully, the injuries he received at the hands of the banda gang were superficial and a fresh rental car was waiting for him when he was released from the Mexican hospital.

With a minimal number of bandages on his face, the pilot had no problem crossing the border with a passport LD had procured and sent by courier to XM's bedside. Safely back on U.S. soil, he checked into the Hilton and was making the most of room service. Despite the wonderful climate, the swimming pool sprinkled with available women, and the variety of dining options street-side, XM Nixon intended to sample every item on the room service menu while he waited for LD, his wealthy benefactor to call again. He'd finished the lunch appetizers and was about to order a burger when her first text came through.

His initial thoughts were of relief. A screw up at the level he'd just suffered was not something he thought he'd survive. The woman rarely handed out second chances. Xavier figured his value as a pilot was his saving grace, especially given that few aviators would take her on as a client.

After a short stint in the Air Force where Xavier discovered he could not only fly better than any of the other recruits, but was also willing to grab the throttle of anything with an engine, he'd answered a newspaper ad and met LD. She was searching for a pilot to fly a seaplane from downtown Manhattan to the Caribbean once a week.

The Caribbean was a loose term that included Cuba, Jamaica, and the Yucatan where XM sat in the cockpit while unknown packages were loaded into the hold. He was instructed in no uncertain terms to never ask what was in them or leave his seat, even at gunpoint, while the seaplane was docked outside the United States.

Each flight had a different copilot seated next to him. Some were men, but the majority were women. They spoke little during the flight. None of the women were interested in dinner. None of the men wanted to go for a drink once the mission was complete.

Xavier accepted the missions without question. The pay was ten times what a commercial pilot made. Dud had taken the danger out of the equation. And having peace and quiet during a three-hour trip from New York harbor to the Cuban capital made flying as easy as autopilot.

. . . . .

The phone rang and Xavier sprawled across the king-size bed to answer it. His limo was here and did he need help with his bags? Xavier told the hotel operator no and hung up the phone. He dumped the plate of cookies into his gym bag and grabbed two hand towels from the bathroom on his way out the door. The galley on LD's Gulfstream was always well-stocked, but he'd learned from experience that the food wasn't there for the crew.

Today's copilot didn't look old enough to shave, much less fly a twenty-million-dollar jet. He nodded at Xavier and went back to his checklist.

"You got much time in this model?" The senior pilot adjusted his seat and looked over expectantly at the kid.

"I've flown everything Gulfstream sells." Flipping the checklist to the next page, the copilot looked up briefly at Xavier. "You?"

"Just this one." Xavier opened his case and took out the pilot's checklist. "These days, I only fly for LD."

The kid said nothing and continued down the page.

"You ever fly for her before?" Rotating his sunglasses to the top of his head, Xavier began testing the controls.

Again, no response from his copilot.

"Look, we've got twenty-one hours of flight time ahead of us. I know you guys are told to zip it and just fly, but I left my finger puppets at home and my imaginary girlfriend is on vacation." Xavier dropped the checklist in his lap and held out his hand. "Xavier Milhous Nixon, but you can call me XM."

The kid leaned the clipboard against the wheel and looked over at Xavier. He sighed and shook the pilot's hand. "She said you like to talk too much."

·　·　·　·　·

The prison where they'd thrown Yan Ling Po wasn't on any of the Moscow tourist maps. No one offered to call the British Embassy and let them know that one of their citizens had run afoul of the law. Sitting on the metal bunk inside his cell, the boy rubbed the knot on the back of his head. He'd landed one good punch to the soldier who was dragging him off the train before someone slammed the butt of a crossbow into his skull.

The remaining slag buns had been shipped under guard to the Moscow Culinary Laboratory. A Russian chef, who was in reality a Kremlin spy, had murdered his French counterpart at their restaurant in Chaumont with a blowgun. He had taken the last three tubs of Boulong's cheese and had been extracted at midnight by a Russian Air Force helicopter that landed in the middle of the A5.

Tasting and testing both cheeses with the most advanced culinary deconstructor in existence, a group of cooks broke them down to their molecular components. Whiteboards were filled with chemical equations and images from an electron microscope scrolled across a bank of computer screens.

A Gordon Ramsay look-alike flew into the lab and screamed in a variety of Russian dialects at the scientists. He insinuated that one of the chefs had the tastebuds of a mountain goat and then stormed out of the lab, slamming the door closed behind him.

Moments later, the activity screeched to a halt as the door was opened by a soldier carrying a dart rifle over his shoulder. Two more soldiers marched in and took up positions on either side of the doorway. Their rifles were held out in front and they swept the room searching for threats.

Coming to attention, they turned and saluted the woman who rolled into the room in a gold-plated wheelchair. Its silent motor and extra wide wheels rolled to a stop in front of the cooks. Her expression was one of annoyance, as though she'd been interrupted while stirring borscht and it was going to burn. Staring around the room, her sneer pierced everyone in the lab. Most seemed to be holding their breath, and no one spoke, even to greet her.

She wore an apron that looked as though it covered her clothing seven days a week. Perhaps she even slept in it. Every color of the rainbow was represented by a stain, including streaks of dried blood. It may have been white when new, but desert sand was now the background color as though the cleanliness had been washed away, never to return.

Gliding across the room in the motorized chariot, she stopped at the table holding the cheese samples and stuck her finger into the beaker on the left. Tasting the cheese, she smiled. "This is Boulong's cheese."

She licked the finger clean and repeated the test on the other sample.

"This is not, but it's damn close." She looked around the room. "How much do we have?"

A chef to her right raised his hand.

"You're not in sixth grade, Boris."

He blushed. "Twenty-nine buns, not counting the cheese in the beaker."

"Not nearly enough." She turned to the soldier who'd opened the door. "Tell the Colonel to go get the rest."

"All of it?"

She nodded. "Every kilo and then burn the place to the ground."

． ． ． ． ．

The Gulfstream had been refueled so quickly when they landed in Hong Kong that Xavier hadn't had time to get takeout. He'd eaten the last of the four-inch chocolate chip cookies two hours ago and was hungry enough to eat a cat. They were cleared to cross mainland China and were less than a hundred miles from the Mongolian border when the radar chirped. His growling stomach stopped abruptly.

"We've got company." Xavier increased the forward range of the scan. "Three jets. Russian MiGs."

The copilot leaned over and looked at the radar screen. "If you stay above them, they can't hit us with rocks."

Brilliant. His first words in four hours and that's all he's got? "I know, but they can out-fly us and they've got grapple bombs."

"Grapple bombs? I've never heard of them."

As soon as you graduate from high school you will. "They're mounted under the wings. Small canisters with a parachute at one end and an iron grapple inside. They get sucked into the engines and the grapple tears the fan blades all to shit." Xavier reset the onboard computer screen. "We're well outside Russian airspace. What the hell are they doing here?"

The Russian jets passed them at supersonic speed. One flew straight at the Gulfstream, peeling up and away seconds before it would have collided. The other two MiGs soared so close underneath their jet that Xavier had trouble holding it level. They came around from behind and the threat indicators lit up on both sides of the console.

"They're coming in to attack." Xavier shoved the throttle to maximum and pulled back hard on the yoke.

"What are you doing?" The copilot's voice was loaded with fear, and Xavier wondered if he'd pissed in his pants.

"A loop. A big goddamn loop."

"They'll follow us."

"Uh, huh."

The kid tightened his seatbelt. "Can we outrun a Russian MiG?" He pointed at the radar. "Three of them?"

"We won't have to." Xavier smiled and reached for the radio. "Hot Pants, Hot Pants, this is Blackbird, over."

The radio hissed for a second and then: "Blackbird, are you on the ground?" It was a woman's voice, soft but commanding.

"Negative, Hot Pants. We have Cossacks on our six. They appear to be hostile."

"Can you keep your shit together for ninety seconds, Blackbird?"

"Yes, ma'am." Xavier slipped the microphone back into its clip. He turned to the kid and nodded. "I hope you like roller coasters."

· · · · ·

Xavier sent the Gulfstream screaming for the sky. It was a maneuver designed to encourage their pursuers to follow. Once into the loop, the Russian pilots couldn't release their weapons. Gravity would work in Xavier's favor. But the trick would only work one time and only if Hot Pants was on her game.

Pulling the yoke back as far as it would go, the pilot hoped the MiGs weren't going to be fast enough to get ahead of them. They were close to the top of the arc and their airspeed was dropping too low for the jet to fly.

With the threat indicators now flashing as though it was the last day of their lives, the young copilot shouted, "Stall indicator!" as the Gulfstream approached its operational ceiling.

Xavier banked out of the loop and began a dive from thirty-six-thousand feet to the barren waste of the Mongolian desert below. The MiGs followed him, closing with every foot they dropped.

They were at nine-thousand feet when the cavalry arrived.

"More jets." The copilot grabbed at the window. "Coming in from our right."

Xavier looked at his watch. "Right on time."

A swarm of Chinese fighter jets–ten of them armed with grapple bombs and air-launched harpoons–closed on the Russian MiGs, scattering the three much smaller jets to the west. They chased the Russians until they were out of sight of the Gulfstream. Xavier hoped they would stay with them all the way to the Caspian Sea.

He leveled the Gulfstream and selected their destination from the computer screen. Blowing out a quick breath, Xavier looked at the kid and tried to hold a serious expression. "We're twenty minutes out. You know how to land this thing, junior?"

Chapter Twenty-One - Competition

Mookie verified everything that Boulong had seen on the Internet. Even with the Pope waving in the background, the farmer had a hard time believing his son had discussed world affairs at that level. Boulong filled in the missing pieces for all involved, describing in detail the destruction of their dock and the failed helicopter attack.

"Who's the woman over your left shoulder?" Widening the image with his fingers, Boulong tried to recall her face.

Mookie smiled. "Everyone calls her LD."

"LD?"

"Lorna Doone, like the cookie." Mookie turned the lens toward the woman. "She's the one who brought me here to convince you that all our cheese has to come to the Vatican."

"To make pizza?" Chuckling at his own joke, Boulong narrowed his gaze. "Why should we give an exclusive to the Catholic Church?"

The woman stepped closer to Mookie's phone. "Because that's the only way to avoid the war."

"By giving all our cheese to the Vatican?" Boulong laughed. "You think the Church has the power to prevent war? No one likes the Pope. I heard that his last public Mass was attended by seven street sweepers and a Jewish couple that was looking for a deli."

"You don't understand." The woman's face was hard, and she pointed a manicured finger at the lens.

"No. You're the one who doesn't understand." Shaking his head, the farmer leaned closer to the camera. "God doesn't eat cheese. God doesn't keep my cows happy. And God sure as shit is not going to dictate who I sell my dairy products to, not as long as I'm the one squeezing the udders."

The woman took a step back from Mookie's cellphone camera, grabbing it out of the boy's hands, and drew a dart gun from her purse. She aimed the gun at the boy's left ear and stared coldly into the lens.

"I'm not someone who makes idle threats, Mr. Boulong. Your cheese in exchange for your son's life. It's a simple equation. Solve it correctly and your boy will be home before sunset to help you make the cheese. Wrong answer and his death will be just the beginning."

Boulong couldn't breathe. He held the phone so tightly that his palm was sweating. Focusing on the woman's face was impossible, and he tried to look away, but her eyes held his gaze. He forced the word "No" out of his mouth and then his throat went dry.

Mookie closed his eyes and held his hands out in front of his chest. Coming up from behind, the pilot grabbed the boy's arms and pinned them tightly behind his back. Mookie struggled, but the man was far too strong.

"It's just cheese, Mr. Boulong." She pushed the dart into the hair on the side of Mookie's head. "One squeeze and your son dies over a dairy product. Is your cheese more valuable than your son?"

"No," Boulong whispered. Again, the only word his brain could form.

"Then we have a deal, Mr. Boulong?" The woman put her arm around Mookie's shoulders.

Boulong tried to nod, but his body wouldn't respond. Blowing out his breaths as though he'd just finished a marathon, the dairy farmer felt himself getting dizzy. Speaking was impossible. The only word that bounced around his head was his son's name. And what was making it even worse, it was being spoken in his ex-wife's voice.

"Well?" The woman was running out of patience. She pushed the boy away and pointed the weapon between his eyes. "I'm going to count to five. One. Two. Three–"

Her count was interrupted by a ringing from her pocket. Lowering the weapon, the woman took a step back from Mookie and answered the call.

"You've got it?" She smiled. "And the woman was satisfied with the arrangement?" Another smile. "Wonderful. Get the hell out of there. Those MiGs will be back with reinforcements and I've run out of favors with the Chinese."

She ended the call and slipped the cellphone back into the pocket of her jeans. "Well, Mr. Boulong, it seems as though we might not need your cheese after all."

"Oh?" Boulong's breathing slowed, and he relaxed his grip on the phone.

The woman snapped the safety in place on the dart gun. "We may have found another source."

. . . . .

The Queen was swimming laps with a kickboard and floaties when Lord Fitzpatrick burst into the royal gymnasium and ran over to the pool.

"The Russians have the cheese!"

She came to a stop in the middle of the pool and stood in the waist deep water. "Boulong's cheese?"

"No, something similar from Mongolia."

"The Mongolians cook barbecue. When did they come up with cheese?" Her Royal Highness pushed the styrofoam kickboard over to the edge of the pool and climbed out. "Can we get any of it? The dinner party is tomorrow night."

The Minister of Defense shook his head. "Not unless you call your friend in New York."

"She's behind this?"

He nodded and pursed his lips. "She called five minutes ago and told me the basics. She said to call her back after your swim."

"Dammit." Reaching for a towel, the Queen of England wrapped herself in it and looked around the ceiling. "I want this room swept for bugs again."

. . . . .

The news of an attack by Russian MiGs reached General Purpose while he was having breakfast. Corporal Tsunami was on the secure phone relaying the message while the General chased two tiny pieces of bacon around the plate with the crust from his toast.

"It was an American Gulfstream. Privately owned but the copilot was Air Force."

Giving up on the bread, the General tapped his finger on the bacon and licked it clean with his tongue. "Our Air Force?"

"Yes, sir. His orders came from the White House."

"Baldy assigned one of our pilots to fly a mission on a private citizen's jet? To goddamn Mongolia?" General Purpose slammed his palms on the table. "What the hell is going on?"

Covering the phone with his hand, Tsunami looked at the General and just shrugged.

Trying to get a grip on the situation, General Purpose added some cream to his coffee and stirred it with his finger. He closed his eyes in deep thought for a few seconds and then looked over at his aide. "How'd they outrun the MiGs?"

Corporal Tsunami asked the question and nodded as he listened to the response. "The Chinese."

"The Chinese attacked the MiGs? The Russian MiGs?" General Purpose pushed the empty plate away and held out his hand. "Gimme that thing."

The voice on the other end of the line came from Jerusalem. Sergeant Zumba had watched the entire episode from a satellite feed and, following established protocol, made his report to the commanding officer. He left out the part where the pilot helped two women onboard the Gulfstream while it was on the ground in Mongolia. The resolution from the spy satellite wasn't clear enough to see their faces, but there was no mistaking the cleavage.

At the General's order, he transmitted the video to the military base in Orlando and asked if he should also send it to the White House.

"They haven't put a monitor on the tennis court, so I wouldn't bother." General Purpose watched the spinning blue circle on the monitor. "How long is it?"

"Ten minutes, sir, but the connection is running slow this morning."

Baldy's streaming porno. "The entire network seems to be bogged down with some major task." He leaned over to Corporal Tsunami and whispered, "Six televisions in his bedroom, and I'll bet he's got a different movie on each one. If the man could only put that much effort into running the government we wouldn't have so many states threatening to secede."

"What are your orders, sir?" Sergeant Zumba was a man who lived for efficiency.

"Put an AWACS surveillance plane over the area to keep an eye on things. Move the satellite closer to Moscow. If the Russians are planning on joining this fracas, we need to know as soon as they strap on their boots." Folding his last piece of toast, the General nodded once. "And reach out to the Chinese ambassador to the United Nations. Tell him I said *arigato*."

Corporal Tsunami raised his eyebrows. "That's Japanese, sir."

"Whatever. Just thank him, okay?"

· · · · ·

The Queen stood on one of the many pigeon-crap-covered balconies of the palace and looked at the gathering clouds. It had been sunny for nearly half an hour and she was working on her tan. Turning to walk back inside, Lord Fitzpatrick met her at the threshold and handed Her Royal Highness the phone.

"It's Ronzoni."

Lifting her crown from the small table by the door, she placed it on her head and took the phone from Lord Fitzpatrick.

"Chef, good afternoon. I trust you had a pleasant flight."

The Chef's voice was taught, respectful, and far too formal for someone he'd known for thirty-one years. "Your Majesty, I shall eventually recover the feeling in my legs from sitting in a coach class seat, but it is always my duty to the crown and I shall not–"

"Cut the crap, Giuseppe. Where are you?"

"In my kitchen, Your Highness."

"Good. A Gulfstream is flying over the pole as we speak. It will be landing at Heathrow in five hours. On board is a cheese that's supposed to be better than Boulong's. I want you to prepare the boar fillet with it and bring me a sample to taste."

"As you wish, sire."

"And Giuseppe, don't try to fool me with Cheese Whiz again. We have lots of room in the Tower dungeon."

· · · · ·

Boulong wiped the sweat from his eyes and stared at the woman. "What about my son?"

"You mean my guest?" She smiled. "I could use some company after the strenuous day I've had." Wrapping her arm around Mookie's waist, the woman pulled him closer. "I'll see to it that he gets home safe and sound. But not right away."

"I...I need him to make cheese."

"Sorry, Mr. Farmer, I need him for something far more important than cheese." She winked and ended the call.

Melinda shuffled over in her bedroom slippers and took Boulong's hands. "Maybe she has a hot tub."

Chapter Twenty-Two – The Magic Kingdom Attack

The janitor was dusting when the threat board lit up and the alarms went off. Ducking under the massive conference table, his first thought was that it was an attack and his ass was ground zero. When nothing exploded, he got up and checked all the buttons, dials, and handsets he'd just cleaned to make sure it wasn't something he'd pushed in error.

Silencing the klaxon was his primary concern. A red button was flashing on the console in front of the illuminated map of the world. The janitor walked over and pushed it with the tip of his broom. Peace returned to the empty conference room, but a smaller red light was now visible about an inch from the South Florida coast. Not having a legend to help him translate the distance, he guessed it was around a hundred miles...give or take.

The klaxon only stayed quiet for a minute. When it resumed its screeching, two more lights on the console began flashing in rhythm. On the threat board, three small green lights appeared over Central Florida and began heading toward the red one in the Gulf of Mexico.

．　．　．　．　．

Two-thousand miles south of the flashing lights and crying klaxon, the Mexican barge Dobby had triggered an underwater sensor designed to alert U.S. authorities of drug trafficking. They'd ringed the peninsula with devices that would detect any vessel larger than a rowboat that was attempting to reach the U.S. shores illegally.

The Dobby, a large barge that was normally used to haul trash out to the middle of the Gulf and dump it, was on a course that would bring it to Marco Island on the west coast of Florida. According to Google Maps, there was a beach large enough to land the ship and roll off the Cessna that had been outfitted with the atomic bomb.

Other than the ship's captain and his mate, the only other person onboard was the Mexican President, but he was still bound and unconscious. The bomb that was originally strapped to the underside of the airplane with duct tape was now resting on a pile of broken lobster traps. Saltwater had loosened the mounting, and the weapon had fallen and almost rolled into the Gulf of Mexico. It was far too heavy for the two men to lift and re-tape, but they figured there would be plenty of help from their former countrymen once they landed.

. . . . .

Approaching the Dobby from the east, three Air Force reconnaissance jets armed with grapple bombs were on their way to identify the threat. At the same time, three men spread across the globe watched in silence as they tried to figure out what was going on.

The President had been interrupted in the middle of his evening "research" into adding sex workers to his healthcare plan due to be rolled out in a few months. He was now in the Situation Room trying to explain to the janitor which buttons controlled the klaxon and how to unlock the liquor cabinet.

At the military base in Orlando, General Purpose was screaming at his underlings in a vain attempt to find out who had given the order to launch his jets. His aide, who had the keys to the vending machines, was distributing candy and singing, "*It's the end of the world as we know it, and I feel fine.*"

And deep within the kosher command center in Jerusalem, Sergeant Gregory Zumba sat back and folded his hands behind his head. He'd just prevented an atomic war.

. . . . .

The jets came in low at a thousand feet above the barge. On the deck, the pilots could see two men waving. One of them had a flag, the other a pitchfork. They couldn't tell from that altitude whether or not it was retractable, but decided that it was a threatening gesture. They banked and assumed an attack formation.

"Taco leader to command, we have the target in view and are preparing to attack."

"Taco leader, you are clear to fire. Repeat, you are clear to fire."

The lead jet inched forward and dipped its nose. "Taco leader to Taco flight. On my command." The jets swooped down to five hundred feet. Seeing the barge fill his bombsight, the pilot squeezed his microphone and the bomb release at the same time. "Now. Drop, drop, drop."

Six five-hundred-pound grapple bombs slipped simultaneously from their mounts on the fighter jets. Moments later, they slammed into the deck of the barge, releasing their sharpened prongs as the wood splintered and caught. The casing of the bombs continued through the ship and pierced the hull. Holes so large that a humpback whale could have swum through them without catching a fin tore apart the flat bottom of the barge, and it began filling with the warm water of the Gulf.

Grabbing a life preserver, the captain and the mate jumped overboard. Neither one could swim and they waved their arms frantically as the fighter jets sped off in the distance. The Cessna slid toward the stern as the barge sank. Bound and seated in the pilot's seat of the small aircraft, the Mexican President took a last gulp of air as water filled the cockpit.

The jets circled once and dipped their wings to let the two sailors know that help was on the way. They went to afterburners, heading east toward Orlando. An afternoon baseball game was starting and the three pilots had money on the table.

·　·　·　·　·

All but two of the bomb-carrying terrorists had been captured. Their red legal bags loaded with fissionable material were taken to Area 51 to be stored in the same salt mines as spent nuclear fuel rods. Police and the FBI dusted the captured terrorists' sandals for clues and found nothing besides athlete's foot fungus.

The pair of suicide bombers still on the loose were standing in line at the main entrance to Disney World, unaware that the first attempt on the Magic Kingdom was now at the bottom of the Gulf of Mexico along with the late President of Mexico.

"I am going to kill the mouse." The younger of the two terrorists slicked back his hair. "He is the symbol of the infidel. He must die first."

"No," argued his partner, "the Queen is our target. It is written."

"The Queen?" The first terrorist laughed. "A woman has no power. It is the man mouse who controls her destiny and he must be put down so that she understands Allah's great plan for the universe."

A little girl standing in line behind the men tugged on the older one's shirt. "You're in the wrong line for Universal." She turned and pointed across the parking lot. "The entrance is way over there."

Smiling, the younger terrorist knelt and asked the girl, "Are you still a virgin?"

Her father, a cross-country trucker who had survived tornadoes, highwaymen, and rotten food, grabbed the terrorist by the shirt collar and lifted him off his feet. "You miserable piece of shit." He pounded his fist into the bomber's face and knocked several teeth out of the man's mouth.

Joining the battle, the older of the two terrorists tried to grab the trucker around the neck. He went airborne as the girl's father flipped him into a fountain. Several other parents standing in the queue saw the girl break down in tears and began beating on the two foreign-looking men with bags, umbrellas, and souvenir plastic crossbows.

Ever-vigilant security forces descended on the line and clubbed the two bombers into unconsciousness. Moving as though they were suspended by a magnetic force, the Disney World police dragged the men into the underground labyrinth of service tunnels before most of the guests had a chance to snap a photo.

In the confusion, someone picked up the two red leather briefcases and disappeared with them. A maintenance man speared the two pair of desert sandals and dropped them into his rolling trash container.

．　．　．　．　．

The President took another sip of his gin and tonic and nodded with a smile on his face. "Hell of a good drink, son."

Stirring his beverage with his pinky, the janitor thanked the President. He'd been mixing drinks at a local pub in his off hours and was giving serious thought to leaving the White House and working full time at the Drink Shack. The hours were better, and they had more than one large screen television. With football season only a few months away, the janitor was going to need to watch all the games at the same time to keep his bookmaking operation solvent.

"What happened to the dots?"

"That's a kill." Taking another slurp of his drink, the President set the plastic cup on some papers and reached for the remote. He tapped rewind and waited until the three green dots were just starting to move across the State of Florida. "Those are F-15s out of McGill. I rode in one once." The President pinched the bridge of his nose. "Puked all over myself. No one told me not to eat breakfast before going up."

The green dots passed over the red, turned, and came back from the opposite direction. The jets slowed, sped up, and went back over the area where the red dot had been moments before. It was gone.

"That'll show 'em." The President winked at the janitor. "I've got some unfinished business in the West Wing." He nodded toward the pitcher in front of the janitor. "One more for good luck?"

·   ·   ·   ·   ·

Sergeant Zumba unwrapped a falafel pita and dipped it into the little container of tahini sauce. Having grown up on the Americanized version of Middle Eastern cuisine, every meal had opened his eyes further to authentic Israeli food. He'd been doing a web search based on the word "kosher" when the Dobby had set off the alarm.

The President had called twice. First to ask who'd ordered the attack and second to make sure the Sergeant told anyone else who asked that it was a Presidential Directive that set the wheels in motion. Zumba explained it in those terms to the irate General Purpose who only stopped screaming when he ran out of breath.

Tearing off a chunk of the crusty bread, the sole occupant of the Jerusalem command center scooped the last of the sauce from the plastic cup and held it on his tongue for a few seconds. It was the best he'd eaten since being transferred.

While the huge glowing threat board was programmed to follow all the military activity around the globe, several non-governmental aircraft were also tracked for various reasons. The Gulfstream that lifted off from a private runway outside of Rome was one of them. It came up as a lavender dot with its designation in capital letters below it. Sergeant Zumba put down the loaded piece of pita and enlarged the area.

LORNA DOONE? Nabisco has a monitored aircraft? He entered the airplane's unique designation into the computer terminal on his desk. *And it's armed?* The sergeant watched as the lavender speck moved north and then turned toward the west. Taking a sip from his can of Dr. Brown's Cream Soda, he closed the styrofoam takeout container and dropped it into the trashcan. *Where are you going, little bird?*

The dot continued turning west, making a long sweeping arc that brought it over the Adriatic Sea. It went "feet dry" crossing into Croatia where it began a turn to the north. Sergeant Zumba finished the last dregs of his soda and tossed the can into the trash. He looked up at the digital clock over the threat board. The lavender dot had been on the move for over ninety minutes. He had to pee.

. . . . .

General Purpose was watching the same lavender dot and asking a similar set of questions. He'd never heard of a Lorna Doone and figured it was someone's code name. Corporal Tsunami had been searching the Internet for a match but kept coming back to either the cookie or a fictitious character from the 1800s.

"It's heading for the Ukraine."

The General shook his head. "No, he would have turned by now. Five'll get you ten he's crossing the Black Sea."

"And going where? Kazakhstan?"

"Maybe, but I'll bet he's going to turn." The General pulled out his wallet and threw a twenty on the console. "Come on, Hideo. I'm already down a hundred."

Corporal Tsunami walked over and matched the bet but held his finger on the money. "North or south?"

"North."

The General won the bet. Moments after his aide lifted his finger off the cash, the lavender dot began a sharp turn to the north. It crossed the Black Sea an hour later on a direct heading toward Moscow.

. . . . .

In the men's restroom, Sergeant Zumba watched the remote screen hanging over the sinks while he washed his hands. *Rome to Moscow. Two and half hours, not a bad flight. But that airport in Moscow?* He spit into the sink and shook his head. *Fasten your seatbelts, ladies and gentlemen. And men? Grab your nuts.*

He walked back into the secure command center and wiped some crumbs off the console. His relief was due in an hour, and she'd already written him up twice for leaving a mess. Flipping the logbook to a clean page, Sergeant Zumba made note of the fact that "Lorna Doone" had landed in Moscow at 1400 hours.

Chapter Twenty-Three – No Substitution Allowed

The cheese sauce was awful. Despite Chef Ronzoni's best efforts, the taste of the tenderloin wasn't even close. Not wanting to be one to appear boorish, the Queen swallowed the piece in her mouth and got up from the table without a word.

The cheese used by the Mongolian horde had a distinct flavor somewhere between moldy bleu cheese and rancid butter. Perhaps it had tasted better fresh. Maybe it had something to do with the flavor of the buns. Chef Ronzoni knew the Queen wouldn't like it, but the threat of spending time in the Tower dungeon convinced him to give it a try.

"You tasted this?" The Queen pointed at the yellow goop on her plate.

"Yes, Your Majesty."

"And yet, you served it to me?"

The Chef nodded and kept his eyes glued to his Crocs.

Turning to her chambermaid, the Queen sighed. "Cancel the dinner. Let the house staff know."

"Shall I tell them to reschedule, Your Highness?"

"No." Walking over to the table, the Queen covered the slices of boar and cheese sauce with her napkin. "Not until we can get the proper cheese."

. . . . .

Boulong sat on a milking stool inside the barn with his head in his hands. All he ever wanted to do was make butter and cheese. He saw the world outside his Paradise as customers. What had he done to turn them into enemies? He'd almost been witness to the murder of his son. Was cheese that important?

Thinking back to the flaming arrow that had been fired at him when he'd first announced the shortage, Boulong tried to understand the mania. He knew his cheese spread was tasty, that chefs spoke of it in ethereal terms. But to the farmer, it was only a product. It was a source of income and, until recently, the only way to heat his hot tub.

Melinda walked over to Boulong and put her hand on his shoulder.

"You're worried about Mookie, aren't you?"

He nodded. "That and the danger we all seem to be in because of my cheese."

"You heard what that lady said." Melinda had been standing off to the side, watching as the farmer had been threatened. "Give the damn cheese to the Pope. Nobody will attack the Vatican."

"And when all the cheese is gone and we start making more? Then what? Are we going to be slaves to the Catholic Church?" Boulong got up from the stool and kicked it behind him. "No goddamn way is that gonna happen."

Mikey joined them, retrieving the small stool and settling down on it. "What do you plan to do?"

"I could lead the cows into the river and let them drown."

Melinda covered her mouth in shock. "You wouldn't do that."

"No, but it's an idea." Boulong shrugged. "If we get rid of the cows, we can raise chickens and sell eggs."

Mikey shook his head. "Everyone has chickens. It would be like trying to sell ski passes in the summer."

"You're both forgetting about Mookie." Stomping her foot, Melinda crossed her arms over her chest. "You've got to make the cheese or she'll kill him."

"I don't think so." Pursing his lips, Boulong paced in front of them. "That boy has some magic in him. There's something about him that women find intriguing."

"Beyond his good looks?" Melinda blushed. "I mean, he *is* quite attractive."

"Ha." Mikey kicked some hay. "His teeth are crooked, and he picks his nose."

"Jealous?" Walking around behind him, Melinda tickled the boy's armpit.

"No." He pushed her hand away. "Stop it."

"Both of you cut it out." Boulong got between them. "This is serious."

Melinda slinked over and kissed the farmer on his cheek. "Okay. Let's be serious. What's first, captain?"

"A pregnancy test." Taking the girl by the waist, Boulong began issuing orders. "I'm going to take the skiff over to the French side and buy a test kit."

She pushed him away and shook her head. "Terrible idea."

"Why?"

"Everyone knows you. It wouldn't be safe." Melinda turned to Mikey. "Mikey can drive the boat. I'll go ashore and find a pharmacy. No one knows me and they won't bother someone with a broken leg and crutches."

Mikey nodded. "It makes sense, dad."

Boulong looked back and forth between them. Finally, he let out a sigh. "Okay. But get the test and get back here. If there really is a war being raged, this island may very well be the only safe place on the planet."

. . . . .

Lord Fitzpatrick had been looking forward to the dinner for weeks. He'd promised a certain young maiden a special seat at the table in return for a night she swore he'd talk about in his sleep for the rest of his life. Not having the same appreciation for cheese as the Queen, he couldn't taste any difference between the slag bun and a grilled cheese sandwich.

"What if you leave off the cheese sauce and just use ketchup instead?"

Chef Ronzoni forced the bile back down his throat. "I'm sorry, Your Lordship, but did you just suggest putting ketchup on a boar fillet?"

"We put it on a hamburger. What's the difference?"

The bile was winning. "Well, for one, hamburgers are ground beef along with a number of filler ingredients."

"So what you're saying is that if a fillet was put through the grinder it would be the same as a hamburger, correct?"

The chef turned his head and spit into his sleeve. "Using your analogy, we could take a whale and convert it into fish and chips as long as we had large enough potatoes."

Lord Fitzpatrick cocked his head to one side and narrowed his gaze. "Brilliant."

I should never have left Milan. Turning slightly to his left, Chef Ronzoni asked the Queen, "Would you prefer hamburgers at the next state dinner, Your Majesty? Perhaps when the American President comes to visit, we could add frankfurters as well."

"Oh no, Chef, no one puts ketchup on a hot dog." Holding his head in his hands, the shock on Lord Fitzpatrick's face was genuine. "We would be seen as commoners, uncouth, slovenly."

Slovenly? Don't drip, Your Lordshit. "Your Majesty?" Chef Ronzoni completed his turn, putting the Minister of Defense out of his line of vision.

"We're not serving stadium food in Buckingham Palace." Sighing, the Queen tried another bite of the boar tenderloin. "No. This just won't do. Giuseppe, give this to the stablehands. I don't even want this mixed in with the regular trash."

"What about that island in the South Pacific?" The chef thought about his friend, XM Nixon. "You could send the RAF."

The Queen shook her head. "No. I believe that Boulong's cheese is irreplaceable. If we're going to use force, let's stay closer to home. Remember the fiasco that happened with India."

Lord Fitzpatrick perked up. "We could attack this evening."

"Should I assume you've already formulated a plan, Lord Fitzpatrick?"

Reaching into the red leather briefcase on the floor by his chair, the Minister of Defense pulled out a folder marked "Very Top Secret" and handed it to the Queen. "Like the American Boys Scouts always boast, 'Be Prepared'."

· · · · ·

Boulong's sail couldn't decide which wind to catch. He connected one cow to a milking station and started on a second one when his mind wandered out of the barn. Leaving only a single tube on the poor cow's udder, he grabbed his binoculars and drove the Gator down to the beach.

The skiff was tied off to the pier on the French side, bobbing up and down in the waves. Melinda and his son were nowhere in sight. Noticing a nail that was not driven all the way into one of the boards, Boulong got out of the Gator and picked up a large rock to sink it.

Several other nails needed finishing, and he worked his way out to the end of the dock, making adjustments even where they really weren't necessary. Boulong tossed the rock into the Doubs and was walking back to the Gator when he remembered that the wash needed to go in the clothes dryer.

Driving through the forest to the house, the tires on the right side rubbed against a fallen tree and nearly tipped the motorized cart. It had been a problem for months that he'd been navigating around rather than move. Getting it out of the path was a two-person job, but Boulong was alone.

He took the towing chain out of the storage box in the Gator's bed and wrapped it around one end of the telephone-pole-size log. Locking the other end onto the tow hook, he got in and gunned the engine. The tree moved less than an inch and then rocked back into its original position.

Boulong tried two more times to get the tree to release its hold on the earth before he decided it really was a two-person job and he'd have to wait until his sons were there to help. Leaving the chain where it lay, he drove up to the barn, suddenly remembering that there was a half-connected cow.

What the hell am I doing? Boulong grabbed a milking stool and sat down, staring at the cow. *I've destroyed the family hot tub, I've buried strangers on the family island, and what's left of my family is standing in front of me, chewing on grass.*

He petted the cow on the nose.

I can't deal with the two sons I've already got. My marriage went up in smoke and my girlfriend shares a generation with my kids.

Getting up from the stool, Boulong walked around to the side of the cow, bent down, and finished connecting the milking tubes.

There's no way. He slapped his thigh. *Uh, uh. No more children. If she comes back and that thing tests positive, she's just gonna have to decide between me and having a baby.*

Taking the stool by one leg, the farmer moved on to the next stall and connected the first and second tube to the waiting cow.

I would never force her to have an abortion. No, sir. That's not my call. But she's got to realize that I just don't have the time to deal with raising another child. If nothing else, at least Sabrina popped out twins and I didn't have go through this child-raising crap twice.

He added the rest of the tubes and went out to the holding pen to bring in another cow when the word "laundry" crossed his mind.

Shit. There's a load in the dryer, too.

Locking the holding pen gate, Boulong went back through the barn and down the slope to the house.

I don't want to lose her, though. He thought about the sex on the cow's back and grinned. *Never would have dreamed of suggesting that to Sabrina.*

Climbing the porch stairs, the beeping of the clothes washer and the marching song that announced dry clothes welcomed him to his chores. Boulong slipped out of his work boots and padded into the house.

. . . . .

He was folding the last load of laundry when a one-line text appeared on his cellphone: "Pregnant!"

Boulong sat down on the dirt floor and cried.

Chapter Twenty-Four - Making Plans

Lord Fitzpatrick's plan would have thrilled Rube Goldberg. Other than a cage coming down at the end to trap a rat, it had all the trimmings of an invasion that a group of elementary school children would design as a class project. Insisting to the Queen of England that his plan was sound added the only missing piece of insanity.

Step one of the madman's design required a dozen large RAF helicopters loaded with paving stones. They would hover a mile north of Boulong's island, where the Doubs was at a narrow point, and discharge their load into the river. Another dozen choppers would follow immediately behind and drop hundreds of bags of quick drying cement.

In effect, the British Air Force would create a damn and the waters around the island would disappear, allowing for an invasion force to march across from the French side.

"Won't it flood the land on either side of the Doubs?" Leaning forward, the Queen pointed out the town on the French side and the Swiss farms bordering the river across from it. "How big an area do you think will be affected?"

"Give or take a few acres, probably seven square miles." Lord Fitzpatrick threw a glance at his military strategist, who was furiously rechecking his calculation on a pad.

"Seven square miles!" The Queen covered her mouth, but the words "Holy shit," slipped out. "The loss of life will be substantial."

Lord Fitzpatrick shrugged. "Collateral damage. It's the cost of war."

The Queen scrolled through the PowerPoint presentation twice before turning to her Minister of Defense with her hand over her eyes. She was reaching the peak of her tolerance and tried to make the man understand just how close he was to a room in the Tower dungeon.

"How do you propose to move troops across a dry riverbed, nearly half a mile wide, that's covered in boulders as large as a Bentley?"

Lord Fitzpatrick switched screens to the second part of the presentation. "We'll build a bridge."

"And where do you expect to find enough timbers to construct a bridge large enough to support troop carriers and tanks?" The Queen's tone had switched to sarcastic. "Giant Lincoln logs?"

"No, Your Majesty, from the trees on the French side."

Enlarging the satellite image of the area Lord Fitzpatrick had just described, the Queen shook her head. "There's nothing but the small town on the French side. I don't see any trees."

Lord Fitzpatrick was getting desperate. "Then we'll take them from the Swiss side of the Doubs."

"You want to invade the last neutral country on the planet and chop down their trees?" Shaking her head, the Queen closed the laptop. "You are truly daft, Lord Fitzpatrick." She closed her eyes and took a deep breath. "Guards!"

. . . . .

Boulong helped Melinda out of the skiff and did his best to smile. "So, you're pregnant."

"For now."

"What does that mean?"

She reached into her backpack and took out a bottle with two pills in it—one red and one blue.

"One pill makes you larger and then one pill makes you small." Melinda hummed the melody and took Boulong's hands. "I've got the next eight weeks to make a decision."

"Whether or not to take the pills?" Squeezing her hands tighter, Boulong tried to hide his joy and failed.

"Don't look so happy, Bouly. This is a really tough decision for me to make."

"I don't have a say?"

Melinda shook her head. "You've already offered your opinion."

"Yo, someone want to give me a hand?" Mikey put a five-gallon gasoline can on the dock and dragged another one closer.

"We'll talk about this later." Boulong kissed his girlfriend and turned toward his son. "Where'd you get the money for gas?" Bending down, he took the second Jerry can and hauled it onto the deck next to the first one.

"I've been saving for one of those computerized exercise bikes." Sliding the last of the cans over so Boulong could lift it, Mikey tightened the lines and hopped onto the pier. "It was going to be the best way to rehab my leg."

Melinda nodded toward the group of cows that had wandered down to the river for a drink. "You could always chase the cows on foot instead of using the Gator and the cattle prod."

"Very funny." Mikey reached for a Jerry can to put it into the Gator. "Why don't you go chase some cows." He pointed at the bovine coffee klatch that was watching them. "Starting with those."

Melinda flipped him the bird and turned to her boyfriend. "I'm going to pick blueberries for a pie. Did you remember the laundry?"

·　·　·　·　·

Mikey waited until the girl had disappeared into the woods before sitting down on two of the gas cans and giving his father the news.

"It's crazy over there. Everyone is walking around with a sword or a knife. I saw a woman pushing a baby carriage. She had a crossbow resting on the handlebar and bolts in a wicker basket next to the child."

"Did you see any soldiers?"

"Oh, plenty of them. It looks like the entire French Army has been mustered." Mikey pulled out his phone and scrolled through a series of pictures. "And look at this." He turned the picture so that Boulong could see it. "An automatic crossbow. It holds six bolts in a magazine. All the user has to do is reset the string with this lever and the next bolt drops into place."

Boulong's eyes opened wide. He used two fingers to enlarge the photo and studied the magazine. "They're trying to increase the killing power." He handed the phone back to Mikey and sat down next to his son. "We finally got rid of the assault rifles and this is their answer. What's next? Compound bows that fire ten arrows at a time?"

Mikey scrolled to the next photo. "No, only eight."

. . . . .

Once Lord Fitzpatrick had been dragged away to the Tower and calm restored, the general and his aides gathered around the prep table to discuss a more sensible plan of attack. It was decided in the kitchen of Buckingham Palace to attempt an amphibious landing on Boulong's island. Knowing that the farmer who lived there had a trebuchet and was skilled enough to take out three helicopters, they didn't want to risk another air assault.

The water was too dangerous for a scuba team and didn't have the depth necessary for a submarine, but inflatable Zodiacs could skim over the rapids and wouldn't be damaged if they hit a rock. Four of the rubber attack boats could be dropped up river by an RAF helicopter which would offer air support as long as it could avoid missiles from the farmer's ancient weapon.

"What are these heavily armed commandos supposed to do once they capture the island?" A general seated next to the large industrial mixer pointed at the aerial photographs. "Milk the cows?"

"They shouldn't expect any resistance." The colonel leading the presentation brought up a slide showing Boulong and his two sons. "There are only three occupants on the island and according to our intelligence, one of them is crippled."

The general wasn't convinced. "From the reconnaissance report I read, this farmer took out the first chopper with a slingshot."

"What do you suggest, General?" The Queen had found a half gallon of mint chocolate ice cream and was digging into it with a soup spoon.

"A HALO drop at one o'clock in the morning. There's no moon and when our paratroopers come whizzing down from ten-thousand feet, the occupants of the island will never have enough time to mount a counter-offensive. Sending our troops across a rickety bridge leaves them too exposed." The general rubbed the back of his neck. "We'd lose half of them before they set foot on the island."

The Queen closed the container of mint chocolate and switched over to mango sorbet. Lately, she'd been having a problem with some of her clothing being too tight. She'd chastised the royal laundry but in private told her handmaid that they should both go on a diet.

"And this, what do you call it?"

"A HALO drop, Your Majesty. High altitude, low opening parachute jump. The plane is too high to be detected by radar and flying slow enough that our troops can safely exit the aircraft. They free fall for over a minute before pulling the ripcord."

The Queen furrowed her brow. The plan had an air of feasibility. "How soon can you put your plan in action, General?"

"Twenty-four hours, Your Majesty. The troops are already on high alert. We just need you to give the order."

"What about Parliament?" She poured several long squeezes of chocolate syrup onto the sorbet and mixed it together. "Shouldn't we at least let them know what we're doing?"

The general shook his head. "And have them spend the next six months debating it? Have you forgotten Brexit?"

"Don't remind me." Reaching for the phone, she dialed the operator and asked to be connected to Ten Downing Street. Protocol required that she notify the Prime Minister, even if she couldn't stand the woman.

"So, is it a go, Your Majesty?" The general held his cellphone in midair, ready to send a message.

"Give me a second, General." Whistling the opening bars of "*God Save the Queen,*" she walked over and put the mango sorbet back in the royal freezer.

The operator came back on the line and announced the Prime Minister.

"Jackie? It's Liz. Listen honey, we're about to go to war with France and... No sweat. We've got this. Don't get your knickers in a twist... No, you don't have to come over here. I'm not going to bring in the press... Of course... As soon as we reschedule the dinner... Yes, dear... Okay... Enjoy the baseball game. I hope your team wins... You, as well."

The Queen dropped the handset into the gold-plated cradle and turned to the General. "Go get the bloody cheese."

Chapter Twenty-Five - Don't Shoot The Cows

The President held his daily schedule at arm's length and frowned at the sheet of paper. His day, already an hour behind according to the printout, began with a briefing about the incident in the Gulf of Mexico. It was followed by a briefing to make him aware that an American citizen who was only known by her initials–LD–was negotiating some sort of cheese deal with the Russian President. The third briefing of the day had been requested by General Purpose, who was currently waiting impatiently in the outer office.

"He flew all the way up here from Orlando? What, we have better pole dancers in D.C.?" The President handed the schedule back to his personal secretary. "I don't have time for all these briefings. Any chance we can put them off a day or two?"

"No, Mr. President, and the Queen is waiting on line one."

"Which queen?"

"England, sir. Queen Elizabeth."

Now what? "Has she been holding long?" The President looked down at the flashing light on his telephone. "Nah, never mind. I'll talk to her." He tapped the button with a pencil and dropped into his chair.

"Lizzy, what's happening, what's going on, how's it hangin', girl?"

"Joseph, have you seen the news this morning?"

"Just ESPN. The Mets lost again last night. Did you bet on the game?"

"No, Joseph, I've been dealing with some much more worldly events." She paused and lowered her voice. "Are you on a secure line?"

The President shrugged. "I'm in the Oval. Aren't they all secure?"

"One can only hope. Listen, Joseph, the situation in France has gotten out of hand and I feel the only solution is military action."

"Don't screw with the French. I hear they have skunks and they're not afraid to use them."

An audible sigh came over the line. "We're prepared for any contingency." Another pause. "Unlike your Marines."

"They held the Eiffel Tower to the last man."

"A conversation for another time. Right now, you need to know that an expeditionary force is being assembled and we intend to take control of an island in the Doubs River that's considered French territory."

"You're invading France? Hot damn, tamale. Can we help?"

Had the President been able to see the Queen's "Oh, my, God" face he wouldn't have asked the question a second time. But he couldn't and he did.

"Really. We've got lots more Marines and they have gas masks. I can have them ready to go with the snap of a finger."

The Queen was as polite as a girl's school headmistress. "Thank you for the generous offer, Mr. President, but we've got the situation well in hand." *You lunatic.* "I will keep your Situation Room updated as to our progress. Good day, Joseph, and keep working on your backhand."

· · · · ·

In the few seconds it took for General Purpose to walk into the Oval Office and say good morning, the President had formulated a plan of his own to deal with France.

"I want to attack the Normandy coast."

"Like we did for D-Day?" The General wrinkled his nose and shook his head. "Why?"

"Beachfront, General." Walking over to the Rand McNally executive-size, Presidential model of its thirty-six-inch globe, the President spun it around and stopped with his finger on Mexico. "People spend more time and more money on beach vacations than any other form of relaxation."

"Including tennis?"

"Tennis is never relaxing, General. Don't kid yourself. Man's true anger and frustration can only be released by swinging a racket." The President lifted his new racket from the Resolute desk and spun it in his hands.

"Granted. But the Normandy Coast?"

"Can we do it? Do you think there will be much resistance?"

General Purpose shrugged. "A collection of AirBnB operators, all the tourist guides, and a bunch of farmers? I don't think we'll have a problem."

"Good." The President carefully laid the racket back down on his desk. "How soon can we attack?"

"What's the rush, sir?"

The President pursed his lips and wondered if he should tell the General about the pending British invasion. It was on the other side of the country, one that was big enough to share. If they wanted the mountains and rivers, he saw no reason not to take the beaches.

"The weather, General. If we can mop this up in a day or two, we still have the advantage of the tourist season and the income it will generate."

"Are you suggesting we annex France as a U.S. protectorate, Mr. President?"

"Just for the summer." The President smiled. "Nobody goes to the beach after Labor Day anyhow."

· · · · ·

A sixteen-man paratrooper team sat in the cargo bay of the RAF transport, waiting for the signal to jump. Their wrist-mounted altimeters were reading ten-thousand-five-hundred feet and the missing oxygen at that altitude was flowing through their masks. The Master Sergeant that would lead them out the open cargo door had given his troops one final order: "Don't shoot the cows."

"We're taking this island to preserve a way of life that's been threatened by a foreign government. The French want to remove the cows and build a bridge to the ski resorts on the opposite side of the Doubs. The Queen considers this island to be of strategic importance to continued free trade in the region. Our mission is to secure the island without injuring the livestock."

The Master Sergeant held up a photo of a Guernsey. "Some of you have never seen a cow before. You might think that the milk you add to your tea is produced in a factory from some closely guarded chemical recipe. This is a cow. Cows produce milk which is drained from this sack that hangs from their bellies."

He held up a second photo, a close-up of the cow's hoof. "Because they do not have an opposable thumb, there is no risk of a cow attacking you with a crossbow or a knife. They do, however, have horns and can inflict serious damage with them if they are provoked."

A paratrooper in the front row raised his hand. "What do you suggest to avoid a cow attack, Master Sergeant?"

"Don't provoke them," was the answer from the Master Sergeant, who pulled his mask back over his face and wondered to himself just how one would provoke a cow.

. . . . .

Mikey was still of the opinion that producing more cheese would quell the war cries. While Boulong brought the processing equipment up to steam, he and Melinda rounded up twenty cows and moved them into the holding pen. Another ten were already connected to milking tubes and a fresh crate of cheese tubs had been dumped into the sterilizer.

A hundred pounds of raw cheese was moved from the aging tank to the mixer where it would be combined with fresh whey to make the magical spread. They'd missed the Friday delivery with all the distractions and Mikey figured that over the next week, they would be able to produce close to a normal batch with the three of them working around the clock.

Not another word had been spoken about Melinda's pregnancy, but Boulong couldn't keep his eyes off her stomach. He was sure he could see some swelling and didn't want Melinda to injure herself making cheese.

"Watch out for that cow." Boulong yanked his girlfriend out of the way of a cow that was kicking some hay.

"I can see him." Pushing his hand away, Melinda shook her head. "Just because I'm pregnant it doesn't mean I've gone blind."

"He could have backed out of the stall and slammed into you."

"Bouly, do you really think the cow is faster than me in reverse?" Laughing, the girl smacked the beast on its rump.

Mikey came in with a cow to replace the one Melinda was mistreating. "It's getting dark outside. Let's finish up with the cows that are already milking and call it a day."

"What about your idea to work all night long?" She rested her head on the cow's back and smoothed its coat.

"The cows need rest." Disconnecting the milking tubes from the cow that was going to be replaced with a fresh one, Boulong urged the beast out of the stall and smiled at his girlfriend. "She remembers you from the other night."

Melinda took a step back and stared at the cow. "How do you know it's the same one?"

Boulong winked at her. "I know everyone in my family."

. . . . .

Five miles west of Paradise, the RAF cargo plane slowed almost to a stall and dropped the steel-reinforced loading ramp. The jump light went from red to green and the Master Sergeant turned to his troops and circled his hand in the air.

Two-by-two, the soldiers walked to the edge of the ramp, spun around and saluted those behind them. Then, taking a long backward step, they jumped into the darkness at eleven-thousand feet.

Having practiced HALO jumps for years, the soldiers relaxed as they passed through clouds, falling to Earth at one-hundred-and-twenty miles an hour. Several of the paratroopers did somersaults, one of them barrel-rolled for a thousand feet. Without the moon to backlight them and wearing flat black nylon jumpsuits, they were invisible to anyone looking up from the ground, even when their chutes were deployed.

At thirty-five-hundred feet, sixteen black chutes opened in unison. A light westerly wind blew the paratroopers off course by less than twenty yards, with all of them landing safely at the northern end of Boulong's largest pasture. Too small for radar, they passed unseen within a quarter mile of the U.S. Air Force stealth bomber that was making an eastbound pass over the island.

. . . . .

Safely on the ground, the paratroopers rolled their chutes into their backpacks and set their dart guns to single-shot. They were armed with the latest innovation from the military gadget lab. A cylinder similar to the one found on a revolver had been mounted onto a spring-powered dart gun. Fifteen steel darts were loaded into the cylinder, which was rotated by a metal strap. In full-automatic, the weapon could fire all fifteen darts in four seconds.

A sniper team climbed an evergreen and established a cover position. The two shooters had modified compound bows that could put an arrow through a two-by-four at a thousand yards. So far, no one had been attacked by lumber, but several studs had been pierced in testing.

The Master Sergeant split his troops into three teams. One would stay in the landing zone and establish a safe perimeter for helicopter extraction. The second team was to head down to the beach they'd seen in the satellite photos and destroy what appeared to be the start of a bridge. He would personally lead the third team on an attack of the two structures that showed up on an infrared scan.

"There are supposed to be three civilians on this island. I want them taken alive." The Master Sergeant looked back and forth between his teams. "And the same goes for the cows."

. . . . .

Boulong got into bed naked, as he had done his entire life. Melinda was still in the bathroom. He'd heard the toilet flush, and it sounded as though she was brushing her teeth. Mikey had chased them out of the barn, promising to get to bed himself as soon as possible. One very stubborn cow was going to need some additional coaxing to come out of the milking stall, and the cattle prod's batteries were dead.

The word "pregnant" had been bouncing around his cranium for the last hour or so and he tried to remember how it was with Sabrina when she was carrying the boys. His ex-wife wanted to have sex as often as she wanted to shave her legs, which was at best once a month. Boulong recalled hearing "No!" far more regularly than "Well, okay, but make it fast."

Sabrina was older than Melinda though when she got pregnant. He blew out a quick breath. *Maybe younger women can handle it better. Man, I hope so.*

The sound of water stopped, and Boulong heard his girlfriend gargle and spit. She came out of the bathroom a moment later wearing nothing but her sneakers.

"Come on. Put your boots on and let's go make love on a cow."

"Are you sure?"

"Are you asking because I'm pregnant?"

Boulong looked up at the ceiling and shrugged. "It's a logical question."

"Asking someone if they want to screw on a cow's back?" She laughed. "If that's logic, then I'm the Queen of England."

Chapter Twenty-Six - The Tequila Shortage

Generalissimo Newsenz had been trying to reach the barge by radio for days. With the Mexican Air Force grounded by a tropical storm that had rushed across the Caribbean and into the Gulf, he had no way of knowing the Dobby was resting on a coral reef under nearly a mile of water. The barge captain and his mate had been taken into custody by the U.S. Coast Guard and were sitting in a cell awaiting extradition.

The guillotine his army had hastily constructed failed on its first test. They'd built a dummy out of cornstalks and hay, using a large melon for the head. The blade stuck and one of the workmen went up a ladder to try to free it with a hammer. He missed with his first swing and fell. The vibration of the ladder shook the blade free and it zipped down, slicing the man's thumb clean off his hand.

In retaliation for closing the border to the U.S., the Generalissimo ordered his troops to begin construction of a wall to keep the American tourists from coming back. He'd had enough of the "lazy Mexicans" and "dirty water" comments to last several lifetimes. In the middle of the evening news, he interrupted the broadcast to announce that all the resorts on the Yucatan Peninsula were now free for Mexicans.

"We don't need no stinking tourists." He sneered into the camera. "Americans can come here, but they will need a brown card and can only stay longer with a visa."

The TV anchor questioned the term "brown card" to which the Generalissimo replied that it was going to be harder to get than a U.S. "green card" and could be revoked for any reason he saw fit.

European, Asian, and even Russian tourists were welcome without restriction. Of course, the only way they could get there would be by ship, as the U.S.

construction company that had been repairing the international airport was now on the other side of the wall.

Hearing that they made excellent housekeepers, Generalissimo Newsenz dispatched the country's only naval vessel to the South Pacific to see if anyone living on Tikopango might be interested in foreign employment. The ship, a destroyer without weapons, was never heard from again.

. . . . .

Those Mexicans living outside the country were stranded. With the border sealed so tightly that jumping beans were bouncing back, anyone who wanted to return was forced to swim the Rio Grande at night. Older émigrés to the U.S. remembered the horrific crossing and opted to renew their green cards.

However, the padlocked border also made it impossible for tequila to leave the country. Produced solely in the Mexican state of Jalisco, the fiery alcohol that was necessary for margaritas, sunrises, and frat parties was now in short supply around the world. Consuming three-quarters of all the tequila produced annually, Mexico's northern neighbor had run out of the beverage within days of the border closing.

The panic that started on college campuses quickly overflowed to summer barbecues, white trash weddings, and Americanized taco trucks that had fought so hard for a liquor license. Summertime was margarita time and without the key ingredient, revelers were forced to eat burritos with Mountain Dew.

Generalissimo Newsenz didn't need to sow discontent on the other side of the border. A lack of tequila had already shoved the first boulder down the mountain. He knew that an avalanche would rumble in his direction. All he had to do was wait for the dust to settle and the Americans would come crawling back with their dry tongues hanging from their mouths.

. . . . .

The President didn't drink tequila. He'd tried it once when he was in college and thought it tasted worse than siphoned gasoline. But it was a popular drink with his constituents and thus required some sort of response from the White House.

He went on national television just before the start of the baseball game and reassured Americans that tequila would be available, even if it meant rationing for a while.

"We all remember the toilet paper and hand sanitizer hoarding. Well, that's not going to happen with tequila. As your President, I will see to it that no one goes thirsty. If need be, we will use our military to make this happen. I don't want to flex American might, but we can't let this situation paralyze our economy. Even at the cost of significant hangovers."

He'd dropped in that last line without telling the speechwriters and chuckled when he read it. The backlash from the American Medical Association, Alcoholics Anonymous, and the makers of Bayer aspirin would last for weeks.

.　.　.　.　.

Unfortunately, the tequila shortage was just the beginning. The American economy was dependent on cheap labor. Labor that had been abused long after slavery had been abolished. Hispanic workers from south of the border were the only ones skilled to handle the unskilled jobs. What they were paid was so far below the minimum wage that most of them made too little to pay taxes.

Maintenance, both indoors and out, was the purview of people who called someplace else home, but were desperately trying to relocate to America. Landscapes, hotel rooms, office buildings, and dirty cars were kept tidy by teams of workers who referred to chickens as "*pollo*" and answered "*sí*" instead of "yes."

The watertight compartments on the Dobby were just beginning to leak when the Mexican community living in the United States went on strike.

First affected were the fast-food chains. Not only were the bulk of their employees immigrants, but so were their customers. Rather than eat greasy burgers and drink beverages that were more sugar than soda, Mexicans went back to traditional home cooking. The dollar meal was reduced to fifty cents, but even that wasn't enough to lure their customers back.

Pristine landscapes filled with weeds. Hotel guests searched vacant rooms for clean towels. Car washes shut down. And a bottle of cheap tequila was sold on eBay for three-thousand dollars. Several attempts to make tequila from agaves grown in New Mexico were dismal failures. Most of the product ended up as bio-diesel fuel.

On the second day of tequila rationing, the President went on national television and criticized the rioters. He ordered the National Guard to protect the larger liquor stores, especially the drive-thrus that had become so popular since the pandemic. And then in a moment of clarity, he issued an executive order that made tequila a Schedule I drug, filling the slot held by cannabis for many years. It was now illegal to own or drink the beverage in any form.

. . . . .

No one in the Royal Family drank tequila...at least not in public. However, they drank gin in quantities equivalent to the American consumption of diet soda. Not having tequila, drinkers in the U.S. turned to the other members of the clear liquor tribe, starting with gin. This, of course, produced a shortage of the only reason for the existence of tonic which led to the closing of the largest soda plant in Europe and more riots.

Forty-eight hours after Generalissimo Newsenz had turned off the tequila tap, the Queen of England reached out to the American President and told him that if he didn't open the border immediately, not only wasn't he going to be at Wimbledon, but that she'd forbid the Rolling Stones from touring again.

The U.S. Mexican border reopened twenty minutes later.

. . . . .

Boulong drank tequila, but only when someone else was pouring. Other than a significant collection of red wine, an unopened bottle of crème de menthe, and several wooden cases of local beer, he didn't keep alcohol on the island.

Their second sexual tryst on the back of a cow was much more successful than the first...at least in Melinda's case. She'd climaxed twice before falling off the cow and onto the gravel path. Boulong was too excited that he'd given her such pleasure to concentrate on his own. No frustration crossed his mind, however. He knew there were lots of cows and plenty of warm nights to come before his girlfriend got too round for bovine-supported sex.

The more he thought about having another child, the more he warmed to the idea. *Wait until Sabrina finds out. Yeah, bitch, I had another kid. Now I'm a two-woman father. Ha.*

He knew where his ex-wife lived. Had her address in his contacts. He'd send her a picture of the baby being born and then another with him, Melinda, and the newborn smiling the way proper families do, moments after the pain of delivery is gone.

You thought I'd never find someone else? Screw you, you miserable cheating bitch. Here's proof.

Had Melinda not been sitting on a log, rubbing her sore thigh, Boulong would have done a King Kong imitation, beating his chest and howling at the moon. Instead, he slipped off the cow's back and rushed over to her.

"Are you okay?"

She nodded. "My ass hurts, but everything else feels so fine that I'm tempted to get back on."

"That's a horse thing."

"What?"

"You fall off a horse and you're supposed to get right back on."

Melinda looked over at the cow. "I think she's done for the night."

"Me, too."

"But you didn't–"

Boulong covered her mouth with his hand. "That's okay. You did, and that's what matters." He dropped his hand to his lap and looked up at the stars. "There's no moon tonight."

"I can see Orion." Melinda pointed toward the west. "See his shoulders and that's his sword hanging down. The really bright star that's his left shoulder is Betelgeuse."

"Like the movie?"

"Yeah. That's why everybody knows how to find Orion, only I think they spelled it different in the movie."

With a sigh, Boulong turned to his girlfriend and took her hands in his. "Soon, we're not going to be able to do this."

"Sit naked on a log and look at the stars?"

He laughed. "No, silly. Have sex on the back of a cow."

"Too bad we don't have a hot tub anymore."

"Are you still thinking about taking the pills?"

Melinda let go of his hands and stood facing him. "I have eight weeks to think about it, Bouly. Can we not make this the only topic of conversation for the next fifty-six days? Yes, I'm thinking about it. You will be the second person in the Universe to know the answer to that question."

"I'm–"

"Oh, yes, you are and don't bullshit me, Bouly. You're spending so much time thinking about me being pregnant and how it's going to affect our sex life that you can't cum." She walked over to the branch where they'd hung their towels and wrapped herself in the larger of the two. "You need to focus on three things right now. First, where is Mookie? Second, cheese. And third is getting us a new hot tub."

Boulong pointed around the evergreen forest. "Show me an oak tree and I'll build you one. All the timber came from up north."

"Build one? Welcome to the twenty-first century, Bouly. Fire up your laptop and go shopping. Everything you ever wanted is available on Amazon dot com."

Chapter Twenty-Seven - Spies

From his position at the top of the rise, a paratrooper radioed that two of the civilians had just gone inside the house. One was still in the barn and he hadn't yet seen anyone else. A thick line of evergreens had prevented the soldier from spotting Boulong and Melinda rocking on the cow, but he did make note of the fact that the man was naked as he climbed the stairs to the porch.

The Sergeant Major ordered the sniper team down from the tree and sent word to the team on the beach to hold off on the demolition until the third civilian could be located.

"We have two targets." He pointed at the barn. "That structure has some heavy equipment parked on the south side and electrical cables strung from a generator on the southwest corner. It's well lit and recon reports that there's a sound of equipment running inside."

The soldier who'd handled the reconnaissance added, "And six cows."

"Yes, mustn't forget the cows." The Sergeant Major adjusted his leather utility belt. "We'll take the large building first and then deal with the house. Remember, these people are non-combatants. Shoot only where you see a threat."

. . . . .

Mikey was having trouble keeping his eyes open. Sixty-four ounces of coffee and all it did was make him pee. He gave a moment's thought to chewing on the un-ground beans, but that would mean walking back down to the house to get them. The last six cows were emptying their udders and could be set free into the pasture as soon as he disconnected them from the milking machine.

He'd left the barn door open as well as the door out to the holding pen. A cool breeze was drying his sweat before it could drip into his eyes. Mikey closed the valves on the whey tank and was about to remove the tubes on the cow closest to the door when the balloons exploded.

Filled with compressed air, thin rubber balloons as big as a medicine ball made enough noise when popped with a dart that one would go deaf for several seconds. That brief interval was perfect for a team of British commandos to storm into the barn and take Mikey and the six cows prisoner.

·　·　·　·　·

The Sergeant Major evaluated the situation and decided to interrogate his prisoner immediately. From the photos supplied by a dairy farmer in England, he was able to identify the equipment in the structure, even going so far as to agree with one of the paratroopers that the structure was a barn.

"Where are the others?"

Mikey folded his arms across his chest. "Arming themselves to chase your ass off our island."

"Arming themselves? With what, cow patties?" The Sergeant Major chuckled at his joke. "We don't want to hurt anyone, son."

"Oh? Crashing a helicopter into our pasture and nearly killing a dozen cows doesn't count?"

"You shot it down."

Shot it down? "Yes, that's right." Mikey nodded. "We're heavily armed. You don't realize it, but you've stepped into cow shit up to your knees."

The radio on the Sergeant Major's utility belt crackled and he unsnapped it to hear the transmission. The demolition team on the beach was under attack.

"Four Russian Zodiacs have beached. Must be at least sixty heavily armed soldiers. They have automatic crossbows. Oh, shit–"

Running to the barn door, the British commandos could hear the zipping of crossbow bolts in the distance. Sounds of battle: people shouting, running footsteps, arrows thudding into wood. And then silence.

The Sergeant Major tried reaching his team on the radio but heard only static. Switching channels, he called the evacuation choppers that were waiting on the Swiss side of the Doubs.

"We're under attack. Russians in Zodiacs have landed on the island. Possibly a battalion. We need air support and reinforcements."

The reply was more static.

Turning to his troops, the Sergeant Major was about to issue orders when a crossbow bolt pierced his radio, yanking it out of his hands. A red dot appeared on the forehead of the soldier to his right and floodlights mounted on top of the house bathed the hillside.

Boulong, in coveralls and combat boots, stepped from behind a tree and aimed the crossbow at the officer.

"There are Russian commandos on the beach holding your men captive. No one has been hurt. Drop your weapons and come out of the barn with your hands in the air. Just as easily as I shot that radio out of your hand, I can put a bolt between your eyes and reload before you hit the ground."

The Sergeant Major hesitated a moment too long and Boulong fired a second time, knocking the dart gun out of a paratrooper's hand.

"I'm not going to tell you again." Boulong put the dot back in the middle of the commando's forehead.

"Drop your weapons." Turning around, the Sergeant Major looked from soldier to soldier until each one had placed his dart gun on the ground.

The farmer called to his son, "Mikey? Get your ass out here."

Inching around the soldiers, Mikey hobbled down the hill and stood next to his father.

"Are you okay?"

He nodded. "But there are still five cows connected to milking machines."

Boulong looked at the Sergeant Major and grinned. "Send someone in there to disconnect those tubes or I'll connect them to your penis and see if I can suck your brains out."

The Sergeant Major pointed at the nearest paratrooper. "You, get in there and remove the devices."

"How?" The soldier shrugged. "I grew up in Liverpool. The only thing I know about cows is that you can eat them."

Laughing, Boulong explained, "Red switch on the top of the unit. Flick it off and the suction will end. All you have to do is pull lightly and the tubes will fall off by themselves."

The soldier looked at the Sergeant Major and nodded. "I can do that, sir."

From behind Boulong and his son came the sound of boots on gravel. The farmer looked over his shoulder. "The Russians are coming."

The Master Sergeant repeated the phrase, but as a question. "The Russians are coming?"

"Yes." Boulong lowered his crossbow. "And I think they want cheese."

·   ·   ·   ·   ·

In the war room at Buckingham Palace, the Queen and her new Minister of Defense had been monitoring the radio transmissions. A large monitor showed the British troops in blue dots and a much larger number of red dots approaching them from the west.

"Sixty-five men and four boats." The Minister squinted at the screen. "What happened to our helicopter?"

A technician seated next to her moved the image to the east. "It's down on the Swiss side of the Doubs. The pilot and copilot are still onboard but they're not responding to the radio."

"You're certain they can hear us?" Adjusting her glasses, the Minister pointed at a large red dot not far from the blue one that indicated the British chopper. "What's that?"

"An aircraft. Probably a bomber from the size of the dot." Zooming in on the area, the technician tapped several keys and looked up at the screen. "It's Russian. A TU-22 bomber. It must have forced the helicopter to the ground and is sitting on it."

The Queen put down her tea and sighed. "How did the Russians know we were attacking?"

"We have a leak." The Minister of Defense got up from her chair and walked back and forth in front of the monitors. "Maybe the war room is bugged."

"We met in the kitchen, Natasha. Who the hell bugs a kitchen?"

"How well do you know the chef?" Counting employees on her fingers, the Minister stopped in front of the Queen. "There's the sous chef, the dishwasher, the pastry chef, the servers. I could go on and on, but you get the idea. Any one of them could be a spy."

The Queen shook her head. "All those people have been on the royal staff for years. We don't put ads in the London Times asking for kitchen help. These people were vetted by your predecessor."

The Minister frowned. "My point exactly, Your Majesty. Where is he now?"

. . . . .

With the British commandos bound and locked inside the holding pen, Colonel Karloff watched his men load Boulong's cheese spread into refrigerated chests.

"You can thank your son for this rescue when he gets home."

"Mookie set this up?" Boulong shook his head in disbelief. "Who did he have to screw to get the Russian Army to come to our aid?"

The Colonel let a sly grin fill his face. "She only goes by her initials, LD. I think it stands for Little Demon."

"I spoke to her." Recalling the woman's face and her evil words, Boulong's heart sunk. "She threatened my son."

"I think her threats were more for your benefit than his." Stepping out of the way of the soldiers carrying the first refrigerated crate out of the barn, the Colonel took a phone call and walked away from Boulong to speak in private. When he returned, Colonel Karloff put his arm around Boulong's shoulders and walked the farmer out of the barn.

"Your son will be home in the morning."

Boulong relaxed. "Is he coming alone?"

"If you're worried that LD will be with him, don't." The Colonel shook his head. "She rarely spends time with men. If your son lasted two nights with her, it's only because she was too busy to look for a suitable woman."

The Russian soldiers returned with a second refrigerated cooler. Boulong walked over and opened one of the tubs of cheese spread and tasted it.

"These need another week before they're finished."

"I will pass that along." Tasting for himself, the Colonel nodded. "Good cheese. When will you have more?"

"More?" Boulong winced. "Not for another two weeks but I need to spread it around. You can't expect to take it all."

The Colonel put his hands on the farmer's shoulders. "Expectations only get good people in trouble."

"What the hell is going on here?" Melinda, wearing a bathrobe and flip-flops, came marching up the hill. "Who are these guys?" She closed one eye and squinted at the Colonel's insignia. "Oh shit, Commies?"

Chapter Twenty-Eight - Beachfront Property

General Purpose leapt from the massage table wrapped in a thin sheet. It was eleven o'clock at night and the message his aide had just read to him about the British attack on Boulong's island was two-hours old. Someone was going to be court-martialed for the holdup. The General planned to start with whoever was manning the Situation Room and go up the chain of command from there. If he was lucky, the moron behind the delay sat in the Oval Office.

Corporal Tsunami held up his hand. "Wait, there's more."

"What? The French counterattacked? The Pope is sending in more Swiss Guards?"

"No. It's worse." Hideo read the note a second time. "Russian commandos took the island by force. They crossed the Doubs in Zodiacs from the French side."

"Any word on casualties?"

"A bull charged one of the rubber boats and an archer killed it."

The General grabbed his clothes and began dressing. "Who's in control of the island now?"

"It doesn't say, but I think we have to assume it's the Russians." Corporal Tsunami handed the paper to him. "This could be the start of a Russian invasion of Western Europe."

"Your President wants us to invade Normandy. Maybe we should start with Geneva first."

"As you found out this morning in Washington, we've already lost the battle for Paris. I think you're right, sir. An attack on France from the Swiss side of the Doubs gives us a significant advantage." Corporal Tsunami reached for the secure phone. "Do you want to call the White House or should I order dinner first?"

General Purpose looked at the time. "Screw it. Go home to your girlfriend and remind her about hooking up my new TV. I'll call Baldy in the morning."

. . . . .

The flight from Dulles to Orlando had been through enough storms to dislodge every joint in the General's body. Tanya had returned along with her wonderful massage skills. She was still pregnant and dancing four nights a week at a club downtown, wearing mouse ears and a tail. Known locally as the number one draw for the gentleman's club because of her ability to spin around the pole in defiance of gravity while swinging the tail, the girl had saved enough g-string money to buy an accordion that she practiced at all hours of the night.

Tanya's plan for the future was to have the baby but give it up for adoption. She never wanted to have kids in the first place, but read an online article that said she could get rich by selling her baby to the right couple. She didn't expect to ever hear from the pilot again and found out that the only way to get to Tikopango was to swim or win the lottery. Her best hope to get out of the pole dancing gig was to get good enough on the squeeze box to join a polka band.

. . . . .

Little did she know that XM Nixon had rented a townhouse on the other side of Orlando. He'd delivered the slag buns, cashed the check that was waiting for him, and flown the Gulfstream to Miami, following LD's instructions. True to his word, Xavier had come back for Tanya. At least, that's the story he was going to tell LD when she asked.

The argument with Lady Doom, as he called her, lasted less than a dozen words out of his mouth. If the look from her eyes was any colder, Xavier might have suffered frostbite on his nose.

"Fathers don't have to spend all their time with a baby. That's the mother's job. You'll still be flying for me and perhaps there'll be a bump in your salary to help you raise a family."

LD turned away from the pilot and said nothing for a few moments. When she continued, her voice had softened. "I never knew my father, but I took revenge on his murderer. My mother never read the book on how to raise a child, so my parents are the streets." She shook her head. "That's not how it's supposed to work. Not for me, and certainly not for your child. You'll be a good a father or a very young, very handsome corpse."

Smiling, LD held his check in the air as though it was a wet dish towel. "Now take this and go back to that woman before I change my mind."

.   .   .   .   .

Having been awakened before dawn and not being able to find her spectacles, the Queen read the communiqué twice, crumpled it, and threw it across her bedroom. "The Russians have stolen all the cheese, and that idiot wants to replay the D-Day invasion?" She looked at the calendar. "He's a week too late."

Catching the piece of trash before it hit the floor, the Minister of Defense shook her head. "He doesn't want a reenactment, Your Majesty. The President of the United States intends to annex the Normandy coast and convert it into beachfront property." She gently lifted the Queen's eyeglasses from the royal nightstand and handed them to her.

"Didn't the last President try that with South Florida?"

"Yes, Your Majesty, but he went bankrupt because he had no funds to back the development." The Minster opened her laptop and sat it on the royal bed where the Queen could see the screen. Tapping a few keys, she brought up a copy of the current President's tax return on the monitor. "This one's loaded."

The Queen slipped her spectacles onto her forehead and scanned the screen. "Good Lord. He pays more in taxes than I earn from the royal salary."

"He was an early investor in cannabis. When the vaccine was discovered, his net wealth increased a hundredfold overnight." She tapped the spacebar and displayed a chart showing the President's astronomical fortune on a graph.

"And now he plans to use those assets to create a northern version of Monte Carlo." The Queen whistled. "It's brilliant."

"Wait a moment, Your Majesty. Are you seriously considering joining his effort?" The Minster of Defense closed her laptop and stared at the Monarch in disbelief. "We can't invade France. They're our allies."

"I beg your pardon. What happened earlier this evening?"

The Minister opened her mouth to reply but suddenly realized that any argument was invalid. The British Commonwealth had already invaded France. But then again, so had the Russians. If the Americans were next, why not get in line?

The Queen smiled. "Right, then. Let's get Baldy on the phone."

· · · · ·

With the exception of the Secret Service and the President of the United States, everyone else in the White House was asleep. It had taken the President two hours and a fresh set of batteries in four of the remotes, but he'd finally gotten all six televisions synched to his laptop. The color was the same on each screen, the audio levels were matched, and every thrust was Technicolor bliss.

He let the phone ring more than a dozen times before an Agent knocked on the door and asked if he was okay.

"Yeah. I got it. Give me a minute. Goddamn it." Muting the televisions, one remote at a time, he got up from the bed and slipped back into his silk robe. Angrily, he grabbed the handset off the cradle. "What?"

· · · · ·

Colonel Karloff was the last one to board a Zodiac. He'd spent over an hour inspecting Boulong's trebuchet and was impressed that it had remained in such pristine condition after all those years. In exchange for the cheese that they'd taken without asking, the Colonel promised Boulong enough oak timbers to build a hot tub big enough for a cow. He would personally select the wood from the Moscow Home Depot and have a military helicopter deliver it before noon the following day.

Boulong tried to negotiate the cheese spread situation with the Colonel, but Karloff told him that he had no say in the matter. He was just following orders from someone many pay grades above him. But he did offer a solution.

"There are ways of making this work if you are creative in your thinking." Taking a seat on one of the boulders that his soldiers had removed from the dock, the Colonel opened a package of beet-flavored chewing gum and offered a stick to Boulong. "Some creative accounting goes a long way."

"Oh?"

"Many businesses in Russia only report a fraction of what they produce." The Colonel looked around to make sure they were alone. "If you make a hundred kazoos and you only tell the government that you've made ninety, then you have some to sell at a much higher profit. Now, I'm not suggesting that you lie about how much cheese your little factory can churn out in a week's time, but you'll be busy building your new hot tub and won't be able to keep track of the count every day."

"And we get to keep all the ones I don't count?"

Colonel Karloff pursed his lips. "Not all of them, my friend."

. . . . .

Her Majesty's long distance conference with the President ran over an hour. Together with the Defense Minister, they'd printed out a map of the original D-Day invasion sites and were referring to them by the names used by the Allied Forces in 1946. To her "Omaha, Juno, Gold, and Sword" he was calling them "Hilton, Hyatt, Marriott, and Motel Six." It was the first time the Queen could remember needing a translator for a foreigner speaking English.

They agreed on using the Liverpool football stadium as a staging point. The season was over and the team had done poorly. As part of the deal, the President agreed to pay for new sod when the operation was over. A combined expeditionary force would be assembled to attack the Normandy coast on Bastille Day–July fourteenth. The President originally wanted to go immediately, but the Queen reminded him about Wimbledon and he next suggested American Independence Day on the Fourth of July.

Not wanting to make it seem as though this was another U.S. annexation, the Queen suggested holding off another ten days and hitting the French on their most important national holiday.

With social media, it was going to be difficult to keep the operation under wraps for very long. The President's suggestion was to dress all the soldiers as painters and workmen. The press would be told that the stadium was undergoing a long overdue refurbishing and to get it done in time for next season, no one but the workers would be allowed inside. The Queen went along with the idea but told him that the U.S. would have to pay their share of the paintbrushes and ladders.

. . . . .

General Purpose called the President while he was having breakfast on his verandah. He managed to say, "Good morning, Mr. President," before the leader of the free world, at least what was left of it, cut him off.

"Frank? Forget the cheese. I spoke with Queen Lizzy and we've got a deal going that will make Trump Tower look like a tent sale."

"Mr. President, I—"

"I want you to pull those Marines out of the Eiffel and tell them to head north to New Miami." The President shuffled some papers. "A Major Zumba will meet them at the train station in Caen. He was promoted this morning and he's got their orders. Supposed to be on the ground there from Jerusalem in three hours."

General Purpose held the phone away from his face and mouthed the words, "He's crazy" to his aide. Putting the President on speaker, he asked as calmly as possible, "Where is New Miami, Mr. President?"

"I've got a team working on updated maps as we speak, General. You might know it as Juno Beach."

"You're really doing this." Closing his eyes, the General could hear his retirement elf whispering in his ears. "Have you spoken to anyone else about this plan, Mr. President?"

"Other than Lizzy? No."

"No one in Congress? What about the Vice President?"

The President sighed. "He left an hour ago for Honolulu. He's going to run for President of Hawaii. Said the weather was the only factor. But I know his knees have been bothering him for some time. Can't run after a well-hit tennis ball for shit."

General Purpose ran a list of important people through his head. It was a shame that the United Nations had shut down so quickly after Dud was announced. So many of his contacts had been shipped home.

One ace remained in the General's pocket. He ushered the pole dancer out of the room and took the phone off speaker.

"Have you called the Vatican, Mr. President?"

A long pause came from the other end of the line. Finally, the President blew out a breath. "Not yet. But he's my next call."

They were the words General Purpose was hoping to hear. "I'll hold off on moving the Marines out of the Eiffel Tower until I hear back from you, Mr. President."

Disconnecting the call, the General, still slathered in massage oil under his clothes, walked out to the balcony and put his arm around Tanya's shoulders.

"Do you know how to speak French?"

She turned and kissed him. "*Voulez-vous coucher avec moi ce soir?*"

Chapter Twenty-Nine - Criminal Charges

The Marines were no longer on the observation platform of the Eiffel Tower. Still nauseous and vomiting from the skunk attack, they had been handcuffed and arrested by the Paris Police. A recent inmate escape had left plenty of space in the holding cells of the local precinct and all forty members of 3rd Battalion, 7th Marine Regiment, Flintstone Platoon were now incarcerated.

They'd been relieved of their weapons, uniforms, boots, and backpacks before being fingerprinted and left with their socks, t-shirts, undergarments, and a case of Air France puke bags. The cops who'd processed the prisoners had separated the women from the men, although most of the female Marines protested loudly, demanding equal treatment.

Standing on the freedom side of the bars, several cops were trying to interrogate the Marines at the same time. While the soldiers stood casually against the far wall, the Parisian police officers shouted questions at them in a combination of French and English. The Marines smiled and waved before turning and dropping their drawers.

Captain Crunch stood as close to the bars as possible and refused to answer any of their questions, ordering his men to give out nothing more than name, rank, and serial number.

After a few minutes of this chaos, a well-dressed gentleman who appeared to be in command walked over to the bars and pushed the cops who'd been asking the questions out of the way.

"You are the commanding officer of these men?"

Captain Crunch hesitated, but then nodded his head.

"I am Inspector Gussone of the Paris Prefecture of Police. I am in charge here."

Looking through the bars at the Inspector, Captain Crunch took a step back and saluted.

"That is not necessary. You understand that you are not prisoners of war?" The man pursed his lips and stared hard into the Captain's eyes.

Another nod.

"You are under arrest for trespassing, littering, and cruelty to animals."

"They attacked us." Looking around for support, Captain Crunch raised his eyebrows and held his hands out toward his Marines. "The Geneva Convention–"

"Does not say anything about skunks, monsieur. On the other hand, French law, section one-forty-five, page seventeen, paragraphs nine through twenty-one deals with willful destruction of national monuments." Inspector Gussone folded his arms across his chest. "It prescribes a minimum fine of two-hundred Euros and a maximum of ten years in prison, depending on the extent of the damage."

Locking his hands behind his back, Captain Crunch walked back and forth inside the cell. Stopping in front of the man, he shook his head. "We don't have eight-thousand Euros, but we're willing to fix anything that we broke."

"Would you like us to drive you back to the Eiffel Tower to effect the repairs or will you be calling a cab?" The inspector cracked up at his joke and pointed at the Marines. "You'll be staying right here for now. We've contacted the American Embassy but they told us to call NATO."

"NATO was disbanded eight months ago." Captain Crunch shrugged. "No one saw a need for them anymore. Even the United Nations is shuttered. I heard that Hilton is interested in buying the property on the East River. Condos there would be worth millions."

Inspector Gussone shook his head, but then looked at the Captain expectantly. "Do you have an American Express card?"

· · · · ·

General Purpose had no idea that the Marines were locked up in the holding cell of a Paris police station. He was also unaware that the only person manning the Marine command center in Jerusalem had been transferred again and was waiting for the platoon in the northern French city of Caen. Sergeant Zumba, now a Major in the United States Marine Corps, was not yet on the General's radar.

It was after midnight all around the world, and the General was more than happy to let this problem sit until morning. He slipped the secure NSA cellphone into the charger and stepped out of his bathrobe. Tanya smiled and held out her hand.

"Are we still going to France?"

"I'm not sure." General Purpose looked back at the cellphone. "I'm supposed to order an attack on the Normandy beaches, but I can't find the Marines."

"You lost the Marines?"

"Not all of them." He shrugged. "Just a platoon."

Tanya laughed. "I was going to say, call out the Marines, but it sounds like you've tried that already."

"I'm not sure it's the Marines that we need right now."

"No? Who then?"

General Purpose pulled back the covers and got into bed next to the pole dancer. "I'll start with a competent shrink for the President."

. . . . .

The President was pleased with his decision. Anything he could do to piss off the French was a bonus in his mind. The Great State of Florida had been threatening to secede and join with their neighbors ninety miles to the south. Most of the residents already spoke Spanish, and it would be a simple task to build a wall on the Georgia-Florida border. When the last member of the Castro clan passed away last year, the Cubans had made an overture to the Florida Governor, offering him the vacant presidency and control over the island nation.

It would take some time to offset the lost tourist revenue and to convince travelers that the beaches of northern France were a better choice and less polluted, but the U.S. Treasury had lots of extra money to spend on an advertising campaign. The President had done some preliminary research before getting on the phone with the Queen. One thing he learned was that there were no sharks in the English Channel. That would be a key selling point in their advertising efforts.

He felt certain that the cheese problem would solve itself, plus with his cholesterol still too far above where his doctor said it should be, cutting out dairy from his diet made far more sense than adding more. If the Queen was so hot on this guy Boulong and his dairy products, the President would give some consideration to helping her out now that she'd come on board with *his* plans.

Closing the curtains in the Presidential bedroom, he switched the six televisions back on and lowered the sound just enough to where he could still hear the moans. It would take a bit longer than usual for him to get the image of the

Queen out of his mind, but the President knew even she couldn't spoil his prurient entertainment now.

. . . . .

Cursing softly, the Parisian police inspector hung up the phone. It was his third call to the U.S. Embassy and his patience was running thin. No one he spoke to had any knowledge of the Marines attacking the Eiffel Tower. At first, he wondered if the Captain he'd questioned downstairs was running some kind of a rogue operation. But the man insisted that he was under direct orders of the President of the United States.

The cells that were holding the Marines were normally used for drunks and stoners who couldn't find their way home. These soldiers weren't impaired but it was obvious that they had no way to get home, even if he were to let them go. They hadn't enough food to feed forty prisoners, and even if they did, the jail wasn't designed for long-term incarceration.

He looked at the clock. It was almost dawn and the tourist crowds would be queuing for their ride up one of the elevators to the observation deck of the most popular attraction in the French capital. When he'd been up there a few hours prior to assist in the mass arrest, the skunks were gone but their foul-smelling flood still festered. Visitors would gag and scurry back down the stairs or the lifts or they might even jump to escape the noxious fumes. Revenue would suffer and he would be blamed.

The officer lifted the phone and dialed the maintenance number for the Paris Parks and Recreation division. Budget cuts and layoffs had affected them as well as every other civil servant in the city. However, they had plenty of mops, buckets, and extra clean uniforms...enough to fit forty U.S. Marines.

. . . . .

Boulong awoke in the middle of a nightmare. Molten cheese was pouring from the barn and flowing down the hill toward the house. He'd rolled the trebuchet around from the back and was trying to cool the cheese by flinging loads of water from the Doubs at it. All the time, Colonel Karloff was standing on the roof of the house and laughing at him.

Getting out of bed, the farmer tiptoed into the bathroom and softly closed the door. He sat down on the toilet, holding his head in his hands.

If I let the Russians take even half the cheese, there won't be enough for my regular customers. Mookie is supposed to be home tomorrow and we'll be able to get up to full production come Monday morning. With Melinda's help, we can increase the production, but we'll still be giving the lion's share to the Russians.

He spun a few sheets of paper off the roll and rewound it.

We can't do that. This farm has been here for centuries, producing butter and cheese for everyone. I'm not going to be a slave for the damn Russians.

Flushing the empty toilet, Boulong washed his hands and snuck back into the bedroom. Melinda was snoring so loud that she wouldn't have heard her boyfriend even if he hadn't stubbed his toe and screamed in pain. Hopping over to the door, he grabbed his bathrobe and hobbled up the stairs.

. . . . .

A few cows were mulling around in front of the house. Most of them were asleep, but a curious brown one wandered over and gave the farmer a whiff.

Boulong petted the cow on its head and gazed into its eyes. "You wanna make cheese for the Russians?"

The cow backed away and shook its head. It might have been chasing a fly, but to the farmer it was all the affirmation he needed. The Russians could get in line to buy his dairy products just like everyone else. Melinda was right. He could replace the hot tub on Amazon. Screw the Russians and their lumber.

He'd need protection, and a single trebuchet wasn't the answer. Both invaders had shown him the vulnerabilities of his Paradise. Boulong's little family wasn't equipped to fight a battle, much less a prolonged war. The failure of the British commandos was a fluke, but he knew they were a stubborn lot and would try again. He'd been bombed by the Americans, so they couldn't be trusted to stand behind him even against their perennial adversary.

Are we really alone in this battle?

The wind was picking up. At least that's what Boulong thought. It got stronger and the swirling dust stung his face and arms. Running for the shelter of his porch, the farmer stumbled with the pain of his stubbed toe and fell face first in the gravel. The gentle wind had been transformed into a gale and he covered his head with both hands.

A roaring came from the slope leading up to the barn and Boulong tried to turn his head to see what was causing it, but the spinning gravel stung his face and he had to look away. At the same speed as it arrived, the noise faded along with the wind and the farmer was able to roll over onto his back.

Mookie, dressed in a black nylon flight suit, held out his hand and smiled. "Hi, dad."

Chapter Thirty - Empty The Collection Tray

Father and son sat on the porch and watched the cows slowly return. Most of them had bolted for the furthest pasture but a few were caught between the open spaces and the forest that led down to the Doubs. The aircraft that had landed on the hillside was known as a VTOL. It was capable of vertical takeoffs and landings from any flat surface whether or not it was level. LD owned the only stealth version of the advanced flying machine and was currently hovering at three-thousand feet while she waited for Mookie's signal.

"I don't understand. Colonel Karloff said she didn't like men."

Mookie shrugged. "Apparently, she'd never had a real man."

Boulong leaned back from his son. "Now that's some bullshit if I ever heard it."

"Does it worry you that there's another stud in the family?"

"I don't know. Should it?"

The boy smiled. "Don't worry, I'm not going after your girlfriend." He looked up at the sky. "In fact, I've got to get my ass in gear."

"You're not staying?"

"No." Mookie nodded toward the clouds. "I promised to show her how to make cheese spread."

Boulong grabbed his son by the shoulders. "You're not giving out family secrets."

"Of course not." Taking his father's hands in his own, Mookie shook his head. "She doesn't know that everything I've been telling her about cheese production is stuff I found on Wikipedia."

"Are you moving in with her?" Boulong squeezed his son's hands in anticipation.

Mookie shook his head. "No. One floor down. She owns the whole building."

"It's not gonna last."

"You say that every time."

Letting go of his son's hands, the father stood and sighed. "I haven't been wrong yet."

Walking over slowly to the brown cow that had been sniffing him before his son's raucous entrance, Boulong turned and cocked his head.

"She arranged the deal with the Russians?"

Mookie nodded. "Yeah. I was there."

"Can she un-arrange it?"

"What do you mean?"

"I don't want to sell cheese to the Russians. I want to sell it to anyone I desire."

"That's not going to happen, dad. LD got paid a lot of money to put the deal together." Mookie got up from the porch steps and walked over to his father. "Unless you know someone with more cash than her."

Boulong blew out his breath and smiled. "From what I've heard, only the Catholic Church has more money than your mysterious friend."

"And the Pope really likes our cheese." Mookie let a sly grin fill his face. "And not for nothing, but I've got his personal phone number."

· · · · ·

Pope Victor had celebrated Mass on Sunday, knowing that his favorite grilled cheese sandwich was going to be made with something other than Boulong's cheese spread. He'd given some thought to having a bagel and lox instead, cream cheese being his second choice. But the Pope had come to expect his lunch a certain way. After all, it was one of the benefits of the job.

His argument with LD, who he called Luscious and Delicious when she was out of earshot, was that the cheese was for the good of all mankind. She didn't buy it. He threatened to have her excommunicated. She reminded him about a certain video that she owned. It was an original and there were no copies. The Pope remembered the movie, the two dwarves, and the gallon of sangria. It wasn't his finest moment.

Mookie had watched LD operate with the precision of a seasoned prosecutor. She took apart every argument the Pope laid out with ease. Her money trumped his religion. His need for Boulong's cheese would only benefit himself. Spreading the cheese among the Russian oligarchs would not only bring them pleasure, but their ensuing good spirits would enrich every Russian's life. He asked her to explain that, but she simply laughed and told the Pope he'd have to figure it out on his own after he retired.

After they'd left and were on their way to Moscow, Mookie had questioned LD's wealth. In a moment of weakness urged on by his massaging her neck, the woman had admitted that while her finances were substantial; the Church had much deeper pockets.

"If you tell anyone, though, I'll cut off your testicles and feed them to my Doberman." LD had pulled Mookie around in front of her and was grabbing his crotch to emphasize her point. "Don't think for a moment that just because you've found a way to pleasure me like no woman has, that we're standing on the mountaintop together. The peak is tiny and it only holds one person at a time."

She pointed out the window as they crossed over the Alps. "The view is exciting from the top, but it's horrifying when you fall." LD leaned across and kissed him. "Don't make me push you."

. . . . .

Boulong's face relaxed. His entire body released the tension of recent events and he smiled at his son.

"The news said the Pope was considering retirement."

"Yeah." Mookie nodded. "He spoke about it when I met him."

"Is it his health?"

"No. I think he's worried about losing his audience." The cellphone in Mookie's pocket chimed and he pulled it out to read an incoming text. "She's getting anxious." He replied that he would need a few more minutes.

"What do you mean about losing the audience? People are still going to church."

"Not according to the printouts he had on his desk." Mookie unzipped the flight suit and slipped the phone back into a pocket. "The Vatican has a server array in the catacombs that would make Bill Gates drool with envy. They collect data from every church in the world and the folks who interpret that data are telling the Pope it's not good."

Boulong frowned. "Now you know why I don't bother with God."

"Ever since Dud, many of the threats that drove people to church on Sunday have been eliminated. Fear has been replaced by hope according to their reports."

Mookie's phone chimed again, but he ignored it. "The Pope doesn't think the Vatican will be an independent city for much longer. Sure, it's got all the tourist attractions, but that's just it. There's talk among the bishops of adding a multiplex cinema, a sushi bar, and ziplines across the main piazza."

"Ziplines?"

"Four of them that will run night and day."

"And the Pope is in favor of all this?" Boulong shook his head. "I can't believe it."

"That's just it." Pulling the phone out of his pocket, Mookie put it on silent but held it in his hand. "The Pope thinks it would be best for him to retire before it all goes to hell in a cannoli shell."

Boulong hadn't danced since his divorce was final. He grabbed his son's hands and tapped a few steps before his injured toe put an end to the joyous performance.

"We don't need money to buy back the rights to our cheese. The Catholic Church will cover the tab." Boulong slapped his thigh. "Bingo."

"How are you going to convince the Pope? LD will upload that video on social media and ruin the man if he gets in her way."

"And the Pope will be forced to retire." Boulong's smile was so wide that tiny pits had formed at the corners of his mouth.

"He's not going to do that, dad."

Boulong winked at Mookie. "He will if you can make him an offer he can't refuse."

"Me?"

"You said you've got his number."

Mookie nodded slowly. "Okay..."

"Did you know that before he went into the clergy, Pope Victor was a dairy farmer?" Boulong held his arms out. "Look at this beautiful dairy farm. Lots of cows. A working cheese processing plant and plenty of room to build a nice retirement cottage for a fellow farmer."

"You're nuts."

"You're leaving, right? Melinda's pregnant and in a few months, she won't be of any use in the barn. It'll take months for the damage to actually force the Pope to hang up his mitre and pallium for the last time. According to Melinda, we can buy anything on Amazon dot com. I figure a nice Quonset hut with a space heater and a king-size air mattress will be just fine until we can build an actual cottage."

Mookie was stunned. "You're going to make the Pope live in a Quonset hut?"

"No. It's for me and Melinda." Boulong shook his head. "Even though I don't believe in religion, I still have some respect for the job. The Pope can sleep downstairs in our bedroom until the cottage is ready."

"Let me make sure I understand this." Taking a step back, Mookie stood with his hands on his hips. "In exchange for buying out the Russians so that you can sell cheese spread to the free world, the Pope is going to accept the embarrassment of a video that even PornHub would refuse to show. And when the Catholic community sends him packing, you're going to put him up in Paradise and let the Pope milk cows."

Boulong nodded. "Make the call and do it quickly." He looked up at the sky and shielded his eyes. "It's getting windy."

Chapter Thirty-One - Party Time

The Queen had called while his staff was prepping for lunch. Chef Ronzoni was pleased: the state dinner was back on and his favorite tennis player was coming. The Chef loved all the American Presidents. They would eat anything he put on a plate and then describe it with such overflowing joy. Most of all, they wanted quantity over quality. Any chef worth his apron will tell you that they're not happy unless their customers are eating.

He recalled Bill Clinton and the man's voracious appetite for pasta. The Chef knew President Chubby, as he called him, would be good for three helpings of any dish with tomato sauce. Chubby had consumed two pounds of meatballs by himself, just to use up the sauce on his plate. Obama, the hot dog king, had shown Chef Ronzoni a novel way to garnish street food that turned the chef's stomach upside down but reminded his honored guest and Chicago native of home. It was the first and last time the one-star chef would ever taste a frankfurter.

Even though he couldn't spell the word correctly and was the king of the boorish Presidents of any country, the most recent of America's former leader's need for cheeseburgers surprised Chef Ronzoni. It was a shock that sent the staff running for the kitchen when the obnoxious President insisted on Boulong's cheese instead of Kraft singles. The man with the odd skin tone slathered every entrée with ketchup, including the boar fillet, but he had an extensive knowledge of champagne. The Chef walked out of his own restaurant when the President asked for Dom Perignon to go with his French fries.

The current Oval Office occupant was a health nut when the cameras were on but a pure carnivore in private. The President had turned down Beef Wellington, ignored Steak Diane, and taken one bite of the best chateaubriand the chef had ever prepared before pushing the rest of it around his plate. But Chef Ronzoni's boar tenderloin with pine nuts and cheese sauce was a cow of a different color.

"He ate a full kilo of meat by himself the last time he was here." The Chef pointed at the cook coming out of the freezer. "Get two more tenderloins and another bag of pine nuts. I guarantee there won't be any leftovers."

"What about the cheese?" His new sous chef wiped his hands on a towel and flipped it onto his shoulder. "We don't have any of Boulong's cheese spread. How do you plan to make the sauce?"

Chef Ronzoni reached under the prep table and pulled a can of Cheese Whiz out of a paper bag. "With this."

. . . . .

Boulong woke Mikey a few minutes after the VTOL departed with his son. It would be dawn in two hours and the farmer was energized. Mookie would make the call. He'd never failed to honor a promise to his father. LD would be a problem, but not one that the boy couldn't solve with his tender touch or whatever parts of his body were necessary to fulfill the woman's desire. He'd started to give Boulong the details, but the father stifled the attempt.

Mookie reminded his father that LD had no genuine interest in the cheese. To her, it was all about money and the art of the deal. She was planning to write a book about negotiations to correct all the bad information that the former U.S. President and reality TV star had insisted was true. If what the boy told Boulong was accurate, she'd go along with whatever the Pope decided, just as long as she got paid.

Having little doubt that LD would blackmail the Pope, Mookie was going to make an effort at finding the video and destroying it, but he wasn't sure if the woman had made copies. He'd insisted that his sexual prowess would be sufficient to make Boulong's plan work and went so far as to offer to buy the Quonset hut on his personal credit card.

. . . . .

Pope Victor had been a radical in the church from the day he first stepped into the pulpit. Gay marriage and the end of required celibacy had already been approved by his predecessor. But the new Pope went several steps beyond and gave his blessing to every union between humans, regardless of sex or the number of people involved. He wasn't a Mormon, but was enamored by the concept of multiple wives.

His own wife had disappeared on a ski trip to the Alps soon after he became a bishop. Efforts to find her body were met with disaster. Apparently, the crevasse she'd tumbled into was over a mile deep and had never been explored. Bishop Victor mourned his loss for nearly a month before getting back into the habit.

It was rumored that most of the nuns in his parish had spent time alone with the Bishop. No one was able to capture the philandering priest until the last night of Lent, five years before he was chosen as Pope. A late night party at a parishioner's house had gotten out of hand. Two dwarves from a traveling circus had been making pizza deliveries to earn some extra cash. The explanation the Bishop gave as to why he was naked, one of the dwarves was wearing his mitre, and how everyone got doused with sangria was accepted without question. The video that was filmed disappeared and it was assumed that it had been erased.

It hadn't, and the only copy was stored in a fireproof vault in LD's penthouse.

· · · · ·

Boulong clicked on the lights in his son's room. "Get up and get dressed." He kicked the foot of Mikey's bed.

"It's not even four." Mikey rubbed his eyes. "What's going on? Another invasion?"

"You missed your brother."

"He came back?"

Boulong nodded. "Yes, but he's gone again and probably for good."

Mikey swung his legs over the side of the waterbed. "What?"

"It's too long a story for right now, but he's got himself a woman."

"Another hooker?"

"No, not this time. I think she's paying *him*." Boulong laughed. "Now, that would be a first."

"So, why am I awake at this ungodly hour of the morning?"

Looking out the window, the farmer smiled. "Because God is coming and we need to have cheese."

. . . . .

Major Zumba had checked into a small bed-and-breakfast on the north side of Caen. He'd waited at the train station for the Marines until dawn before giving up. Trains ran with military precision in Europe. If they hadn't arrived at the designated time, he figured they'd missed a connection or gotten on the wrong train.

Before going downstairs for breakfast, the newly promoted Major sent a text to his replacement in Jerusalem. The sergeant who'd arrived at the Marine Command Center while Zumba was packing removed his orders from a red leather briefcase and had set up at the console without speaking a word.

> Zumba: "Arrived yesterday at 2245 hours. No Marines as of 0800 this morning."
>
> Jerusalem: "Who is this?"
>
> Zumba: "Major Gregory Zumba. You replaced me yesterday."
>
> Jerusalem: "You forgot to leave me the Netflix password."
>
> Zumba: "It's taped to the bottom of the keyboard."
>
> Jerusalem: "Got it."
>
> Zumba: "Where are the Marines?"
>
> Jerusalem: "On top of the Eiffel Tower."
>
> Zumba: "They were supposed to be here."
>
> Jerusalem: "The password doesn't work."
>
> Zumba: "Those are zeros, not the letter O."
>
> Jerusalem: "Got it."
>
> Zumba: "I need you to reach out to Flintstone platoon and get them here ASAP."
>
> Jerusalem: ...
>
> Zumba: "Did you get my last text?"
>
> Jerusalem: ...

Major Zumba dropped the phone in the middle of his bed and went down for coffee, croissants, and runny eggs. *I should never have given him the password.*

. . . . .

General Purpose was also wondering what had happened to 3rd Battalion, 7th Marine Regiment, Flintstone Platoon. The morning news had a report of a serious skunk problem in the French capital that had delayed the opening of the Eiffel Tower until the afternoon. The reporter said a team of American volunteers were assisting in the cleanup, but there was no accompanying video.

"Hideo, call base operations and schedule me on a flight to Paris."

Corporal Tsunami looked across the booth, holding a glass of freshly squeezed orange juice in midair. "Just you?"

"Is your girlfriend going to hook up my television this weekend?"

"She said it would be Sunday afternoon, but yes, she'll get it done."

The General smiled. "Okay, you can come."

"What about me?" Tanya grabbed the General's arm. "You said I could go to Paris the next time you went."

"Not when it's official military business, sweetheart."

General Purpose's secure NSA phone rang and he looked at the image of the President on the screen. *Now what?* Reluctantly, he tapped the button and smiled. "Good morning, Mr. President."

"Frank? Pack your bags. You're coming to London with me."

"What about Normandy, Mr. President?"

"That's why we're going, Frank. Lizzy's throwing a kickoff dinner and she wants all the commanders there to discuss the invasion."

The invasion of a place that's already been invaded, conquered, and settled. Thank God he's not thinking about colonizing the moon. "I'm not so sure a public gathering is a good idea. The original D-Day attack was the best kept secret of the war."

"War? Who said anything about war? Jesus, Frank, don't get all military on me now. This is going to be a small expeditionary force that will land and assume control of the beachfront without a single shot being fired."

"I'm sorry, Mr. President, but do you really believe the French people will simply surrender and hand over the deeds to their property?"

"Oh, come on, Frank. The French are always the first to surrender."

General Purpose shook his head and mocked choking. "Is she serving that gamey tenderloin crap with the cheese goop?"

"The boar tenderloin? You bet."

Oh, wonderful. The General whispered to his aide, "Make sure you pack the Alka Seltzer and the Imodium." Blowing out a long breath, he closed his eyes. "We should land at Andrews Air Force Base before sunset, Mr. President."

"Great. Bring your tennis racket. We don't leave for London until late afternoon tomorrow. We'll have plenty of time for a match."

Chapter Thirty-Two - Getting Ready

Melinda made breakfast for Boulong and Mikey when she rolled out of bed just before nine in the morning. Shredding some of the aged cheese in the pantry, she'd whipped up scrambled eggs and melted the cheese on top while the eggs were still in the frying pan. Having cut squares of the mixture, she laid them on toast with a slice of ham on top.

"They're not the same as you'd get from Mickie D's arches, but at least they're homemade." Melinda placed a tray of the hot sandwiches on the workbench in the barn and took one for herself.

"What happened last night? I dreamt an airplane landed in the front yard."

Boulong finished connecting the cow in the last stall and wiped his hands. "If all goes well, we'll be getting company on the island."

"How many?" Melinda looked at the tray and wondered if she could cook for a crowd.

"Just one. An old German dairy farmer." Boulong grinned, but then looked away. "If you're gonna take those pills, I suggest you do it before he gets here."

Taking a few steps back from her boyfriend, Melinda smiled. "I swallowed them this morning. No baby for Boulong."

Boulong was stuck between confusion and relief. "I thought we were going to discuss this."

"And I decided I wasn't ready to be a mother." Melinda struck a modeling pose. "Plus, I don't want to lose this sexy body."

"So, we're back to trusting the birth control pills?"

She smiled. "You can always get fixed, Bouly."

. . . . .

On the other side of the Atlantic Ocean, the President was fixing things as well. He'd gone downstairs to the Situation Room and instructed the janitor to get the place ready for war. All the beer had to go and the extra apps that had been loaded onto the smart TVs had to be removed, including their passwords.

Sergeant Zumba's plaque on the back of his chair needed to be replaced, although the President wasn't sure how to find someone to take the seat. Of the remaining Joint Chiefs, the Admiral of the Navy was vacationing in the South Pacific on Tikopango, and the Air Force General had moved to Colorado, where he was running a skydiving school.

The President knew there were lots of officers hanging around Andrews Air Force base that would jump at the chance to participate in war games with actual soldiers. He grabbed a couple of Marine guards and ordered them to head over to the military air base and find some willing players.

. . . . .

It was necessary to inform Congress that military action was planned so the President called his executive secretary into the Oval Office to take a memo.

"We are losing states and with them, the tourist revenue that is crucial to our economy. Since the announcement by the Governor of Florida of their pending vote on the issue of secession, California, Oregon, and Washington have begun making plans to form a west coast country to be called either New Pacific or Cannaland. Until the next major earthquake, they will control all of the beaches west of the Mississippi."

His secretary held her pen in midair. "I'm sorry, Mr. President, but aren't there beaches in Texas on the Gulf of Mexico?"

"Hey! Who's President here?"

She put her pen back to the pad and looked up at her boss. "I beg your pardon, Mr. President."

The President continued his memo. "They will control all the *good* beaches west of the Mississippi, seeing as how everything on the Gulf is still screwed up from hurricanes and oil spills." He looked at his secretary and smiled. "Happy now?"

She nodded.

"Okay." The President looked out the window, thinking about the gist of his message and how to word it. "Okay," he said again and then continued with the memo.

"As a nation, we must be ready to continue our roll as the lifeguards to the free world. So it is, my fellow Americans–"

His secretary shook her head.

"What now?"

"You're not giving the State of the Union, Mr. President."

He blew out a quick breath and shook his head. "Fine, cut that last part." Walking over to the window behind his desk, the President rubbed a smudge and then turned back to his secretary. "Screw it. Just tell them that we're attacking France and if they don't like it, they can kiss my ass."

· · · · ·

Boulong heard the helicopter and ran from the barn with a retractable pitchfork in his hands. He stopped and turned away from the dust and wind as the chopper bounced to a landing in front of his house. Colonel Karloff jumped from the open door and waved. On the opposite side of the Russian MI-38 cargo transport, four airmen began unloading wooden planks.

"You know the Pope?" Karloff's eyes were so wide that Boulong thought they were going to roll out of their sockets.

"Not me. It's my son."

The Colonel nodded. "A lot of money has changed hands over the past four days. You must make some very exotic cheese here."

Boulong pointed toward the barn. "Fresh every day. Would you like to try some?"

"No thanks." Colonel Karloff held his stomach. "Dairy gives me gas." He looked over at the growing pile of lumber. "You'll be able to build a much larger dock than before. Have you thought about a getting a bigger boat?"

"It's been on my wish list for years." Gazing over at the empty space next to the house that would soon contain a Quonset hut, Boulong shrugged. "But it'll have to wait a bit a longer."

Not wanting to seem ungrateful, the farmer had given Colonel Karloff a hundred pounds of frozen steaks and a freshly slaughtered goat. Lambs, rams, and goats roamed the island freely, but Boulong's family had rarely eaten them because of all the excess beef. The four-legged lawnmowers were superb at keeping weeds at bay. Plus, several of the Swiss chefs who purchased his cheese would buy every ounce of butchered lamb he brought to their side of the Doubs at a premium price. Mikey had killed the goat that morning after finding it stuck in the field where the British helicopter had crashed.

The animal had wandered into the wreckage and slipped on the greasy deck. Its two front legs were badly mangled and Mikey put it out of its misery with a crossbow bolt to the head. He was going to butcher and freeze the meat as a special first night dinner for their soon-to-be arriving long-term guest, but Boulong had heard the Pope was a closet vegetarian. Either way, they had lots of extra goats in Paradise.

. . . . .

Next Friday's dairy load would be close to normal. Colonel Karloff had left two of his commandos on the island to fill in for Boulong's missing son. All was well with the boy who'd telephoned the Pope in the middle of the night. Whatever tools Mookie had used, the Russians had agreed to settle for slag buns.

Along with the measurements of a bed that could hold three couples, Mookie had sent his father a picture of the sunset from his new digs in New York City. Centered in the image was the remaining shell of Trump Tower and the cranes that were dismantling it.

Everything was cool with Luscious and Delicious. He didn't even mind wearing a lavender bathrobe all day long, but she didn't have a pair of desert sandals in his size and he was walking around barefoot. All of her friends were waiting when they arrived. He'd never seen so much champagne, but couldn't get past the taste of fish eggs, with or without the little pieces of toast.

Boulong replied with a thumbs-up emoji and was about to put the phone in his pocket and get back to work. However, one last text arrived from his son in America and he read it, laughing so loud at the end that he almost caused a stampede.

"The women love my accent, but they all want to know what it's like to have sex on the back of a cow."

The words were followed by a new line and then a row of question marks.

Boulong replied with a single smiley.

Epilogue

The retired Pope had insisted on taking the Quonset hut. He'd spent too many years surrounded by people and wanted to spend the rest of his life alone with no one but God and a few friendly cows. A plumber from the French side was brought over to install a toilet and sink in the bathroom that Boulong and Mikey built into one side of the hut. Amazon delivered a combination heater and air conditioning unit that the Pope kept at comfortable levels for a former German dairy farmer.

It wasn't the Vatican, but no one outside of Paradise, the entire Russian Army, and two lovers in Manhattan knew he was there.

. . . . .

Dairy production doubled and then tripled. Victor, who refused to respond to the word "Pope," still had friends in holy places. The influx of cash during his first month in Paradise was enough to add five more milking stalls and an extra whey tank.

They worked as a team with no need for a leader. If Mikey needed a break to massage his sore leg, one of the other three would jump in and keep the cheese processing equipment running. When it rained and they needed to open the gate of the holding pen and let in the cows that were ready to milk, Victor had no qualms jumping behind the wheel of the Gator without a hat on his head.

His only regret was not being able to go ashore to help sell the butter and cheese that they produced. It was too much of a risk that someone would recognize the former Pope and his life of solitude would shatter. Boulong's island was both a paradise and a prison.

Dinner at Buckingham Palace had been a disaster of biblical proportions. Worried that the Queen would taste the cheese sauce and know that he'd made it from a can, Chef Ronzoni had used ground cannabis flour in the sausage rolls they'd served during the cocktail hour. By the time the main course was placed on the table, everyone was so stoned that they would have eaten cheeseburgers and praised his creativity.

Of course, the dosage was enough to send hormones into overdrive and mi-lords and mi-ladies were soon ravaging beasts who had no interest in food. The dining hall was trashed. Curtains were ripped from their rods and revelers were drinking wine from bottles, buckets, and navels.

The Queen, long past any desires of the flesh, stumbled into the royal swimming pool and was last seen floating on her back surrounded by several ducks who had wandered in through the open door.

. . . . .

Xavier Milhous Nixon visited every gentleman's club in Orange County, Florida in search of Tanya the pregnant pole dancer. She, of course, had traveled to London with General Purpose and his aide, but hadn't been invited to the Buckingham Palace gala. Wandering the streets of Chelsea, she stopped to watch a small theater troupe as they performed the last act of Hamlet.

Intrigued, she waited until the crowd had dispersed and walked over to the actor who seemed to be in charge. She told the man that she was Blaze Star, an acrobat from the United States who was thinking about relocating. The leader of the group introduced himself as Theodore Boulong and said she would be welcome to join and could stay at his place if she needed lodging.

. . . . .

Having exhausted his search, XM had driven down to Miami from the center of the state and was at the private airport, working through the Gulfstream's preflight checklist. He put the clipboard on the ground to answer LD's call.

"I just got a phone call that someone is running preflight on my jet."

Xavier took a deep breath. "I need to get away for a while, clear my head."

"You're taking the pregnant pole dancer with you?"

"No." Pausing, Xavier knew there would be only the truth with his wealthy benefactor. "She's gone to London, just like you said."

"And had the abortion. Just as I predicted. You should have gone after her."

"I gave it some thought, but it never would have worked out." Clicking his ballpoint pen over and over, XM Nixon looked at the gleaming black jet and grinned. "Sometimes running away makes more sense. Look how you turned out."

"Running is rarely the answer, especially when there's a woman involved. And you want to borrow my Gulfstream to make your escape? Don't you think it would have been nice to ask first?"

Xavier shrugged. "I'm only taking it to San Diego."

"You'll bring it back?"

"No, but I'll leave the keys in it."

"That's fine. Where are you going?"

The pilot sucked in another deep breath, held it for a few seconds, and then blew it out. "I'm gonna find a yacht that's heading to the South Pacific and see if I can hitch a ride. I liked that little island where you sent me for the cheese."

"Tikopango? I hear it's turning into a real tourist destination. Marriott is negotiating for their Tiko Hut."

"Well, maybe I can convince the Tikos to keep the place native."

"I heard a woman aviator tried that a bunch of years ago." She sighed. "Good luck, XM."

. . . . .

The combined British and American Expeditionary force never invaded France. Major Zumba's report was short and to the point. When it was leaked to the news media, he was praised not only for his brevity but also for preventing a major investment calamity.

With the arrival of the Marines, two days past schedule and wearing City of Paris Maintenance uniforms, the mission formally got underway. It was late, so they reconnoitered the Normandy beach after midnight by the light of the full moon.

Several of the Marines were surfers from Hawaii, who took one look at the rocky shoreline and pebbled beach and said no one would ever want to lay there and sunbathe. To add to the uselessness of the Normandy beaches, the waves were too small to surf, the water even in mid-June was freezing, and there were so many fishing boats that the place smelled worse than an unwashed latrine.

Speaking from a podium in front of Air Force One, the President claimed that he had no knowledge of the supposed plan to invade one of their closest allies. He put the blame on what he called "cheese terrorists" who had attempted to start a war over rising dairy prices at home that he was fighting to control.

He thanked General Purpose for putting an end to the attempted invasion and was going to pin a medal on him, but the commanding general of the U.S. Armed Forces was nowhere to be found.

Across the English Channel, General Purpose and Corporal Tsunami were sitting outside an Amsterdam "coffee shop" and smoking a pipe filled with ground hashish. Madness had peaked and the General needed to walk away from it for a while. Hideo's father was still slicing fish at a sushi bar in Rotterdam, and his mother was making up the bed in the spare room for their guests. It was only an hour drive, but a Marine helicopter was waiting for them across the street.

Thankfully for both men, the secure NSA cellphone was under a pile of magazines in a toilet in Buckingham Palace.

. . . . .

The day the border between Mexico and the United States reopened, the Border Patrol Agents were expecting a massive traffic jam, as American tourists returned to reclaim their beach loungers and tequila. It was less than a trickle. Once again, America had been attacked by a foreign nation and threatened with atomic extinction. It would take time for patriotic Americans to see our southern neighbor as a friend.

Maybe we didn't need taco trucks and their homemade salsa. Perhaps refried beans really were ground up cow guts. Let the bandas go party in the Yucatan and eat all the yuc they could swallow. For now, Mexico was as uninviting as Mongolia in winter.

. . . . .

And the virus that started it all? Covid hit a mutational wall and lost its power to harm humans. Only one species on the planet was threatened by the final iteration of the disease. By the millions, the insect that was supposed to survive a nuclear holocaust succumbed to the microscopic killer. Around the world, cockroaches crawled into the sunlight and died. Their tiny corpses could be seen floating in rivers and lakes. Piles of them a foot deep were shoveled against curbs in New York City. Snowplows and bucket loaders had to be used to collect them.

Covid was vanquished without the need for any more vaccines and with it, Dud was gone with the wind. The friendly microbe had nothing to eat once all the gunpowder and nitrocellulose had been consumed so it became cannibalistic. The Dud bugs went after their brothers and sisters, and within a few months, all the invaders were nothing but harmless Dud poop.

About the Author

Ricky Ginsburg is one of those writers who sees a flock of birds heading south for the winter and wonders what they talk about on their journey. While much of his writing has elements of magical realism and humor, he also has a serious side, but keeps it in a small plexiglass box under his desk.

Note from the Author

Word-of-mouth is crucial for any author to succeed. If you enjoyed *Boulong's Cheese*, please leave a review online—anywhere you are able. Even if it's just a sentence or two. It would make all the difference and would be very much appreciated.

Thanks!
Ricky Ginsburg

Thank you so much for reading one of Ricky Ginsburg's novels.
If you enjoyed the experience, please check out our recommended
title for your next great read!

The Blue Macaw

Ricky Ginsburg

"With diamonds, rare birds, football and numerous other
twists and turns, the complex story moves to
a quick and satisfying end."
-Gemma B. Publishing

View other Black Rose Writing titles at
www.blackrosewriting.com/books and use promo code
PRINT to receive a **20% discount** when purchasing.

CPSIA information can be obtained
at www.ICGtesting.com
Printed in the USA
FSHW012132270421
80846FS